AFTER
THE
SUMMER
RAIN

Praise for the works of Gerri Hill

Moonlight Avenue

Moonlight Avenue by Gerri Hill is a riveting, literary tapestry of mystery, suspense, thriller and romance. It is also a story about forgiveness, moving on with your life and opening your heart to love despite how daunting it may seem at first. Gerri Hill's stories will always make me feel as though I'm in a book lover's paradise because her beautiful descriptions of nature and the landscape in Corpus Christi made me feel as though I was seeing everything firsthand. In addition, she creates the most down-to-earth and adorable characters ever. This author really went above and beyond to give me an enthralling mystery that I gleefully devoured for hours on end and I am keeping my fingers crossed with the hope that Gerri Hill would write a sequel to this outstanding story.

- The Lesbian Review

This is a real murder mystery book. It is in the same vein as a Sue Grafton or JM Redmann type of mystery. There is a lot of surveillance and following the clues. Besides the mystery this is a slow-burn romance. It is very slow-burn but I loved every second of it. I'm not sure what it was but I thought the chemistry was great. It kept building and building and eventually they started to put out sparks together. If you are a mystery fan don't hesitate to grab this. This was a treat to read and I hope we will be seeing a book 2 soon.

- goodreads, Lex Kent's Reviews

Moonlight Avenue is another perfect example of why Hill is a master at her craft! This book appears to be the start of a series, at least, I'm really hoping it is because I'd love to see more from this team in the future! The crime takes the main stage in this book, but the romance isn't exactly a back burner. I like to think of it as a pleasant side story. It's hard for authors to lace romance into true crime novels, but Hill handled it very well and set these two up with enough chemistry to make it interesting. Just read the book. It's another classic Gerri Hill crime novel, and you won't be sorry for picking it up!

- goodreads, Bethany's Reviews

...is an excellent mystery novel, sheer class. Gerri Hill's writing is flawless, her story compelling and much more than a notch above others writing in this genre. I really enjoyed the interpersonal relationships in this story. They were well observed and natural. The case they were working was full of twists and turns and had me desperate to find out more. I loved it and would be interested to find out what happens next for these characters if Ms Hill decides to make this a series. Highly recommended.

-Kitty Kat's Book Review Blog

The Neighbor

It's funny... Normally in the books I read I get why the characters would fall in love. Now on paper (excuse the pun), Cassidy and Laura should not work... but let me tell you, that's the reason they do. I actually loved this book so hard. It's was light, cute and gave me all the feels. It was exactly what I needed after the emotionally hard book I read before. Cassidy and Laura together are hot stuff and I reckon it's the build up to them being together that got me all flustered when it did actually happen. Yes it's a slow burn but so beautifully written and worth the wait in every way.

- Les Reveur

This is classic Gerri Hill at her very best, top of the pile of so many excellent books she has written, I genuinely loved this story and these two women. The growing friendship and hidden attraction between them is skillfully written and totally engaging. This isn't a new story or a clever plot, but it is so exquisitely done that it is totally absorbing. Laura needs to accept who she is and let go of who she thought she was. Cassidy has to work out who she'd rather be; a conflict reflected in her friendships, real and false. A 40 something romance, genuine and real, women we can relate to and empathize with, laugh with and relish. This was a joy to read.

- *Lesbian Reading Room*

I have always found Hill's writing to be intriguing and stimulating. Whether she's writing a mystery or a sweet romance, she allows the reader to discover something about themselves along with her characters. This story has all the fun antics you would expect for a quality, low-stress, romantic comedy. Hill is wonderful in giving us characters that are intriguing and delightful that you never want to put the book down until the end. If you're lounging by the pool, on the beach, or just soaking up the last days of summer in some tropical location, this is definitely the book to read. Follow Laura and Cassidy as they see, truly, just how close love can be.

- *The Lesbian Review*

About the Author

Gerri Hill has thirty-six published works, including the 2017 GCLS winner *Paradox Valley*, 2014 GCLS winner *The Midnight Moon*, 2011, 2012 and 2013 winners *Devil's Rock*, *Hell's Highway* and *Snow Falls*, and the 2009 GCLS winner *Partners*, the last book in the popular Hunter Series, as well as the 2013 Lambda finalist *At Seventeen*.

Gerri lives in south-central Texas, only a few hours from the Gulf Coast, a place that has inspired many of her books. With her partner, Diane, they share their life with two Australian shepherds—Casey and Cooper—and a couple of furry felines.

For more, visit her website at gerrihill.com.

Other Bella Books by Gerri Hill

Angel Fire
Artist's Dream
At Seventeen
Behind the Pine Curtain
Chasing a Brighter Blue
The Cottage
Coyote Sky
Dawn of Change
Devil's Rock
Gulf Breeze
Hell's Highway
Hunter's Way
In the Name of the Father
Keepers of the Cave
The Killing Room
The Locket
Love Waits
The Midnight Moon
Moonlight Avenue
The Neighbor
No Strings
One Summer Night
Paradox Valley
Partners
Pelican's Landing
The Rainbow Cedar
The Roundabout
The Secret Pond
Sawmill Springs
The Scorpion
Sierra City
Snow Falls
Storms
The Target
Weeping Walls

AFTER THE SUMMER RAIN

GERRI HILL

BELLA
BOOKS

2019

Bella Books, Inc.
P.O. Box 10543
Tallahassee, FL 32302

Printed in the United States of America on acid-free paper.

First Bella Books Edition 2019

Editor: Medora MacDougall
Cover Designer: Sandy Knowles

ISBN: 978-1-64247-071-0

CHAPTER ONE

"Where are you tonight?"

Melanie looked out into the black darkness of night... waiting. The coyote pair, which she'd named Goldie and Rick, was usually singing by this time. Goldie, because she had the lightest colored coat Melanie had ever seen. And Rick...well, just because.

But the night remained quiet and still, and she thought that perhaps this would be one of the rare evenings when they wouldn't come close and serenade her.

Some people hated, even feared, the coyotes, saying their barks and howls gave them chills. To her, their song was hauntingly beautiful—and oh, so lonely. She knew all about that, didn't she? Maybe that's why she embraced it so; it reminded her of darker times. It reminded her of Adam. It also reminded her that she'd gotten past all of that.

She shifted in the rocker and took a sip of the hot tea she'd laced with honey. Down by the creek, she heard an owl softly hooting. A few beats later, its mate answered. She leaned back and closed her eyes. Sometimes she wished she could sing like the coyotes, call like the owls... Call to someone. Call and have them answer.

She opened her eyes. It felt different tonight. *She* felt different tonight. She felt like...like change was coming.

She tilted her head, looking into the night sky. Had her heart...her soul been calling to someone?

Had someone answered her call? Was someone coming?

Yes, sometimes when she was feeling particularly lonely—like tonight—she wished there was someone. What would it be like to have a lover out here in this secluded place she'd called home for the last seven years?

What would it be like to have someone?

She closed her eyes, letting her heart call to whom it may.

Would someone answer?

CHAPTER TWO

"When's the last time you've slept?"

Erin glanced at the trash basket beside her desk, noting the mound there of empty Red Bull cans. She dismissed her sister's comment with a wave of her hand.

"Last night, of course. What's up? Kinda busy."

Joyce walked closer, peering over the desk, her head shaking slowly. "You can't live off caffeine during the day and booze at night." She glanced at the dirty ashtray beside her laptop. "And cigarettes, Erin? Really? In the office? What is wrong with you?"

"Oh, I don't know," she said sarcastically. "Perhaps I'm a bit stressed. I'm juggling ten houses, two of which are in the final month, two more that just got started, and three that are already behind schedule." She stood up quickly, her chair rolling back and banging against the wall behind her. "I'm late. Time to go browbeat some contractors."

Joyce held her hand up. "Not today, sis. Dad's here. Meeting."

"Meeting?" She shook her head. "I don't have time for a meeting. It wasn't on my calendar."

She went to walk past her sister but found her father standing in the doorway. He was a large man, tall and bulky. His once dark hair was showing gray at the temples. The moustache and goatee that he'd had her whole life was now totally gray.

"Family meeting," he said, motioning with his head. "Brent is already in the conference room."

Erin blew out her breath. "Dad…really, I don't have time. I've got a million things to do. I've got—"

"A meeting, Erin. You've got a meeting. Now."

The tone of his voice indicated it wasn't up for discussion. That didn't prevent her from glaring at Joyce. The gentle smile Joyce gave her in return only fueled the irritability that had been eating at her all day.

All day? Try all week. All month. Hell, all *year*.

She took in a deep breath and closed her eyes. No. She had no time for a meeting. There were deadlines. There were contractors to yell at. The end of the quarter was fast approaching and she…

She what? She was already far ahead of her brother and sister in sales. What was driving her this time? Was she trying to break her own record?

"Erin?"

She glanced up, finding her father waiting. She nodded, then grabbed her phone before slamming her laptop shut.

* * *

As was the norm, Erin sat opposite Joyce at the table. Brent, the youngest of the three, sat at the end, twirling a pen between his fingers. She didn't know why. He never bothered taking notes. Her father sat down at the head of the table and scooted his chair closer. What was missing, however, was his secretary Carol Ann. There was never a meeting of any kind that she didn't attend, jotting down notes on her laptop as if her life depended on it.

"I'm making some changes." Her father folded his hands together on top of the table. "Overdue changes, I might add."

Erin arched an eyebrow but said nothing.

"Where's Carol Ann?" Brent asked as he dropped his pen on the table. "You know, she always sends an email with the recap of the meeting."

"No need. This won't take long." He cleared his throat. "I'm discontinuing the bonuses you all get on the number of projects that are completed within each quarter. From now on, everyone gets the same salary."

Erin's eyes widened. "*What*? Then what's the point?" She stood up quickly, nearly knocking her chair backward. "I bust my ass," she said loudly. "They produce half of what I do. Why should they get the same salary?"

"This competition has gotten out of hand," he said evenly. "You're likely to have a heart attack and die on us before you're forty. Now sit down, Erin."

Erin felt her hands shaking and she didn't know if it was from caffeine or anger. She pulled the chair closer with her foot and sat down again. Her head was starting to pound and she rubbed her temples.

"I didn't mean to imply that you would get the same pay. There will be a salary and there will be quotas to meet. Instead of getting a bonus for completions, you'll be docked for incompletions. Simple."

"Wait a minute," Brent said. "That's not fair."

"Of course it's fair. I should have done this years ago. Perhaps then the three of you would get along better and act like siblings instead of competitors. When Randy and I ran this business, there was never any of this squabbling that you all do. I'm sick of it."

"When Uncle Randy was involved, the company was in debt up to its ears," Joyce reminded him. "Thank God he didn't have any kids or we'd be fighting with them too."

Erin shook her head at Joyce's callousness. Randy was her father's only sibling. She'd still been in college when he was killed, crushed when a forklift lost its load of lumber. Of course, at the time, the lawsuit was the only thing that saved the company. Randy had no kids, no, but there had been two ex-wives who'd tried to cash in on his death.

"I'll have Carol Ann send the particulars out to you all. This isn't up for discussion. Now—Brent, you may be excused."

"Why do they get to stay?"

"Because, as usual, you are lagging far behind them. You only have four projects, Brent. Four. All four are behind schedule. Why don't you go work on those?" He held his hand up when he would have protested. "You're dismissed."

Brent shuffled out of the room, tossing daggers with his eyes at both her and Joyce. Her father stood up and went to the bar, pouring them all a glass of water.

"Erin?"

"Yes, sir?"

"You're not going to like what I'm about to say, but this too is not up for discussion."

She felt her brow furrowing. *Now what?*

"You need a break."

"A break? Like...a vacation?"

"A lengthy vacation, if you want to call it that."

She felt panic about to set in. What? Was he firing her?

"We're worried about you," Joyce said gently. "You don't sleep, you don't eat. When's the last time you've looked in the mirror, Erin?"

"What are you talking about? I sleep. I eat."

"You live off of Red Bull, bourbon, and cigarettes. You're a shell of yourself. You're wasting away to nothing."

"I'm not—"

"Nobody wants to work with you anymore, Erin," her father said bluntly.

She turned to her him. "What are you saying?"

"The contractors. You push too hard. You're on their ass every day. No one wants to work with you. We can't afford to lose contractors, Erin."

"The more I push, the quicker they get finished. They can go off to another job sooner. It's a win for both of us."

Her father came and sat down beside her. "I'm worried about your health, honey. Joyce is right. When's the last time you've truly looked at yourself in the mirror? Because I'll be frank. You look like hell. Your eyes are bloodshot. You smell like cigarettes and booze. You're going to kill yourself if you don't stop." He shook his head. "Why in the world did you start smoking?"

Joyce, too, came around the table, sitting beside her. They had her surrounded and she felt like she was suffocating. Yeah, she'd looked in the mirror. She didn't recognize herself. And yeah, she felt like hell too. So she had a drink at lunch? She needed it. And in the evenings? Yeah, she may have a drink or two in the evenings. Or three or four. But what was she to do? There was stress to deal with. There were deadlines. There were projects to complete. There were contractors to yell at.

"I found a place," Joyce said. "For you to go to."

"A…a place?" She pushed away from the table, escaping the claustrophobia from being between the two of them. "A *place*?" She pointed her finger at Joyce. "You're out of your goddamn mind if you think I'm going to rehab or something. Christ. I have a few drinks when I get home from work. Who doesn't?" She paced across the room. "And yeah, I keep a bottle at my desk. The stress gets to me sometimes." She opened up the cabinet above the bar, pointing to the shelf with four bottles of booze. "We all do it. I happen to know that you keep a bottle of scotch in your credenza," she said to her father.

"Yes. And that same bottle of scotch has been in there months now. It lasts me longer than a week or two, Erin."

"I don't have a goddamn drinking problem!" she nearly yelled. "And I'm not going to goddamn rehab!"

Joyce stood up. "I didn't say anything about rehab. But Dad's right. You're going to kill yourself. And as much as we fight and bicker here at the office, I do still love you. You need to get away, Erin. Get your life back. Put things back into perspective."

"I have things in order and my life is fine, thank you very much."

"You're only lying to yourself. You have *nothing* but this job. Nothing. It consumes you. Your friends have disappeared. Your—"

"They have not."

"Who's still around, Erin? Who? When's the last time you've been out to dinner with someone? To a party? To a movie? To a friend's house? When's the last time you've been on a *date*?"

"A date?" She stared at Joyce. A date? She didn't date because... Because there was... What was her name? Joyce must have seen the confusion on her face.

"It's been months since Jessica's been around." Her voice softened. "You didn't even know she was gone, did you?"

She looked away. "I've...I've been busy. I've—"

"You've been killing yourself," her father said. "My fault. This stupid competition thing that I dreamed up—I should have known. You got my drive, Erin. And my stubbornness. Brent got none of it, as you both know. I thought this would be a way to push him along, keep up with the two of you." He shook his head. "I had no idea what this would do to you, though."

She ran a hand through her hair. "I'm fine, Dad."

"You're not fine, Erin. You're not going to talk your way out of it this time." He paused. "I'll fire you if I have to."

She felt a lump in her throat and she tried to swallow it down. "Fire me?" She would shrivel up and die if he did that. She had nothing else. She had no one. This job... Joyce was right. She had nothing *but* this job. "Okay." She blinked several times, shocked to feel tears threatening. "I'll...I'll do whatever you want."

He nodded at her. "Three months."

Her eyes widened. "Three *months*? I can't be away three months." She pointed at the door. "I've got ten—"

"I know what your projects are. I'm going to personally handle them while you're away. This isn't negotiable, Erin. This is final."

Was he serious? She turned her back to him and squeezed her eyes closed, trying to make sense of it all. Her mind was a jumbled mess for some reason. Might have been that shot of bourbon she'd had a while ago instead of lunch. Apparently it had gone straight to her head.

"Erin?"

She turned back around. "You can't make me do this. I'm a grown-ass woman. You can't send me away as if I'm a child. Not for three goddamn months!"

Joyce came over to her. "It's like a vacation, Erin. God knows you could use one. It's in New Mexico. It sounds lovely."

"New Mexico?" She narrowed her eyes. "*New Mexico?*" She shook her head. "No. No, no, no. No way. I'm not going."

Her father pushed away from the table with a weary sigh and stood up. "I'll let you two iron out the details."

"Didn't you hear me? I'm not going!"

He stared at her, his eyes hard. "Go there, Erin. Or we'll arrange a clinic somewhere—a rehab, as you said—where you can have counseling. That would have been my choice, but Joyce suggested this. These are your two options. It's your decision on which you choose." He pointed at her quickly, then motioned to the door. "You're not staying here. I've already had your access removed, disabled your accounts, passwords—the works. You're out of here. Effective immediately."

She felt her breath leave her, felt her throat close up. "Dad? Please?"

"I'm sorry, Erin. I love you too much to watch you become... become *this*," he said, motioning to her. "You're...you're a mess. I hardly recognize you." He moved closer to her. "I'm sorry to be so blunt, honey. I really am. That pretty, carefree girl you once were, that easy, happy woman you grew up to be—she's long gone. You look...You look ten years older than you are. The stress is etched across your face, your eyes are lifeless. You've shriveled up to next to nothing. Your unhappiness shows, Erin. It's there for all to see. This *job* isn't worth it. We've tried for the last year to get you to slow down. Nothing's worked." He held his hands out.

"So I'm sorry, but yes, I'm forcing you—grown-ass woman that you are—to take a break. Three months. Your sister found a place that she thinks would be great for you. You should hear her out." She stood stiffly as he hugged her. "I love you. I know you don't like me very much right now, but I love you." When he pulled away, his eyes were serious. "This is hard for us too, Erin. But it's for the best." He gave a rather curt nod and turned and left them.

Her hands were shaking as she pulled a bottle from the cabinet, intending to pour herself a stiff drink. Joyce stopped her.

"Please don't. I want my little sister back. And you—you're not her anymore."

Erin buried her face in her hands. How had it come to this? When did she become so obsessed with beating the numbers? Beating Joyce? When did she become so obsessed with the job?

"I'm good at what I do," she said weakly.

"Yes, you are. Too good. Maybe that's the problem. You can juggle multiple projects. You can coordinate and manage the contractors like no one else. You can negotiate contracts in your sleep. You've got it down to a science. But you can't control the weather. You can't control lumber prices or whether stone gets delivered on time. You can't control *everything*, Erin. Sometimes, we get behind. You used to be able to handle that, you took it in stride. But now? You push and push and push, trying to catch up until you break everyone around you. Dad was telling the truth. The contractors—they don't want to work for you anymore. You know why, Erin? Because you make them miserable. No matter how much money they make, how much you make, everyone is still miserable. Including you."

She sank down into a chair, suddenly so very tired. She'd slept for a few hours last night—two, maybe three. She'd been poring over spreadsheets, trying to find a way to get those three houses back on track. Poring over spreadsheets like she'd been doing for the last few weeks. She took a deep breath, leaning her head back as she stared at the ceiling. Yes, how had it come to this? When had she turned into this crazy, hard-to-get-along-with, demanding workaholic? When had she turned into this person that no one liked?

Was that why Sarah had left her? Not just left, no. She'd been in such a hurry to get away, she'd left more than half her things behind in her haste. She didn't leave the dog behind, though. Nope. She took the little yappy thing with her when she flew off to the East Coast to be with her new lover. Who knew she'd miss the stupid little thing so much?

She looked over at Joyce, who was watching her thoughtfully.

"I have been miserable," she admitted quietly.

"I know. It's been well over a year, Erin. You're killing yourself."

She closed her eyes for a second, looking inward. "Okay. So tell me about New Mexico."

CHAPTER THREE

The bright sunshine felt good on her skin as she pedaled along the bumpy dirt road toward Stella's house. It felt good, but she'd rather be at home, alone. She hated these monthly get-togethers with "the tribe," as Stella called them. But after all these years, she'd grown to tolerate them.

She'd moved to Stella's Eagle Bluff Ranch seven years ago last month. Even before her little cabin was built, she'd broken ground on her garden, as she'd been instructed to do. Growing your own food, being resilient, was one of the requirements to living out here.

"Womyn's land," Stella called it. She'd purchased the land—all seven hundred acres of it—over forty years ago and had retreated from society along with her lover at the time. They'd both been from Los Angeles and didn't know the first thing about living off the land. Sustainable living had always been rule number one, however.

Rule number two? Women only. At first, lesbians only. In the last twenty years, she'd relaxed that rule, but there were still only two straight women who lived there. Stella had other rules too. Being vegetarian. She'd adapted to that rule, even though occasionally she'd eat fish when she was lucky enough to catch a trout in the creek. And like the other women here, yes, she'd retreated from society, but she wasn't completely cut off. She had satellite—she had Internet and TV. Not that she used either all that much.

"Hey, Mel," Angela called from Stella's front porch. "Thought you were going to be a no-show."

Melanie leaned her bike against the porch railing, noting that the white paint was starting to chip in places. She loosened her backpack and smiled at Angela as she walked up the steps.

"I wouldn't miss it for the world," she lied. "It's one of the few times I get to see everyone."

"We have two guests coming next week. Stella wants to go over that before we have dinner."

"Two?" She frowned. "It's not my turn, is it?" she asked hopefully. She hated when she had to host.

"No. It's Lindee and Pat's turn and then Rachel's."

Melanie nodded with relief. "Right." Then she laughed quietly. "Rachel? Poor guest."

"I know. But Rachel would get her feelings hurt if we skipped her."

Rachel was the oldest of the group at eighty-two. She'd lived out here thirty-nine years. Alone for thirty-eight of them. Rachel's hobby was knitting. And inevitably, when it was her turn to host the guest, she tried her darndest to teach them to knit and sew and even quilt. She also ate nothing but beans and vegetables. Every day. Every meal.

The others usually took bets to see how long a guest would last with Rachel before requesting a change. Two days was usually the max. She'd seen some run after only one day.

"There you are. Come in, come in." Stella beckoned, waving them inside.

Everyone else was already there, crowded into her living room. There were seventeen ladies who called Eagle Bluff home. Melanie was the youngest at thirty-seven. Angela was the closest to her in age at fifty-six. The others were all in their sixties and seventies, including Stella at seventy-five.

"I just love this time of year. It's so nice to have guests with us, isn't it?" Stella glided gracefully across the room, her lithe body belying her age. "We have two coming next week. One has been scheduled for months already, but the other just contacted me on Thursday. Well, her sister contacted me." She stood in front of the fireplace, getting everyone's attention. "She is booked with us for three whole months," she said to gasps from some of the women.

"Three months? Whatever for?" Valerie asked.

"Well, I didn't ask, of course. Maybe she's interested in joining us out here and is looking to get a feel for it." Stella waved her hand. "Doesn't matter, does it? At five thousand dollars a month, that will surely help our coffers, won't it?"

Melanie had found that most of the guests who came to Eagle Bluff were looking for a spiritual connection of some sort, looking for some meaning in their lives. Very few came here for what Stella had originally intended—an extension of rehab. Stella had started hosting guests after her niece had stayed two months, way back in the late eighties. Her niece had been in rehab for drug use, and Stella's sister had been afraid she'd relapse. Since no drugs or alcohol were allowed out here and they were more than an hour's drive to a town of any size, Stella had offered to put the niece up for a while. It had been such a success—and money was tight—that Stella started advertising in some of the gay papers in nearby large cities. It had never taken off quite like she had envisioned, but they had enough guests each year, mostly during the summer and fall, to add to the "coffers" as Stella called it. Enough to keep them afloat, anyway. She knew a lot of the houses needed repairs, but there weren't enough funds for that.

"Lindee, I've got you and Pat lined up for our first guest, Melissa Haywood. She's coming to us all the way from Seattle. She'll be with us for three nights. I'll be picking her up on Monday." Stella cleared her throat. "Rachel? Are you up for a guest?"

"I believe it's my turn, isn't it? I so look forward to having the company. And for three months? Won't that be delightful?"

Melanie smiled at her words. No way would someone last three months with Rachel. Her smile faded. She knew that it would be her turn after Rachel, which meant she'd be hosting the guest for the bulk of the three months. She wondered if Stella had intentionally set it up that way. Lindee and Pat—her partner of forty-something years—were also in their seventies, but she supposed it would be asking a lot for them to host someone for that long. Most of the guests who came out here rarely stayed longer than a week.

"Erin Ryder," Stella continued. "She's coming to us from Houston. I'll be picking her up on Thursday. Now—who wants to ride with me and do their monthly shopping? We can split it up. Some on Monday, some on Thursday."

Melanie looked out the window, letting the conversations around her fade to the background. It had taken her nearly a year to get used to doing her grocery shopping only once a month. That was when she'd still been trying to cook based on her old lifestyle. Now? Now she did pretty much what the others did—ate seasonal and out of her garden. She'd also become very proficient at canning vegetables so the wintertime meals weren't quite as meager as they'd once been.

She looked at the puffy white clouds outside the window, wondering when the daily afternoon rains would come. The monsoon season usually didn't start until July. Living here along Eagle Creek, they weren't quite as dependent on the rain as other places. But the rain provided relief from the heat, and it filled the smaller creeks, which were usually dry by the time the monsoons came. It would be nice to take her morning walk along Mule Creek while listening to the water trickle over the rocks. By late August, the summer rains would dwindle to short, quick showers, and by early September, they'd be gone completely.

"You're awfully quiet," Angela said as she nudged her arm. "Everything okay?"

Melanie gave her a quick smile. "Yes."

"I made a berry pie. What did you bring?"

"A squash dish. My yellows are really coming in."

"I got my garden in later than you, I think. I've only picked one so far."

And so it went. Melanie got swallowed up in the group, all asking—and telling—how their gardens were faring so far, who had lost a chicken to the coyotes, whose momma goat gave birth, who had vegetables to trade and so on. That was usually the extent of their visiting at these monthly dinners.

These were her people now, her tribe. They all got along well enough, she supposed. She often wondered, if Stella didn't hold these, how many of the ladies would gather on their own. There were five couples. The rest were single. Most everyone had been here for decades except for her and Angela. Angela had joined them two weeks after her fiftieth birthday, three days short of Melanie's first-year anniversary. How many times during that first year had she wondered if this had been a mistake or not? How many times had she been ready to throw in the towel?

"Melanie, honey, I need your help one day this week, if you're free."

She nodded at Rebecca. "Of course."

"I've got those limbs hanging over the garden. They've gotten so big, they're shading my corn."

"I'll take care of it for you."

And she would. She was the youngest and most able-bodied. She and Angela did most of the heavy lifting, helping out where needed. She knew Stella worried about them all getting older with no "young blood" coming up the pipeline.

It had been six years since Angela had moved there, the last to join them. Out in the real world, times were different now. There weren't that many wanting to escape from a heterosexual society like Stella had done all those years ago when she and her lover had retreated out here where they could live free and open, without any prejudices or homophobia. Things had changed, though, and gay marriage was legal. The reasons for moving out here now would be completely different than the reasons Stella, Rachel, and the others had come for.

The reasons might be different, but the outcome was the same.

To escape.

Isn't that what she had done?

CHAPTER FOUR

"You really didn't have to come with me."

"Dad strongly suggested it." Joyce glanced at her. "He was afraid that when you landed in Albuquerque instead of heading south you'd take off for Vegas or something."

She looked out the window as Joyce drove them into the Gila National Forest. It was prettier than she'd been expecting, although she really hadn't had time to research the area. She hadn't had time to research anything, really. It seemed like once she'd agreed to this—forced—vacation, Joyce had had her packed and on a plane in a matter of days. She hadn't spoken to her father since that day in the office. He'd tried to contact her, but she ignored his calls. Her emotions were still too…too raw.

"Have I told you that I don't want to do this?"

"About a hundred times."

"I'm worried about my projects."

"Dad can handle them. He managed quite well before we all came on board."

She let out a loud sigh as she again stared out the window.

"Looks like Colorado," Joyce mused.

"I wouldn't know."

"That's right. I forgot your idea of a vacation is New York City or some faraway beach destination crawling with tourists. Carl and I went to Colorado three years ago, you know."

"I remember. You took some train or something."

"From Durango to Silverton. Fantastic views. This makes me want to go back."

Yeah, she'd rather be heading to a crowded, touristy beach right now. Not the East Coast, though. That brought back too many memories. Sarah was the one who had loved the city. They traveled there twice a year, and yes, that's where Sarah had met her new lover. Erin doubted she'd ever want to return to New York again.

"This is kinda out in the middle of nowhere, isn't it?"

"I think that's the point, sis."

"I'm going to go stark raving mad if I'm stuck out here for three months. I can't believe you talked me into this."

"You know what the alternative was."

"Why couldn't you have found a beach resort in Cancun or something?"

"So you could do what? Lay on the beach and drink rum for three months? Dad was insistent that you get away somewhere safe. Somewhere where you can clean up—physically and mentally."

"I know you both think I have a drinking problem, but I don't. I've managed the last two days without a drop."

"I'm not saying that you needed a twelve-step program or something, Erin, but you were using alcohol to cope with your stress and that's never a good thing. Not when you have such enormous stress as you had. Self-induced stress, I might add."

"I'm competitive, what can I say?"

"It was more than that and you know it. You went overboard. You made a lot of money, you made our company a lot of money, but at what cost?"

"I'm well aware of what the cost was."

"You're talking about Sarah, I suppose?"

She nodded. "Of course I'm talking about Sarah. She was the love of my life. I lost her."

"Oh, Erin, she was *so* not the love of your life."

"She was, yeah. And I ran her off. Not only did she no longer love me, she no longer even *liked* me."

"You did it for her."

"Did what?"

"Changed, Erin. You changed because of her. *For* her. You became this…this person that none of us knew anymore. She's the one who wanted the big house. The elaborate pool. The new car every other year. The four expensive vacations you took annually. She's the one who pushed you to work every day. She always wanted more and you tried to give it to her. I'm sorry to be so blunt, Erin, but—emotionally—she sucked you dry. I don't think there was any love involved. She was a taker, not a giver." Joyce reached across the console and squeezed her arm. "I had hoped that when she left, you'd change back to your old self, but no—it got worse. Much worse."

Was that how it had been? Her working longer, harder, trying to please Sarah? No. She'd done it willingly. She wanted those things too. She liked the big house, the pool, the new cars. She liked dashing off to New York City twice a year. She loved the cruises they took to the beach resorts in Mexico. They had fun. It was always fun with Sarah.

"It wasn't Sarah's fault."

"Why are you defending her?"

"I know you never liked her."

"No one liked her, Erin. She was using you. Everyone could see that except you."

"No!" Erin said forcefully. "She didn't use me. I loved her. She broke my heart when she left."

Joyce stared at her and slowly shook her head. "I wish you could see what she did to you. She *used* you, Erin. She turned you into…into *this*," she said, motioning at her.

"She loved me. For a while…she loved me. I know she did."

"She zapped the life out of you, Erin! Look at you! I'm taking you to some remote ranch in New Mexico, for God's sake, so you can sleep and eat and…and detox!"

Erin looked at her sharply. "Detox? So you and Dad really thought I needed rehab?"

"Dad did, yes. In your case, I think the detox is more for caffeine than booze," she said, looking at the Red Bull Erin was holding. "I think you're addicted to those things."

"I am not," she lied.

"You'll find out soon enough, I suppose."

"What does that mean?"

"Like you said—it's in the middle of nowhere. I don't think you'll be able to run to a convenience store on the corner and get your fix."

* * *

Three hours later, she stood in the parking lot of a local grocery store, her eyes darting between four gray-haired, smiling women and Joyce. She shook her head slowly.

No, no, no, *no!*

There was no way she was getting in a vehicle with them. No way was she letting them take her away to some remote ranch in the middle of nowhere.

No way in hell. Nope. She wasn't doing it.

She looked at Joyce and shook her head. "No."

Joyce met her gaze. "Yes."

CHAPTER FIVE

"I see you checking your phone, dear. Did your sister not tell you?"

Erin looked over at the woman driving—Stella. She raised her eyebrows. "Tell me what?"

"We don't get service out here for cell phones."

"*What?* Are you kidding me?"

Stella smiled broadly. "It's part of our rustic charm. A few of us have phone lines, though. If there's an emergency or you want to talk to your sister, you can use my phone."

"These young people with all these fancy gadgets they bring with them. Not a one of them works out here," came a voice from the back.

Erin glanced over her shoulder at the three elderly ladies in the backseat. She didn't remember their names. She'd been at a complete loss for words when Stella and her crew—all gray-haired grannies—had met them in Silver City. They'd been to the grocery store, they'd said, and the older model Suburban's third seat had been filled with bags. Colorful, homemade shopping bags that she assumed the ladies had sewn themselves.

She had looked at Joyce, on the verge of begging her not to leave, on the verge of tears. But Joyce had hugged her tightly and told her she loved her.

"See you right back here at this spot in three months. Right at this spot."

"Please don't leave me here," she'd whispered. *"Please?"*

"It's going to be fine, Erin. The time will whiz by. Work on your health," Joyce had said. *"In here,"* she said, touching her chest. *"And in here,"* she added, touching her head.

Then Erin had been whisked away, her luggage stowed in the back. Stella, surprisingly strong for her size, had tossed her bags on top of two sacks of what she'd called "hen scratch." Whatever that was.

"So, really… No cell service? No Internet?"

"What's Internet?"

"Oh, Rachel. Remember when Melanie was explaining it? You *go places* on computers."

"Melanie set up our website, Rachel. She showed it to us all one day, remember?"

Erin grabbed the bridge of her nose and squeezed. Where in the hell were they taking her? No cell service? No freaking Internet? How could they possibly *live* like that?

She looked again at the driver. Stella. She was small, petite, her gray hair cut short above her ears. She moved gracefully, though, and she seemed rather spry for her age, which she'd proudly announced to Erin when they'd met. Seventy-five. The ladies in the back were surely in their seventies as well. She turned her head, finding all three looking at her, all smiling.

"You get to bunk with me," the oldest of the three said. Rachel. The one who didn't know what the Internet was. "We're going to have so much fun, Erin. Do you knit? Sew?"

Erin breathed deeply as she turned away. Knit? She was so going to kill Joyce. She'd be lucky to make it three days out here, much less three damn months.

"What is that you're drinking, dear?"

Erin glanced at the Red Bull she had shoved between her legs. "It's a…an energy drink."

"Energy?"

"Caffeine."

"Like coffee?"

"No. This is…well, this one is cranberry. It's sweet. Like… like juice, I guess. It helps you stay awake."

Stella blinked at her. "Why do you need help staying awake?"

"Because I don't always get enough sleep, I guess."

"I sleep dusk to dawn," Rachel supplied. "Same as the chickens."

"You don't have chickens anymore, Rachel."

"Well, I know that, of course. I'm just saying…"

Erin cleared her throat. "So, what is it that I'll be doing out here?"

"Doing? Well, living, of course," Stella said with a smile. "Hopefully better than you were. Your sister indicated that you had some healing to do."

Healing? She should have researched this place before she'd agreed to it. Joyce had only hit on the highlights. Of course, like she'd said. What was her alternative? But really, what *was* this place they were taking her to?

"What I mean is, what do you offer here for amenities? Is it like a dude ranch or something?"

"Dude ranch? No, no, no." Stella gave her a good-natured smile. "Our guests come here to get away from their life for a while. Most find they connect with their spiritual side. Or a higher power. There's no stress out here, Erin. We live a simple life, but it's so rewarding. You'll have time to meditate, to take long walks, to read. To do whatever you please. Well, within reason, of course. We're a loving community and we all help one another out. Rachel, your host, is eighty-two. It would nice if you helped her in her garden, for instance."

"Garden?"

"Yes, her vegetable garden, although it's very small this year. She doesn't keep chickens anymore, like Valerie said, but everyone shares with one another. Now, we do have a few rules, Erin. I assume your sister went over it all with you."

"Rules? No, she didn't mention rules."

"Oh. Well, the most obvious rule: No men are allowed. Now, some of our ladies have family members—brothers and such—and they're welcome to visit, but they can't stay on the ranch overnight. Women only."

"Women only?"

"Yes. It's womyn's land. And there are absolutely no drugs or alcohol allowed either. Why, I haven't had a sip of alcohol since I was in my twenties. And we are a compassionate, peaceful group too. We don't kill or eat animals. Animals are our friends."

"You're all…vegetarian?" she asked weakly.

"Oh, yes. Your body will love you for it, Erin. You'll thrive out here. And I don't mean to be rude, dear, but you could stand to put some meat on your bones." She laughed. "Meat! See what I did there? We don't eat it!"

I'm going to *kill* Joyce, she thought as she turned away from Stella's smile and the laughter coming from the backseat. She stared out the window broodingly. No meat? No booze? No Red Bull? Did they even drink coffee?

They were between the mountains now, and the terrain was brown and arid here with only a smattering of trees. Joyce had made it sound like she'd be staying in paradise, along a lush, flowing creek with high mountains all around. A vacation in paradise, she'd said. There were mountains around, yes, but there was no lush green paradise to be seen. And Joyce had conveniently failed to mention Stella's *rules*.

She leaned her head against the window, her chest tightening with emotion. She was alone. She was depressed. She felt like crying. She closed her eyes tightly, afraid she *would* actually cry. She was thirty-three years old. How would she explain tears to these women?

She opened her eyes again when she heard the Suburban's blinker. Stella slowed, then turned to the right. She stared out at the passing scenery, noting the dry, arid brown was changing again. Tall pine trees now lined the road and there was a river beside them, its water bouncing over huge rocks on its way down the mountain. Joyce had been right. There were no convenience stores to be seen.

"We follow the river nearly ten miles before we get to our property," Stella said. "The river doesn't flow on our land, but Eagle Creek does. It's a nice creek, almost as big as the river here. We'll cross a bridge a little ways up, right where the creek meets the river. Our property is on the other side of the bridge. As a rule, we venture into Silver City once a month at least. Other than that, we live out here in peace. It's so beautiful. You're going to love it, Erin."

Love it? Oh, she was so *not* going to love it. What in the world was she going to do out here for three months? No alcohol? No meat? No steaks or burgers? No cell phone. No *Internet*?

Jesus. Where were they taking her? To hell?

CHAPTER SIX

Melanie sat down and leaned back against the tree—a large ponderosa. Her tree. After seven years, she'd nearly rubbed the bark smooth where she rested. It was her usual stopping place when she took this particular walk along the dry creek bed. Fred, the old mutt of a dog that she'd inherited when she moved here, plopped down beside her.

Fred was a nondescript white dog with half his tail missing. He was at least fifteen years old. He wasn't particularly friendly or sociable, but he always alerted her whenever predators came near her little farm. When he was around, that is. She may have inherited him, but he made the rounds, staying a night or two, then moving on to someone else's house. When he was around—like this morning—he followed her when she went hiking. When he'd had enough, he simply turned around and went back home.

Yes, home. The little cabin she'd built had become her first true home, she admitted. It wasn't that long ago that she feared she'd never find peace, much less a place to call home.

When she had escaped Phoenix, she thought she'd go someplace greener, wetter...cooler. She wanted to take at least a year, maybe two, to get her head on straight. She smiled, remembering when she'd said those very words to her therapist. The solution seemed simple enough: quit her job, sell the house and everything she owned, and live somewhere on the cheap. Her idea of cheap and real life didn't mesh, though. She'd stumbled upon the idea of living remotely—on womyn's land—after reading an article about a group of lesbians living in Kentucky. She'd researched it and it had sounded ideal. She'd contacted them, had even gone out to visit. But she found it too different from what she was used to. Too green, too wet... too buggy. And the women? Much like here, actually. Sixties and seventies. She didn't get a good feel from it, however. More research landed her on Stella's doorstep a month later.

She took her straw hat off and tossed it on the ground beside her, pausing to run her fingers through her damp hair. The breeze felt good and she leaned her head back, looking up into the trees. She spotted a fuzzy tuft of thistle floating lazily overhead and watched as the light wind carried it along, missing pine boughs by inches as it stayed afloat. It flitted across the dry creek, finally getting stuck in one of the thick junipers on the other side. She stared at it for a moment longer, wondering how far it had traveled. As she stared, the wind lifted it again. She smiled as it floated out of sight...continuing on its journey. With a contented sigh, she picked her hat up and settled it back on her head.

She stood up then and nudged Fred with her hiking stick. "Coming or going?" He struggled to his feet, then shook himself. She motioned back down the trail from which they'd come. "Go on home."

He watched her as she walked on, then she saw him lie down again. Apparently he was going to wait on her to return. She really didn't have time for a hike. She'd picked a huge basket of green beans that morning and needed to start her canning. There always seemed to be something to do, but she'd been craving a hike. Mainly because she knew her free time would be limited fairly soon.

Because Stella had warned her that she didn't think the new guest—Erin Ryder—would last more than a day with Rachel. That meant she would be dropped in Melanie's lap sooner rather than later.

"I get the feeling she didn't come here willingly," Stella had told her when she'd come by to visit. "When I left her at Rachel's place earlier, I thought she was going to cry. She seemed completely lost and so, so sad. It almost broke my heart."

"Why come at all if not willingly?"

"I don't know. Her sister brought her to Silver City. It appears that the sister did all of the planning. Why, Erin didn't even know about our rules, for goodness sake. She seemed shocked. And no cell phone service? Why, you'd think the world was coming to an end."

Melanie smiled as she walked on. Yeah, she knew that feeling. If she hadn't fallen in love with the place, that may have been a deal breaker. She had been as attached to her phone as anyone. However, she'd found if she hiked to the top of the bluff behind her house—and the weather conditions were perfect—she got enough of a signal to call someone. Not that there was anyone to call. Not anymore. She'd been away too long now.

Internet? Yes, she was the only one out here who had it. Satellite Internet was better than nothing, but it was sometimes slow and sometimes nonexistent, depending on the weather. And she and Angela were the only ones to have satellite TV, which she rarely turned on except during the long winter nights. Stella still made use of the old antenna on her house, which got her all of two stations. Some of the others didn't have TV at all.

But that was another of Stella's rules—no sharing the Internet with guests. They were here to "get away from all that nonsense" was her mantra. And actually, that was usually the case. Stella was always upfront with the guests before they came. No cell phone service, no Internet, no nothing.

"Maybe she's sick," Stella had offered. "Maybe she got a bad diagnosis. Cancer, maybe. Wouldn't that be awful?" She'd waved her hand in the air. "I suppose you'll find out soon enough, dear. I fear Rachel is going to run the young thing off."

"Young? How young?"

"Oh, honey, at my age, everyone is young. She did look a bit unhealthy, though. Thin as a rail, clothes just hanging off her. Hard to say how old she is. Such a shame. She was probably once very pretty. I hope we can help heal her."

Melanie took a deep breath and looked up into the sky as she released it. There were enough of them here that they usually only had to host once per year, two at the most. If Stella lowered her cost, she'd probably have more customers, but the high prices kept the "riffraff" out, she claimed. And of course, if she actually advertised, they might have more guests too. Most of their visitors were from word-of-mouth or repeat customers and the rare ones who stumbled upon their rather simple website. Honestly, Melanie was thankful Stella didn't do more. She'd become somewhat of a hermit, she supposed. Having to host complete strangers for a week at a time—or even a long weekend—took her out of her comfort zone.

Three months?

Oh, she really didn't know how she was going to last three months. Her cabin was too small for extended company. She'd only added the second bedroom and tiny, tiny bathroom to the plans after Stella had insisted. Most of the guests, though, were never really underfoot. They went out on their own, hiking and exploring, usually only coming back in for meals.

There was the one time she'd hosted a couple, both in their fifties, who wanted to experience the farm life. They thought maybe they might want to move out there some day. They hadn't been interested in hiking. They'd been interested in the garden. Melanie had put them to work and after three days they'd decided that living in El Paso wasn't so bad after all.

She wondered what Erin Ryder would be like?

"Guess I'm about to find out."

CHAPTER SEVEN

"No."

"It's not hard to learn, Erin. Why, in the three months you'll be here, you could have a whole afghan knitted. Maybe even two, if you really work at it," Rachel said with enthusiasm.

Erin pushed the beans around on her plate, a plate that Rachel had fixed for her. Besides the beans—which were bland and tasteless—there was squash and broccoli, all cooked to a soft mush. Nothing else. There wasn't even a saltshaker on the table. She put her fork down.

"I think I'm full, Rachel."

"Full? Why, you haven't eaten even half of it. No wonder you're so thin," she fussed. "As Stella said, we need to get some meat on your bones."

She stood up anyway and picked up her plate. "What should I do with this?"

"Don't you want to save it for later? Seems a waste to throw it away."

Erin put the plate beside the sink. Rachel could do with it as she pleased. "I'm going to bed."

"Bed? It's not even seven o'clock."

Erin ignored that comment and shuffled off to her room. She closed the door, then leaned back against it, staring at her bags, which were still at the foot of the bed. A bed that was covered in a godawful flowery spread. She wasn't really surprised when a tear ran down her cheek. Instead of wiping it away, she moved onto the bed. She curled into a ball and clutched a pillow to her.

Her mind felt heavy. Her body felt heavy. So heavy, she was afraid the weight might crush her. After Sarah left her, she didn't think she could possibly be any lonelier than she'd been. But right here, right now…

This felt different somehow. Much worse. Maybe because she was out of her element, away from home, away from work, away from…who? Her friends? No. As Joyce had said, there were no friends anymore. Who did she have? Her dad? Joyce? Was that it?

Yes. That was it. Them. And the job. But right here, right now she had no one, not even the job.

She closed her eyes, no longer trying to keep her tears inside.

* * *

"I'm sorry, but I can't stay with her," she said as quietly as she could the next morning. Stella had come to check on her, and while Rachel poured them all a cup of coffee, decaf no less, Erin had leaned closer. "You've got to get me out of here."

"Of course, dear. You're paying a pretty penny to be here. I won't ask you to stay somewhere if you don't want to."

A pretty penny? How much *was* she paying? Joyce had taken care of everything. Truth be told, if Erin had to look at a map, she wouldn't even know where she was.

Stella leaned closer too. "What is it that you don't like, dear?"

Erin blinked at her. It would be easier to tell her what she did like, which was nothing. "She served me beans and broccoli for dinner last night. We had the exact same thing for breakfast. She only has decaffeinated coffee and my head is about to split in two. There is no TV. She wants me to *knit*," she finished. "Please. I need someplace else."

"Here's your coffee," Rachel said, putting a cup in front of her. Rachel turned to Stella, nearly beaming. "I think I've just about got her talked into knitting. We're going to have so much fun."

If her head didn't hurt so much, she would almost feel sorry for leaving. Rachel was obviously lonely and wanted the company. But her head did hurt and she didn't feel sorry for her. Her hand was shaking as she took a sip of the useless decaffeinated coffee which had been diluted even further with cream. God, why hadn't she stashed some Red Bulls in her bag?

Stella patted Rachel's hand lovingly. "Rachel, dear, I hate to do this to you, but I'm going to have to pull Erin away from here."

Rachel's face fell. "What do you mean?"

"Well, she…she—"

"I hate beans," Erin said bluntly. "I hate decaf coffee. I hate broccoli. I might use the knitting needles as a weapon."

"But…"

"I'm sorry." She rubbed her temple. "I'm having major caffeine withdrawals—and I'm likely to go postal if I don't get a real cup of coffee. Soon. Very soon."

Rachel frowned. "Go postal? I don't understand."

"I think she means she's going to throw a hissy fit and maybe start throwing things or something. Or worse, come after you with the knitting needles."

Rachel touched her chest, her eyes wide. "Oh, my."

Thirty minutes later, they were in Stella's truck bouncing down the crude road, leaving Rachel standing on her porch, watching them.

"I'm sorry," Erin said again.

"Nothing to apologize for, dear. Rachel has lost her zest for cooking, I'm afraid. She cooks up a big batch of beans every Sunday and eats on that all week. It suits her, but I'm afraid she doesn't realize that she needs to offer her guests something more."

"Why did you put me with her then?"

"Well, it was her turn."

"Her turn?"

"We take turns hosting, you see. Whoever's turn it is, they get a percentage of the money you're paying—since they're providing you with room and board—and the rest goes into the general fund. That money is used on repairs and such, whatever is needed."

"And that's your sole source of income?"

"We make out just fine. Expenses are minimal, for the most part."

"So...I don't really even know what this place is. My sister kinda found you."

"I figured as much. I own all the land. I bought it with my grandmother's inheritance. Seven hundred acres. When we accept someone new to the tribe, they're free to pick out their homestead. They're then responsible for their house, however they choose to live."

Erin frowned. "Why?"

Stella frowned too. "Why what, dear?"

"Why would someone live out here? Move here?"

Stella laughed. "I moved here forty-three years ago. Being a lesbian out there in the world," she said, motioning out the window, "was a scary thing back then. You couldn't live openly. I understand it's different today, but I wouldn't know, really. The only time I get off the ranch is when we go to Silver City to shop or to pick up guests."

"So you're all lesbians? Even Rachel?"

"Yes. Well, that's not actually a requirement any longer. A woman is a woman, I say. We have only two, however, who aren't like the rest of us. They're both in their late sixties now and perfectly content here with us."

"How many live here?"

"Seventeen of us left. At one time, we had nearly thirty. But some moved away—they missed family—and others passed on.

There's not much new blood coming in. That's why we were so excited when Melanie came here. She was a pretty young thing, barely thirty when she joined us. Then Angela came six years ago, I think it was. She's young too. Not yet sixty." She sighed wistfully. "The rest of us, we're getting on in age. Some, like Rachel, can barely tend to their gardens. I worry what's going to happen to us all. And God forbid if Mel or Angela moved away. I can't even think about that."

The main road curved to the left around a large pine, but Stella took a smaller, less used road to the right, hitting a hole that jolted them both. Stella glanced at her, a smile on her face.

"Are you...one of us, Erin?"

Erin grabbed the dash as they bounced through another hole. "One of you? Are you asking if I'm gay?"

"Lesbian, yes. In my day, gay referred to men."

"I see. Yes, I'm a lesbian. I assume that's why my sister picked this place. She thought I'd fit in."

"Are you looking to escape the world out there, Erin?" she asked almost excitedly. "We'd love—"

"No, no, no. This isn't for me, Stella. I'm a city girl."

Stella scoffed. "I was born and raised on the outskirts of Los Angeles. And Valerie, believe it or not, was from Manhattan. You can't get any more city than that."

Erin shook her head. "Sorry, no. I'm just here to do my time, then I'm gone."

"Do your time? Are you in trouble with the law?" she asked sharply. "Because your sister never—"

"No. I'm in trouble with my father. And my sister. Not the law."

"So you have a three-month 'sentence' then?"

"Something like that, yes."

"What did you do to land you out here?"

Erin stared out the window, noting they were following the creek again. She turned to Stella. "I guess I...I was trying to kill myself."

"Oh my."

CHAPTER EIGHT

Melanie wasn't really surprised to see Stella's old truck coming down the lane. She glanced at the coffeepot, which was nearly empty. She poured what remained into her cup and went about making another pot. Fred barked a couple of times, alerting her to company, then he headed back to his spot under the rosebushes.

She'd already tidied the cabin and got the guest room ready. She had a soup on the stove at a low simmer. She'd found soups to be a good starting point until she found out what her guests liked. Unlike most of the others who simply made their normal meals, she tried to be a little more accommodating to her guests' tastes.

With one more glance around the cabin, she went to the door, pausing to look at herself in the small mirror that was on the wall. She brushed at the blond hair that fell into her eyes and automatically tucked it behind one ear in what she knew was a nervous gesture. Then she took a deep breath and opened the door just as Stella was coming up the steps.

Melanie's gaze went past Stella, landing on a tall but very thin woman. Thin…gaunt almost. She had dark circles under her eyes and her brown hair hung limply—lifeless—around her face. Melanie stared at her for a moment, recognizing something—herself, perhaps?—in her dark eyes. She looked lost. Melanie wondered if Stella's guess that she was ill might indeed be correct. The clothes she wore appeared to be two sizes too large for her.

"Good morning," she said pleasantly.

"Good morning, dear." Stella stepped aside. "This is Erin Ryder. Things didn't work out with Rachel, I'm afraid. Erin, this is Melanie West. Everyone calls her Mel. I hope you'll be more comfortable here."

Melanie held her hand out to greet the other woman, but the woman's dark, hazel eyes looked past her. "Do you have any coffee? Real coffee? Please?"

Melanie lowered her hand with a quick glance at Stella. "Real coffee?"

"Not that decaf crap," the woman said bluntly.

"Oh. Yes."

Stella leaned closer. "Caffeine withdrawal. Headache. It's not pretty," she whispered loud enough for Erin to hear.

"I see. Of course." She pushed the door open fully. "Come in. I just made a fresh pot."

Erin walked in ahead of them both, heading directly for the kitchen and her coffee. Melanie closed the door, watching; Erin's hands were shaking as she poured a cup. The cabin was open, nothing separating the living room from the kitchen except a breakfast bar, as she called it. It could also be called a lunch and dinner bar as that was her only table.

"What's wrong with her?" Melanie whispered to Stella.

"I'm not sure. She's a little…well, grumpy."

"Great," she murmured.

"Let me get her bags, dear."

"I'll help you." Melanie glanced back at the woman who was leaning against her counter, holding the cup of coffee between both hands as if it was a life-sustaining elixir. And perhaps it was. She had a feeling this was going to be a very long three months.

"Oh, Mel. Now you know how Rachel is," Stella said as they walked off the porch. "Her and her beans. Poor Erin there got served last night's dinner for breakfast too."

"Yes, we all know how Rachel is. Why do you still continue to let her host? They never last. It seems to have gotten worse in the last few years."

"I know, but she so looks forward to the company."

Melanie laughed. "She must know that she runs them off. And this one? She looks…I don't know, frail—yet tough at the same time."

"She told me that this was a jail sentence for her. She doesn't want to be here, but it's something her father and sister are making her do." She leaned closer to her, her voice quiet. "She must have tried to commit suicide or something."

"*What?*" she asked sharply, her breath catching. "And you're dumping her off with me? I don't make a very good therapist, Stella."

"Who should I leave her with then?"

"How about Angela?"

Stella shook her head. "No. Angela has no patience."

"And I do?"

"Of course you do, Mel. We're all demanding of your time. There's so much we can't do anymore. You always come when we ask, never complaining."

"That's completely different. This? I don't do drama well. And this one? If she doesn't want to be here? There's going to be drama."

"Oh, Mel…you can handle her." She patted her hand reassuringly. "Perhaps you should skip beans for dinner, though."

With a sigh, she watched Stella drive off. Suicide? No. She could not handle that. She absolutely could not handle that. Then she turned to stare at the door. *Her* door. She took several deep breaths, then picked up two of the three bags of luggage and went inside. She found Erin Ryder still in the kitchen, staring out the window. Melanie followed her gaze, seeing the chickens scratching in what was left of the spring grasses.

"So…I'll take you to your room if you like." The woman—Erin—turned, and Melanie was shocked to see her blinking back tears. She set the bags down. "Are you okay?" she asked gently.

Erin cleared her throat before speaking. "Out of my element, I'm afraid." She wiped at a tear, embarrassment showing on her face. "I… Thank you for the coffee. I'm sorry I was so abrupt earlier."

Melanie raised her eyebrows. "Caffeine addiction?"

She nodded. "Besides coffee, I'm used to downing half a dozen Red Bulls a day." Then Erin paused. "Do you know what Red Bull is?"

Melanie laughed and picked up the bags again. "Yes. We're not completely cut off from the world out here. It's a disgusting tasting energy drink that I used to drink myself. You won't need that here. If you're tired, go to bed. Take a nap. Sleep in the hammock."

She went into the small bedroom and put the bags on the bed. When she turned, Erin was standing in the doorway.

"It's small, I'm afraid," she apologized. "But there's a private bath." She opened the door. "Shower only, but private."

Erin glanced into the bathroom and nodded, but said nothing.

"I'll bring in your other bag."

"I can get it."

They stood there looking at each other in silence, then Melanie moved to walk past her. "I understand you didn't get breakfast. I can scramble some eggs for you if you'd like."

"Actually, that would be wonderful, if you don't mind. I didn't eat much dinner last night." Erin moved the hair out of her eyes with a sigh. "I don't normally eat much anyway, but I usually have other things to occupy…"

"Other things?"

"Nothing."

Back in the kitchen, Melanie poured herself a cup of coffee. "I try to be accommodating regarding meals. Is there something you like more than others? Potatoes more than rice? Beans or tofu? Certain vegetables you don't like?"

"I like my steak medium rare. That's about the only way I eat beef. Or the occasional hamburger. I really prefer chicken."

Melanie's eyes widened. "What?"

A ghost of a smile touched Erin's face. "Kidding. Stella informed me that wasn't going to happen. You're a *compassionate* group out here."

"Are you saying you didn't know you'd be fed vegetarian fare?"

"I'm saying I didn't know a lot of things before I got here."

Melanie took a sip of coffee, then took the pan out of the drain, the pan that she'd used that morning for her own breakfast. She didn't know whether she should come right out and ask the woman why she was here or just pretend it was a normal situation. Because normal, it was not. Her usual guests were brimming with enthusiasm, barely wanting to take the time for chitchat in their haste to get outside and experience the solitude—the quiet—the peacefulness of this river valley.

Before she could ask, though, Erin went out to the porch to retrieve her remaining bag, and she took it silently into the bedroom. With a shrug, Melanie cracked two eggs into the pan, then took the lid off the soup and stirred it, then turned it off. She'd let it sit, undisturbed until lunchtime. The flavors would have ample time to mesh by then.

The scrambled eggs seemed like a meager offering, so she took out the masa and made a corn tortilla, flattening the dough ball in her press before heating it on the cast iron griddle she always used for her tortillas. She put the eggs inside and added a dollop of the green salsa she'd made two days ago. She hoped it wasn't too spicy for Erin. Not everyone liked things as hot as she did. She was about to take it into the bedroom but decided she didn't want to start that habit.

"Breakfast is ready," she called, placing the plate on the bar. "I'll be out in the garden if you need something."

She went out the kitchen door without waiting. She didn't like her space to be invaded in the first place. Hosting a guest was something she only tolerated, much like Stella's monthly dinners. Having a guest who wasn't overly friendly or enthused about being there would make for a dreadful experience, no doubt. Especially if she had…well…emotional issues.

She had a fear that Erin Ryder was going to expect to be entertained. Melanie had no plans to do any such thing. As far as she was concerned, the woman could sit in her room all day, bored to tears, if that was what she wanted.

CHAPTER NINE

Erin devoured the taco, the green sauce nice and spicy. She'd seen the chickens outside earlier and assumed that's where breakfast had come from. She didn't know the first thing about chickens or egg laying and she had no desire to learn. She took her plate to the sink and set it inside, wondering if she should wash it or not. The pan that Melanie had used was soaking in the sink and she simply put her plate on top of it.

She stood there at the window looking outside. It was only then—when she heard a bird singing—that it registered that the window was open. She glanced around, noting all the windows were open, letting in a gentle breeze from the outside. She also noted there were no curtains on the windows. She assumed there was no air conditioning and she wondered how hot it got inside the house during the summer. Of course, it was already June and it was still very pleasant. When she'd left Houston, it had been hot and humid, feeling like mid-summer. Up here though, the air was dry and much cooler.

She caught a glimpse of Melanie in what she assumed was her vegetable garden. She was pushing a wheelbarrow loaded with straw or something. Erin turned away from the window with a sigh and went back into her bedroom. It was smaller than the one at Rachel's, but at least she had her own bathroom. The room was...neutral, she thought. The bedspread was a brown and beige checked pattern, the curtains a light brown, the rug a darker brown. There was even a dark brown throw pillow on the bed. She wondered if this room had curtains—as opposed to the rest of the house—because it's where guests stayed. She sat on the edge of the bed, also wondering what in the hell she was going to do for the rest of the day.

That thought struck her as funny. Rest of the day? What about the rest of the week...the month?

She closed her eyes and lay back. At least she was away from Rachel and her knitting needles. Melanie seemed...well, normal. If you could call it normal to live out here, that is. She seemed close to her own age, maybe a little older. That was a plus although she wasn't sure why. It wasn't like she was trying to make friends with these people.

And she was cute. Surprisingly so. Why would someone like her—attractive, normal—be living out here, with all these elderly women, away from everything? Away from people?

She got fully on the bed and rested her head on a pillow, suddenly feeling tired. At least her headache had subsided. It was now just a dull ache, not the pounding that was threatening to split her head in two earlier.

CHAPTER TEN

Melanie finished off her bowl of soup, wondering if she should wake her guest or let her sleep. She normally ate her lunch between noon and one, not being a stickler for time, really. She'd been afraid Erin would be hungry so she'd come in promptly at noon to reheat the soup and was surprised to find her sound asleep. She'd been curled on her side, clutching a pillow in her arms. She wondered if the tightly held pillow offered her some comfort. She watched her through the open door for a bit, again having a sense of déjà vu. She could picture herself in that bed so easily. She wondered what troubles Erin was dealing with. She'd finally eased the bedroom door closed and gone back outside for another hour, continuing with her chore of piling pine needles around the tomato plants. That was one thing on her list to accomplish before the rains came. One of the compost piles was ready too. She'd tend to the peppers and beans tomorrow, heaping mounds of compost around them before topping with pine needles.

She let out a weary breath. There was a never-ending list, it seemed. Funny how it seemed to repeat itself each year, she thought wryly. Oh, she didn't really mind the chores. It kept her busy. Kept her focused. Kept her fed too. The days, the weeks, the months...and yes, the years still ticked by, though. Hard to believe she'd been out here seven years already. She was a seasoned veteran now. Back that first summer—it was a miracle she'd survived. She knew next to nothing about gardening. Thankfully, Stella and the others had been willing teachers. That...and the Internet. She didn't want to brag, but she was damn near an expert organic gardener now. And now, it was she who the others called when they had pest problems or yellow spots on their tomatoes or wilt on the squash blooms or aphids on the strawberries or worms on their young cabbage plants.

Speaking of strawberries, she'd picked a bucketful that morning. Instead of freezing them, she'd kept them out, thinking she might make a pie or a cobbler for her guest. Now that she'd actually *met* her guest—Erin—she doubted she'd be appreciative of a homemade dessert. Oh, well. She wouldn't mind a strawberry pie herself. Why else did she plant them each year if not to indulge?

She put her bowl in the sink and filled it with water, then, after pausing to stare at the closed bedroom door again, she went to her desk in the far corner of the living room and pulled out a notepad, scribbling a quick note. She left it on the bar, then with another glance at the door, she shrugged and went back outside.

* * *

Erin woke with a start, disoriented for a moment. What time was it? She rolled over, not finding a clock on the nightstand beside the bed. She didn't wear a watch; she relied on her phone for that information. She sat up and rubbed her eyes, noting the sun still high in the sky as it shined into the bedroom window. She peeked out, seeing Melanie out in the garden. God, what could she possibly be doing out there for this long?

She went into the bathroom and washed her face. Her headache seemed to have returned and she stared at herself in the mirror, wondering when—if—she'd ever look like herself again. Her father had been right. They didn't recognize her. *She* didn't even recognize her.

She'd lost weight in the last year, but she hadn't bothered getting new clothes. The shirt she wore now, the slacks, they both swallowed her. She ran a hand through her hair, hair that was much longer than she normally kept it. Longer because—in the last year—she hadn't bothered to get it cut or keep it styled. She hadn't bothered with a lot of things. It was like she'd stopped caring what she looked like. Sarah wasn't around anymore. What was the point? The time and energy she'd spent on Sarah… Well, she had to focus on something else, something other than the fact that Sarah had left her. The job. She'd had only one thing on her mind—the job. Only one thing that she took the time for. Building and selling houses. Nothing else. Not her appearance, not her health. The job. And now the ten projects she'd been juggling for Ryder Construction were being handled by her father, a man who'd been out of the project management business for four years.

She could only imagine the mess he'd make of things. And when she got back, she'd have to work overtime to straighten it out. Three months? She supposed he couldn't screw up too much in three months. Of course, it remained to be seen if she'd have any contractors left who would work for her.

With a heavy sigh, she turned away from the mirror and her hollow eyes. She was supposed to forget about work for a while, wasn't she? She was supposed to waste away here for three long months, doing absolutely nothing.

God. She'd be batshit crazy by the time Joyce picked her up again. With another deep sigh, she went out into the living room, spying a piece of paper on the bar. She walked over to it, eyebrows raised.

"Help yourself to soup."

"Soup?" she asked dryly, a bit disinterested.

But she was hungry. She lifted the lid on the pot, bending down to sniff. It smelled good enough. She filled the bowl that had been left on the counter and took it to the bar. It actually was pretty good. She poked around the stuff, finding potatoes and carrots, squash…broccoli. She pushed the broccoli aside, then scooped it up anyway, surprised that she liked it. She wasn't really much of a vegetable eater. She mentally rolled her eyes. In the last year, she hadn't been much of an eater, period. Takeout, when she thought to stop on her way home. Pizza delivery some nights. Not much else. Well, other than her nightly cocktails. Joyce had guessed right, though. She was going to have a much harder time weaning herself off caffeine than booze. She glanced at the coffeepot, but it was empty, clean.

She ate mindlessly as she looked around. It was a simple house, nothing fancy. Guessing at the square footage, she'd say a thousand, maybe a little more. The living room and kitchen were combined in the main part of the house. The door at the opposite end must be Melanie's bedroom. There wasn't another door so she guessed she had a private bath in there. The outside-facing walls were logs, surprising her. When they'd first driven up, she assumed it was log siding, not actual logs. It was kinda rustic and homey…if you liked that sort of thing.

She let her spoon clank into the bowl, surprised that it was empty. Without much thought, she went to the pot and picked up the ladle, scooping another helping of soup into her bowl. She leaned against the counter to eat, her gaze landing on a desk. A desk and a laptop. Her eyes widened. Melanie had set up their website, Stella had said. Melanie must have Internet then.

She quickly finished her soup and put the bowl in the sink, then hurried to her room. She dug her phone out of one of her bags, going quickly to the settings. Yes, there was Wi-Fi available. Her excitement tempered a bit as a password was required. She looked out the window, seeing Melanie petting a goat.

A goat?

She moved to the window, calling out.

"Hey…Mel." She held up her phone. "I need the Wi-Fi password."

Melanie walked closer to the house, then shook her head.

"No. Sorry. Can't."

"*What?* Why not?"

"Rules."

"*Rules?*"

"Stella's rules." Melanie turned to go, walking toward a shed of some sort.

"Wait! She's not going to know if you give me the password."

"I'll know."

"What? No. Wait."

But Melanie ignored her, disappearing inside the shed. Erin rubbed her forehead, hoping to ward off the fast approaching headache. Rules? She tossed her phone on the bed, then went outside, using the kitchen door instead of the front. She was immediately surrounded by clucking chickens, one of which pecked at her leather shoe.

Do chickens bite?

She stood completely still, wondering if she should make a run for the shed Melanie had disappeared into or take cover back in the house. The shed was closer, but the door was closed. What if it was locked? What if the chickens attacked?

She was butted from the back and the scream was out before she could stop it. The chickens scattered as she lurched forward. With her heart hammering in her chest, she spun around, finding a goat—a gray and white floppy-eared goat—staring at her, its nose wiggling as if trying to decide if she was friend or foe.

"Do not...attack me," she whispered. "*Please.*"

"Rosie—leave her alone."

Erin held her hands up. "Will it bite?"

"She'll eat the shirt off your back if you let her." Melanie walked over and rubbed the goat's face. "Go on, Rosie."

"Do...do the chickens bite? I thought they were about to attack me."

Melanie smiled and took a straw cowboy hat off her head. "They're looking for a handout, that's all. I take it you've never been on a farm before." Her fingers brushed the blond hair away from her face.

"No. City girl. I never even had a pet." She relaxed a little as the goat—Rosie—wandered off. "So...no Internet? Really?"

"Afraid so. The website makes it very plain. No cell phones, no Internet, no TV at most of the houses." She tilted her head, studying her. "You did *see* all that, right? On the website?"

"I did not. My…my sister arranged all of this. And as soon as I see her again, I'm going to kill her."

Melanie laughed appropriately, assuming she was joking. At that moment, she wasn't sure if she was or not.

"It's not so bad. It's very freeing, really."

"How do you even know what's going on in the world?"

Melanie shrugged. "Mostly don't care." She held up an empty bucket. "I'm about to pick green beans. You want to help?"

"Pick green beans? What does that entail?"

"You bend over and pick the ones that are ready." Then Melanie nodded. "Ah—city girl. You've never seen a garden before, have you?"

"About the closest I've come to a garden is the produce section at Whole Foods." Erin shoved her hands into her pockets. Back when she used to shop with Sarah, that is. Back when they used to be happy and would enjoy staying in and cooking together. Back when things were normal in her life. How long had it been since Sarah had left her? More than a year. It was right after Christmas. Damn. A year and a half already. Seemed like yesterday. No… Seemed like a decade ago.

"So…no on the green beans then?"

Erin looked at her thoughtfully. "I'll trade you green bean picking for the Wi-Fi password."

Melanie gave her a half smile. "I can manage on my own then, thanks. Enjoy the rest of your afternoon."

She walked off without another word, and Erin watched her for a moment as Mel plopped the hat back on her head. She turned, seeing movement by a tree. There was a red glass… thing hanging there. Tiny birds buzzed around it and she smiled. Hummingbirds. Had she ever seen a real live hummingbird before? She watched for a few moments as four or five fought for a spot at the feeder. Then she let out a deep breath and made her way back into the house. Once inside, she realized she hadn't thanked Melanie for lunch. Or breakfast, for that matter. Where were her manners?

She shrugged. As Stella had said, she was paying a pretty penny for room and board. She didn't suppose a "thank you" was required.

She went back into her room, intending to unpack her bags. Instead, she sat on the bed and stared out the window. She could only see the edge of the garden from there and Melanie wasn't in her line of view. She turned in the direction of where the hummingbird feeder was, but it too was out of sight. With a weary sigh, she lay back and closed her eyes, suddenly feeling very tired.

CHAPTER ELEVEN

"It's none of my business, of course…But you've pretty much slept the day away."

"I believe you told me that if I was tired, I should take a nap."

Melanie stabbed several green beans with her fork. "So I did. Is it because you're not high on caffeine?"

Erin flicked her gaze at her. "High? Is that what it's called?"

Melanie cut one of the small potatoes in half before eating it. She should just come right out and ask her, she supposed. Things between them couldn't possibly get any more strained. She was tired of worrying that she would open the bedroom door and find her…well, not alive.

"Are you depressed?"

"Wouldn't you be?"

Melanie put her fork down. "Look, it's obvious you don't want to be here. The reason you're here in the first place is still a mystery, but regardless, you're here. And if you treat every day like you did today…You'll drive yourself mad if you don't get out and do something. Take a hike. Walk along the creek. Throw scratch out for the chickens. Muck the goat stall. Pick eggs. Help me in the garden. There are countless things to do here. Get outside in the sunshine. You'll feel better."

Erin eyed her. "What makes you think I don't feel good?"

Melanie was too polite to say that she looked like hell. "*Do you feel good?*"

"I don't know what feeling good is like. I feel like crap, honestly. I haven't gone a whole day without a Red Bull in years. I have a pounding headache that hasn't eased. My body is in shock. I haven't had a drink or a cigarette in five days."

Melanie wrinkled up her nose. "You smoke?"

"No. Not really. It was just…something to do." Erin cut into the squash casserole. "This is pretty good."

"Thank you. You'll be sick of squash soon enough. They're coming in like crazy."

Erin motioned to the plate. "I notice there aren't any beans."

"Stella warned me to stay away from them. At least for today. Being vegetarian, beans are a staple, though. You can expect burritos at least once a week."

Erin nodded. "I liked the green sauce you put on the eggs. Nice and spicy. And I don't really hate beans. Rachel's presentation was…well, rather tasteless."

"Yes, I know. She brings them sometimes to our monthly dinners."

"What dinners?"

"Stella has a gathering at her house once a month. It's a potluck, nothing more, but it gives everyone a chance to visit and catch up, and this time of year, exchange vegetables."

"So you don't really see everyone out here very often?"

"Not often, no. Some do. Most of the others live closer together, closer to Stella. I'm back here by myself. I…" She smiled quickly. "I'm a bit of a hermit, I'm afraid."

"A hermit? Guess me being here is cramping your style, huh?"

"To say the least."

"Why are you a hermit?"

Melanie met her gaze. "Why are you here?"

Their stare ended in a standoff, neither feeling the need to answer the question, apparently. The rest of the meal was eaten in silence.

* * *

She was used to the quiet, used to being alone, but the silence seemed exaggerated tonight. Erin had gone off to her room shortly after dinner. She had at least offered to help with the cleanup and washing dishes, but Melanie had waved her away. She wasn't used to having someone in her kitchen. She, in turn, had offered the TV to Erin. Erin had seemed to consider it for a moment, but then she'd shook her head and murmured a quiet "good night" before closing the door to her room.

She'd spent a little time on her laptop, feeling a bit guilty for getting online when she'd refused to give the password to Erin. She'd almost given in, despite Stella's rule. As Erin had said, Stella need never know. But she feared if she gave it to her, Erin would never step foot outside. She'd live the next three months in her room, online, coming out only for meals and coffee.

Which maybe wouldn't be so bad; she wouldn't have to deal with her then. Like Stella, she wondered what her story was. Why was she here? And how could her father and sister *make* her come out here, for three months, no less? That thought, of course, made her wonder if Stella's words were true. Had Erin really tried to commit suicide? And if so, why? Depression? That seemed obvious.

She knew all about suicide, didn't she? She also knew about depression. That seemed like so long ago. Who knew potatoes and sunshine would cure her?

Her therapy sessions had shifted from a couch to a garden. The chickens and goats were her therapists now as she talked freely to them. Whatever demons she'd had were long gone, though. Well…buried, at least. She rarely even thought about that lonely time in her life. Rarely thought about Adam. Not consciously, at least.

She was physically alone now, but she was no longer lonely. Mostly. Oh, there were times when she wished there was someone here, someone to share her life with. But being alone and being lonely were two completely different things. She didn't feel the need to surround herself with people like she'd once done. Her interactions with the ladies once a month were usually enough for her. Stella, much like old Fred, made the rounds, though. At least once a week, she'd drop by for morning coffee and they'd visit for an hour or more. She didn't mind her company…in small doses. But she had her routine, which worked well for her.

She was up before dawn most mornings. As her coffee brewed, she would take ten or fifteen minutes for meditation. Coffee—when the weather was nice—would be taken to the front porch. She'd sit in the rocker, mentally planning her day as the sun rose from over the bluff on the other side of the creek. Before starting breakfast, she'd walk out to the chicken house and open it up, letting the hens into their fenced yard. The goats were next and she'd open their stalls, letting them out to mingle with the chickens.

Breakfast was usually potatoes and vegetables or rice and vegetables that she'd top with scrambled eggs most mornings. Chores began immediately after that and she'd be outside until noon or so. When the sun was high enough in the morning, she no longer feared Goldie or Rick would come by and she'd let the goats and chickens out of their fenced yard. They never wandered off very far from the cabin and shed. Her only worries then were the goats eating her rosebushes.

During the summer months, a lot of her afternoons were spent canning the vegetables she'd picked in the mornings. If she had a particularly good yield—like the yellow squash she had now—she'd put some aside to share with the others. And if she was feeling lazy, she might put off afternoon chores for a soak in the creek. She had a spot she liked to go to, and she'd ride her bike upstream a half-mile or so where some deeper pools were. Her favorite spot, however, was the hot springs. It was another half-mile upstream, but her bike couldn't make it.

It was steep and rocky and quite an excursion to get there. Most of the relaxation she got out of the soak was forgotten as she had to scramble over and around rocks to get back down to her bike. Still, it was something she did a handful of times a year.

Stella had told her "back in the day" they all used to go to the hot springs together, carrying lunch baskets with them. It was a once-a-month day trip, she'd said. Since Melanie had moved there, she wasn't aware of anyone else using the springs. Of course, the trek would be too much for most of them now, except perhaps Angela.

She moved into the kitchen, opening the cabinet where she kept her cups. She took out her favorite—a heavy blue ceramic—and filled it with water she'd had heating in the kettle on the stove. She plunged an herbal tea bag into the cup, absently dunking it, watching as the water turned from clear to light brown.

After lacing it with a dribble of honey, she took the cup out to the porch and sat in her rocker, the creaking sound of the wood so familiar she hardly noticed it. She took a sip of her tea, then put the chair in motion with her foot. There was no moon this evening—it had already set in the west. While she enjoyed a full moon—it was a beautiful orange as it rose over the bluff—she liked the darker sky. She never got tired of seeing the millions of twinkling stars overhead. She sometimes sat out for hours on end, watching them move lazily across the sky.

She turned her thoughts to her guest, wondering how they were going to manage three months. She couldn't *make* the woman go outside. She supposed she was going through withdrawals…and not just from overdosing on caffeine. She'd been taken from her world—in the city—and thrown out here in the middle of nowhere, against her will apparently, to a place where nothing was familiar. Erin must be feeling cut off from everyone and everything in her life.

Melanie knew that if Erin would simply quit fighting the situation she found herself in and embrace it instead she might actually enjoy herself. And that, of course, would make things a whole lot better for both of them.

But again… She couldn't make her go outside and sit in the sunshine. She couldn't make her get in the garden or throw scratch to the hens. She smiled then, remembering the look of terror on Erin's face as Rosie and the flock of hens had had her cornered. *Wonder what she'll do when she meets Bandito?* The donkey, while friendly enough, loved to push you around with his head, demanding a carrot. He had been inherited along with Fred. They'd belonged to a lady who had died seven or eight months before Melanie had moved there. Stella had strongly suggested that Melanie move into her house, but it hadn't appealed to her. It was within a stone's throw of Valerie's house. She did, however, agree to take the white dog and the miniature donkey.

With one last look into the sky, she got out of her rocker. She listened to the night sounds for a bit, hearing the faint yips and howls of the coyote choruses that were echoing along the bluff. They must be hunting far upstream tonight. It was probably a good thing that they weren't closer. If Erin was sleeping with her window open, they might scare her half to death.

CHAPTER TWELVE

On the morning of her sixth day in purgatory—the word she'd begun using for her so-called vacation—Erin had something rather odd occur to her.

She felt...different. For one thing, it was seven o'clock and she was awake. Not only awake, but up and dressed. Dressed for what, she wasn't sure.

The other mornings, by the time she'd crawled out of bed, Melanie had already been outside. Each morning, her breakfast had been left in the microwave for her to heat as she wanted. Spicy fried potatoes with peppers and onions one morning. A rice and bean taco another. Eggs. She'd eat, then crawl back to her room where she'd hide until well after lunchtime. Again, her cold meal would be waiting for her. One day, there was even strawberry pie left out for her. However, by the time dinner rolled around, she'd had enough of her own miserable company, and she forced herself out of her room to share a usually quiet meal with Melanie. Last night she'd actually accepted Melanie's offer of TV and stayed up to watch a medical drama with her.

And now this morning?

She felt different. She felt...well...*good*. Whatever that was supposed to feel like. Her head wasn't pounding, for one thing. And as she was brushing her teeth, she noticed that the dark circles under her eyes were gone. She also noticed that her cheekbones didn't seem to be quite so prominent. Her hair, though, was still... Well, it looked like crap, she thought as she tucked it behind both ears.

She paused at her bedroom door, however. She heard Melanie in the kitchen, imagined her cooking breakfast. She'd been rude, she knew. She wanted to say that wasn't really her, but it was, wasn't it? For the last year or so—yeah, she'd been a bitch to basically everyone.

She took a deep breath, then opened the door. Her presence was obviously a shock to Melanie. She paused in mid-pour, the coffeepot suspended in air as she stared, eyebrows raised.

Erin cleared her throat. "Good...good morning."

Melanie blinked at her, then nodded. "Good morning." She resumed her coffee pouring. "You want a cup?"

"Yeah. Please." She shoved her hands into the pockets of her slacks, surprised at her nervousness. "I...I owe you an apology."

The expression changed on Melanie's face, but she didn't look at her as she pulled another cup from the cabinet.

At her silence, Erin moved closer to the bar. "I've been... well, rather difficult."

At that, Melanie met her gaze. "Difficult? You haven't really been out of your room long enough to be called difficult."

"I've been rude."

"Yes, you have. I'll give you that." Melanie handed her a cup, the steam rising off the top. "I think I've gotten used to it. Some people are just...rude," she said matter-of-factly.

Erin smiled at that. "Yeah, I've gotten used to it too, apparently. That's not who I am. Who I used to be," she corrected.

Over the rim of her cup, Melanie met her eyes. "You're up early."

Erin shrugged. "Woke up. Feel good."

A quick nod. "Okay. Does that mean you're not going to spend the day holed up in your room?"

Erin put her cup down. "I…yeah…I need to do something. I think I'm slept out. I had a lot of catching up to do. My two, three, sometimes four hours a night caught up with me, I guess."

"God, how could you survive on that little sleep?"

"Obviously, I didn't. Six or more Red Bulls a day will keep the motor going, though. I'm testament to that."

Another nod. "So you finally crashed?"

"Crashed and burned."

A quick smile. "Okay. So you're ready to do something?"

"Yes."

"Good. You can start by helping with breakfast."

Before she knew what was happening, a cutting board was placed on the bar and a rather large knife was slid her way. She assumed they were having those spicy fried potatoes as onions, an assortment of peppers and, yes, red-skinned potatoes appeared.

"Chop," Melanie instructed as she pulled out a cast iron skillet and heated it on the stove. "Onions first."

Erin did as instructed, her mind flashing back to a time when she'd help Sarah in the kitchen. Joyce's words were still fresh in her mind.

She used you.

Had she? She sliced the onion in half, then paused. Sarah liked nice things, sure. And Erin had provided them. That didn't mean she'd used her, did it? They were happy. She frowned. They were *both* happy, weren't they? Yeah. They were. At first.

"You know how to chop an onion, right?"

Erin blinked, chasing away her thoughts. "Sorry."

Melanie drizzled olive oil in the pan, then reached over to scoop up the onions that Erin had managed to chop, adding them to the pan. They sizzled when they hit the hot oil. She chopped the rest of the onion, then started on the peppers, watching as Melanie cut and cubed potatoes.

Before long, everything was in the skillet and Melanie put a glass lid on top and turned the heat down a bit. They both leaned against the bar and sipped from coffee cups.

"What do you do?"

"Do?"

"In real life," Melanie explained. "Job?"

"Oh. My father owns a construction company. New homes. Houston. But we advertise statewide so we'll contract anywhere."

"Big company, then?"

"Big enough. My sister and younger brother work there also. It's still a family business." That made Erin wonder how her projects were doing. "I…I was lead project manager. I was usually in the office by six each morning. Didn't leave until eight or nine. Worked at home. Grabbed a few hours' sleep. Rinse and repeat."

"No wonder you crashed." Melanie added more coffee to her cup, then offered Erin some. "I take it eating wasn't a part of your day? I'm sorry, but you're very thin. Not my business, of course, but unhealthily thin."

"Eating took time away from work."

"So—all work, no play?"

Erin looked away, glancing out the kitchen window. "No play for the last year and a half, for sure."

"Why?"

Erin gave a slight shrug. "Things changed."

"Bad breakup?" Melanie guessed, then she quickly held up her hand. "Again, absolutely none of my business." She took the lid off the pan and set it aside as she stirred the potatoes. "Feel like getting outside today? Sunshine on your skin will do wonders for your mood."

Erin was thankful she'd changed the subject. "My mood needs improving, huh?"

Melanie only smiled as she took eggs out of the fridge.

"Okay, I suppose it does. What do you have in mind?"

"The goats' stall needs mucking, for one."

"Okay, so don't know what that means but…your goat tried to attack me, remember," she reminded her.

"They don't attack. They don't bite. They're mostly pests, if anything."

"How many do you have?"

"Three. A momma—Carly—and her twins, Rosie and Nora."

"Interesting names."

"Carly was already named—and pregnant—when I got her. Rosie got her name because she loves to nibble on the rosebushes. Nora..." Melanie shrugged. "That was the name of my favorite teacher when I was in school."

"So...mucking a stall? What does that mean?"

Melanie smiled, a smile that was...well, Erin didn't really know what it was. Sly? Scheming?

"I'll show you. It'll be fun."

So less than an hour later—after stuffing herself with two soft, flour tortillas filled with crispy fried potatoes and scrambled eggs smothered in spicy green sauce—she found herself standing in a smelly stall with a shovel in her hand. She finally knew what that smile was all about.

"Seriously? The first chore you give me is scooping up goat shit?"

Melanie laughed quickly as she dropped off the wheelbarrow beside her. "Dump it in the compost pile when you're finished. I'll be in the garden. Compost pile is out there too." She paused, looking at Erin's slacks. "Are you sure you don't want to change into something less...dressy?"

Erin glanced at the beige slacks she'd put on and then at her leather loafers. She lifted one corner of her mouth. "I'm afraid I didn't exactly pack for life on the farm." A loud noise coming from behind them made her jump and nearly run for cover. Melanie didn't seem concerned in the least.

"What in the world is that?"

"That's Bandito. And he's braying. Surely you've heard a donkey before."

"Not in real life, no."

"I'll introduce you later." Melanie pointed at the stall. "Time to work."

She wrinkled up her nose as she picked up the first scoop of straw and goat poop. The goats—the girls, as Melanie called them—were out with the chickens in a fenced pen. The gate to the stall was closed, but two faces were squeezed between the slats, watching her. They were kinda cute, she admitted, especially since they were on the other side of the gate and couldn't get to her.

She filled the wheelbarrow to the top and still had half of the stall to go. She wheeled it out to the garden where Melanie had said the compost pile was. Erin found her on her knees, digging in the dirt around a tall plant, the familiar hat on her head covering her blond hair.

"What are you doing?"

"I added compost around them, now I'm mulching with pine needles."

She looked around the garden for the first time, not having a clue as to what most of the plants were. Actually, she didn't have a clue as to what *any* of the plants were.

"First time in a garden, huh? Tomato plants."

"This is a pretty big plot. What do you do with all of this?"

Melanie took her gloves off and slapped them together, knocking the dirt off. "I eat what's in season, I have a pressure canner so I put up quite a bit, especially green beans and tomatoes, and I freeze a lot too." She stood up. "And I give some away. Not everyone out here is still able to keep up a garden like they used to. Rachel, for instance. I think this year she only planted a few tomato and squash plants."

Erin looked around again, the rows neat and tidy. "This is what takes up most of your time then?"

"I find it relaxing, really. There's always something to do. Pull weeds, hoe, mulch, water…and the best part—harvest. But yes, I practically live out here."

"So you were a gardener before you moved here?"

"God, no." Melanie laughed and took the wheelbarrow from her. "I at least knew what a garden looked like, but no, I hadn't grown one before. The first few years here were…Well, let's just say I would have starved if not for some handouts from the others."

Erin walked behind her, guessing her height to be five-five, five-six, maybe. Not overly tall, really, but certainly not petite.

Her blond hair was pulled into a ponytail, away from her face. The tank she had on couldn't hide the fact that she wore no bra. The tank also revealed arms that were used to working; her biceps were well defined as she tilted the wheelbarrow onto an already high pile of what she assumed was the compost. Beside it was a pitchfork and Melanie stabbed it into the pile, turning and mixing.

"There's more in the stall, I'm assuming."

Erin nodded. "This was about half."

"Do you mind getting the rest? That'll finish off this composting site then."

"What does that mean?"

"I won't add anything else to it. I'll start a new one. This one needs to sit and cook, as they call it. I turn it a couple of times a week, keep it watered. It'll be ready in time for next spring." She pointed to another spot of moist, rich soil. "Those two over there are ready. That's what I'm using around the plants now."

Erin nodded, not really understanding any of what she was saying. Seemed like it would be a whole lot easier to go to a grocery store to buy veggies.

She dutifully picked up the wheelbarrow again and headed back toward the stall, but the sound of a dog barking stopped her.

"You have a dog?"

"Occasionally. Fred. He and Bandito came as a package. He only lives here part-time, though." Melanie took her hat off and wiped her brow with her forearm before moving toward the gate. "I assume that's Stella coming to check on you."

Erin saw Stella's old truck coming up the lane. She was glad she was up and about this morning. She wondered what Stella's reaction would have been had she found her still in bed. She was the paying customer, she reminded herself. If she wanted to stay in bed all day, it shouldn't be any of their concern. But Melanie's words rang true. The feel of the sun on her face, on her arms, seemed to be having some magical effect on her. And, she admitted, it did feel good to do some physical work outside in the bright sunshine.

It occurred to her then just how dark her life had been. She was usually in the office before the sun was even up. And it was well past dusk when she got home. The only time she was outside was when she had to go to a site to prod the contractors along. Even then, she'd be in one of her power suits, impeccably dressed. That had been Sarah's doing. Before Sarah came into her life, Erin lived in jeans and company T-shirts. And out at a project site, she fit in perfectly well. But Sarah had convinced her that if she wanted to be the best, if she wanted to have the power, then she needed to dress like it.

So she did. She dressed the part, she acted the part. And she got things done. Not by sweet-talking, cajoling, and gently coaxing them along. No. That was how she used to manage. Now? Now she yelled, she pushed, she coerced, and she *forced* them. Where she used to be buddies with the contractors—laughing and telling jokes and even sharing a beer at the end of the day—she'd become someone they dreaded to see on a project site. Because if she showed up, then something wasn't going as planned, something was behind schedule, something was *wrong*. And someone got yelled at.

She closed her eyes and turned her face up toward the sun, letting its warm rays soothe her. It felt good. She felt good. She opened her eyes again, smiling up into the bright blue sky. Yeah… She felt *good*.

So she pushed thoughts of her job away, turning her attention instead…to goat shit.

CHAPTER THIRTEEN

Melanie offered to make coffee, but Stella declined.

"I already stopped over at Angela's. I think I've had enough." She leaned closer. "Where is she?"

Melanie smiled. "Mucking the goat stall."

Stella's eyes widened. "Really? She didn't seem the type."

"I know. She's in khaki slacks and brown, leather shoes. But at least she's up. If you had come yesterday, she would have been in her room. Actually, today is the first day she's been up, first day outside."

"What has she been doing?"

"Sleeping, I guess. I'll admit, she looks more human today. Her eyes are bright, alive. I don't mind saying, I was a little concerned." She joined Stella at the bar, leaning against it instead of sitting.

"Has she been eating?"

"Yes. Alone, mostly. But then this morning, she was like a completely different person. She got up in time to not only eat breakfast with me but help cook too."

"Cook? Oh, Mel, you know I don't like to make our guests tend to their own meals. They pay enough as it is."

"She's not a normal guest, Stella. She's not here to go out soul searching or to seek the meaning of life. She's not even here to vacation and relax. I still don't know *why* she's here in the first place. She won't say."

"Well, I got a call from her sister last night. She seemed concerned that she might try to escape or something."

"Escape? It's not like she's locked in a jail cell, is it?" Melanie pushed away from the bar. "I don't really like being a part of this, Stella. Erin is here against her wishes, essentially. If she asked me to take her to Silver City, I would. We can't hold her here against her will."

"But her sister made it clear—"

"We are not a prison," she said again.

Stella surprised her with a narrowing of eyes. "So you're saying I should find her another host?"

Melanie paused. This would be her out, wouldn't it? Yes, send Erin to someone else... Someone else could babysit her, worry over her, cook for her... Keep her locked away from the world for three months for whatever reason. All she had to do was say yes.

But she didn't. She thought back to that first day when Erin had been standing in her kitchen, staring out the window...tears in her eyes. *"Out of my element, I'm afraid."* She'd looked so lost and lonely, yet there was still a trace of defiance in those dark hazel eyes, even in her weakened state.

And today? Today she had actually been pleasant, friendly. That was a first, really. But still...three months? Did she want company for three months? Would the money she'd get for hosting be worth it? It had nothing to do with the money, she knew. It had to do with having someone in her space, her house, her life, for three whole months.

"Well, should I?" Stella asked again.

Melanie shook her head. "No. It's fine. She can stay with me."

"Her sister expects us to house her for three months. I don't know what the significance of three months is, but she stressed that, Melanie." She leaned closer, her voice quiet. "That's a lot of money to add to the coffers. A lot for you too. We don't want to run her off. Money has been so tight these last few years."

Melanie smiled and nodded—as Stella expected her to—keeping her response to herself. She knew that the group fund could use some cash, and of course, so could she. But whatever reason it was that Erin Ryder was here, they weren't qualified to offer anything other than room and board. This sister, and even Stella, seemed to think of this stay as some sort of therapy for Erin.

If Erin elected to make it therapy—solo hikes, meditation, self-reflection—then that was her business, but Melanie certainly wasn't going to offer any kind of counseling.

"Now...I guess I'll go say hello and see how she is." She paused at the door. "I'll swing by next week and check on you."

* * *

Erin was coming out of the garden, having dumped the last of the goat poop onto Melanie's compost pile when she saw Stella making her way over. She put the wheelbarrow down, glancing toward the house, but Melanie remained inside.

"Well, there you are, dear. Look at you...in the garden!"

Erin smiled at her. "I don't suppose I'm exactly dressed for gardening," she said, looking down at her slacks and shoes.

"Did you not bring any jeans, Erin?"

"To be honest, I'm not sure what's all in the bags. Joyce—my sister—packed most of it for me. I haven't unpacked everything yet."

"Oh? I know Melanie has a cute little dresser in there. Is it not—"

"No, it'll be fine. I just haven't...Well, I'll probably do that today."

"Okay, good. You'll be here three months, dear. No sense living out of a suitcase. Make your room into a home for you." She leaned closer, conspiratorially. "Now, what about meals? Have they been to your liking? No beans?"

"Meals have been fine. I wouldn't mind some chicken every once in a while, but—"

Stella gasped. "Chicken?"

"And we had beans last night. A spicy, cheesy burrito with onions and spinach and stuff. Very tasty."

"Okay. Good, then. I had hoped you'd like it better here. Melanie is probably close to your age. You'll have more things in common." She grinned. "And she doesn't knit!"

CHAPTER FOURTEEN

"So you never said how your visit with Stella went."

Erin paused in her onion chopping. "She was checking on me. Wanted to make sure you were feeding me properly. I told her I keep hoping to find chicken on the menu one night."

Melanie laughed and pointed at the cutting board. "Don't tell her you're doing food prep. The guests aren't supposed to help with meals."

Erin went back to her chopping. "I offered to help." She paused again. "I haven't been in a kitchen—to cook—in over a year and a half. It…it feels good. Thanks for letting me in your space. I guess you're used to having your kitchen all to yourself."

"Yes. I've been here seven years. You are the first guest to be in my kitchen for something other than eating."

"How often do you have to host people, as you call it?"

"Usually once a year, never more than twice. And it's rare that someone stays more than a week. Long weekends, normally. Three, four nights, most."

"You've been here seven years? Did you come willingly?"

"I did. I was living in Phoenix at the time so it wasn't a drastic move for me." Melanie held up her hand. "And no, I don't want to get into the whys and hows of it." A quick smile. "But what about you?"

"Why am I here?"

"Yes."

Why was she here? She knew the reason her father and sister sent her here, but was that really the reason?

"You were right. Bad breakup."

Melanie gave her a sympathetic look. "Sorry. I suppose it was recent then?"

Erin looked up from her onions. "Why would you think it was recent?"

Melanie scooped up the onions she'd cut and added them to the pan that was sizzling with oil. "Well, you're here. I'm assuming someone broke up with you." She looked at her. "Is that why you tried to commit suicide?"

Erin's eyes widened in shock. "*What?* Suicide?"

"I'm sorry," Melanie said quickly. "I have no right to bring it up. It's just that Stella said—"

"Stella? I never told Stella that." She thought back to their conversations, finally nodded. "Oh."

"Oh?"

"She wanted to know about my three-month sentence. I told her that my father and sister thought I was trying to kill myself." She shook her head. "Not literally." Then she paused. "Or maybe I was. Trying to kill myself with work and Red Bull and booze and cigarettes and not sleeping and not eating." She shook her head. "God, that's depressing."

"That'll certainly do it. Slowly, of course."

"It's been a year and a half since she left."

"Oh, I see. No kitchen duty since then, huh?"

"We used to…stay in and cook. Quite a bit. At first, anyway. The more I worked, the more free time she had. She'd take dinner out with friends since I usually got home late."

"Does *she* have a name?"

"Sarah."

"So she had time on her hands? Did Sarah leave you for one of your friends?"

"No." Erin put the knife down and wiped her hands on a dishcloth. "We used to go to New York twice a year. She loved the city. She met someone on one of those trips. They had an online affair afterward, apparently. Then when we went back, they hooked up. For two years they did that."

"Why an affair? Why not leave you right away?"

She'd asked herself that a hundred times. She knew the answer. Joyce had given her the answer. "Because we had a big house, a nice pool, nice cars, vacations to the Mexican beaches. I guess she wasn't in a hurry to give that up."

"You were together a long time then?"

"Not quite six years. I guess I should say four, since two of those years she had a lover on the side." She motioned to the onions in the pan. "They're going to burn."

Melanie quickly stirred them, then moved them from the heat. "How old are you?"

"Thirty-three. Why? Too old to be forced into this so-called vacation?"

Melanie nodded. "But none of my business."

Erin let out a breath, watching as Melanie added chopped squash and peppers to the onions. "Might as well get it all out," she said, almost to herself. "My father threatened to fire me. This was my alternative. Well, this or a rehab clinic, apparently."

"Do you need rehab?"

Erin smiled. "Does any addict think they need rehab?"

"But you're not really an addict, are you?"

"You seem to be the only one who thinks that." She pushed away from the bar. "I was certainly addicted to Red Bulls. I thought my head was going to explode those first few days."

"And booze?"

Erin shrugged. "I wasn't a drunk, if that's what you're asking. I think it was just something to do in the evenings, when I was alone. Have a cocktail or three while I worked on my laptop, anything to keep my mind occupied. Skipped breakfast, had a Red Bull. Skipped dinner, had a drink."

"Then sleep for a few hours?"

"A few, yes. Then start the process all over again."

Melanie shook her head. "And you did this for over a year? You're damn lucky you *didn't* kill yourself." She motioned to the potatoes on the bar. "Slice those very thin."

"What are you making?"

"*We* are making a casserole. I'm going to blend some tofu to make a cream sauce."

"Cheese?" she asked hopefully.

"Lucky you, I have a weakness for cheese. It's full of fat and so not good for you, but I have yet to give it up. I'm working on that. Once or twice a week is about all I allow myself."

"Were you a vegetarian when you moved out here?"

"God, no. It was hard at first. When we'd go into town shopping, I'd often think of buying some chicken or ground beef or something and sneaking it back to the ranch." She laughed. "Stella must have suspected because she often would inspect my bags."

"So you never did?"

"No. Cold turkey—so to speak—was the easiest way. Like a Band-Aid. Yank it off and be done with it." She looked at her and winked. "That's not to say that I don't fish the creek for trout occasionally."

Erin smiled as she continued slicing the potatoes. "You shouldn't have told me. Now I have something to blackmail you with."

"If you keep my secret, maybe we can try our hand at fishing in the morning. Fresh trout is delicious."

"And Stella's never caught you?"

"No. I know her routine. She comes by usually only once a week and normally between nine and ten in the morning." She picked up the potatoes and added them to the pan. "Of course, she's worried you're going to try to escape, so she may come by more often."

"Escape, huh?"

"Apparently your sister called her last night and planted that seed in her mind."

Erin laughed. "Yeah, Joyce would think that."

Melanie took a block of cheese from the fridge and handed it to her. "Shred that for me, would you? Less than half of it." She bent over and opened one of the cabinets at the bar, pulling out a blender. "For the tofu sauce," she explained.

"How long did it take you to learn to cook this way?"

"Not long. It was sort of sink or swim. I don't do a lot of elaborate dishes, but sometimes I'll splurge, like tonight."

"So this casserole is for my benefit then?"

"I usually keep things fairly simple. Cooking for one doesn't require much. Rice or potatoes, beans…veggies. That's most of my meals. If I could only kick the cheese habit."

"Don't you get lonely out here by yourself? Eating alone all the time."

Melanie seemed to consider the question. "No. That's not to say I didn't at first. In fact, pretty much the whole first year was iffy." She paused. "But, yes. Sometimes I do get lonely." Mel gave her a quick smile. "It passes, though. Eventually."

Erin wondered if that was hard for her to admit. She was obviously independent and it had been her choice to live here, away from everything and everybody. "So tell me how this works. Someone wants to move out here, Stella has to approve it. Then what?"

"Not just Stella, but at this point, I think they would accept anyone, as long as they were female. As you may have noticed, most of them are over seventy."

To the blob of tofu in the blender, Melanie added seasonings, then turned it on. Erin watched a smooth, white sauce take shape. When the blender stopped, Melanie nodded at her cheese pile. "That's plenty."

"So you built this cabin then?"

"Yes. I had the choice of moving into one of the vacant houses. There are still two that are in fairly good shape, but I wasn't interested in either. Most of the ladies are pretty clustered together on the front side of the property, near Stella."

"And you're a hermit so you wanted to be far away?" she guessed.

"I wasn't a hermit when I moved here, no," Melanie said with a laugh. "I was simply seeking solitude, really. I had some… some healing to do," she said evasively. "So I hiked all along the creek until I found this spot. It just…felt right. I've got the bluff behind the house to the west that offers protection from storms. Then the creek right here. And the small bluff behind the creek makes for a beautiful sunrise. I can see the mountains from my windows."

She shrugged. "It felt right. And I did live temporarily at one of the vacant houses while this was being built. That alone convinced me that I'd made the right decision to live back here by myself." She smiled. "I've grown to love these ladies like family, but when I first moved here, they were nosy as hell."

Questions sprang up in Erin's mind, but she reined them in. Was it any of her business what sort of healing Melanie had to do or why she moved here? "They were nosy and you were private?"

Melanie met her gaze. "I didn't have anyone. I grew up in foster homes, so I was used to being on my own, alone. So yes, private."

Again, none of her business, but she didn't think Melanie would have offered that information if she wasn't prepared to talk about it. She asked the obvious question. "Why foster homes?"

Melanie poured the sauce into the pan, mixing it with the vegetables, busying herself with the casserole. So much so that Erin thought she wasn't going to answer. She finally stopped her movements, looking at her again.

"My mother was fifteen when I was born. At that time, she was only a pothead. The cocaine, the heroin, the crystal meth… that all came next. She pimped herself out for money, used the money for drugs." She swallowed. "Her parents weren't much better. When I was six, he died of an overdose, right there on the kitchen floor. Police came, saw the condition of the house, the condition of me….took me away," she said rather matter-of-factly.

"Wow," Erin whispered. "You remember all that?"

"Most of it, yes. I can still see my grandfather on the floor, can see her—my grandmother—kneeling beside him, mascara streaks on her face from crying. And my mother, sitting at the table, a needle in her arm."

"I guess you do know what an addict looks like. God, how awful."

"Yeah, it was." Then she shrugged. "I didn't know any better, really. I cried when they took me away."

"Did you ever see them again? Your mother?"

"A handful of times. To her credit, she tried to get custody of me on and off over the years, but…well, she couldn't stay clean. When I was older, when I got out of the system—when I was working—she started coming by again."

"Wanting money?" she guessed.

"Yeah."

"Did you give it to her?"

"No. She was a mess. And I…I was involved with someone. He was squeaky clean. He started calling the cops whenever she'd come by. She eventually stopped."

Erin's eyebrows shot up. "He?"

"Yes."

"But I thought…Stella said everyone here…"

"Yes."

CHAPTER FIFTEEN

Melanie tried to keep the smile off her face but couldn't hide it any longer. She gave in to it, finally letting laughter bubble out.

"I know," Erin said, standing at the bank of the creek, holding the rod and reel as if she was gripping a baseball bat. "I know."

"Never been fishing, huh?"

"Never been fishing."

"Isn't that odd?"

Erin shrugged. "My dad wasn't really into all that. We rarely left the city. And if we did, it was to the beach in Galveston."

Melanie pointed at her clothing. "Pressed slacks? Starched shirt? Brushed leather?" She shook her head. "Do you know how dirty you get fishing?"

"I didn't find any jeans." At Melanie's arched eyebrow, she explained. "My sister did most of the packing. I guess she thought I was coming to a country club or something."

"Well, if you wear those kinds of clothes for three months, they'll be totally ruined. Shorts?" she asked hopefully.

Erin shook her head.

"So, we'll make plans for a shopping trip. If you want to, that is."

"Like into civilization?"

Melanie laughed. "Silver City, where they picked you up. That's the closest town of any size. It's usually a once-a-month trip, but we can go anytime, really."

"Why only once a month?"

"Oh, that's just the way Stella started it way back when and it's kinda stuck." She opened up the canvas tackle box. "It was hard at first. I was used to going to the grocery store on a whim. I couldn't make it a whole month, but it's well over an hour's drive to get there." She pulled out a jar of the power bait. "Took me at least six months before I felt comfortable. Now? It's no big deal. I've learned to live off what the garden produces and I only need a few staples…dried beans, rice, coffee, flour for my tortillas or masa for corn, that sort of thing." She waved her hand. "Other than, you know, paper goods and such."

"So what's that?" Erin asked, motioning to the power bait.

"It's supposed to mimic salmon eggs." She opened the lid, revealing the pinkish red balls.

Erin leaned closer to inspect them, then wrinkled up her nose. "They smell."

"Uh-huh."

She assumed Erin would want her to bait the hook, but she plucked one out of the jar and held it up, her gaze going to the hook.

"So just stick it on there?"

"You're going to want two or three. Cover most of the hook."

She stood back, watching as Erin studied the mechanisms of the reel with a slightly tilted head. She flipped the metal bail wire up and down, then looked over at her.

Melanie nodded. "When you flip it up, it releases the tension for you to cast."

She was about to offer to show her how, but Erin moved to the edge, holding the rod out with one hand. However, she was holding the rod with the spinning reel on top, not the bottom.

"I've seen this done on TV. You just kinda…flick it out there, right?"

"You want to cast it upstream, then let the water bring it back to you downstream. Trout swim upstream to feed."

The first cast was not pretty and only went a couple of feet into the water. She again studied the reel and Melanie stood back patiently, debating whether to offer instruction or not.

"You've got it upside down," she finally said. "The reel should be on the bottom."

"Really?" Erin turned it around, then seemed totally lost. "Okay, so I guess I'll need a little help."

Melanie moved forward, taking Erin's hand and placing the reel foot between her middle fingers. "Like that. It's all in the wrist. When you open the bail, you hold the line against the rod with your index finger," she said, placing her finger on top of Erin's, pressing up to hold the line. She looked up, finding Erin watching her instead of their hands. She gave her a slight smile, then continued. "When you cast, release the line just past the top of your throw, then close the bail, like this," she said, moving the metal wire back down. She stepped away. "It took me several days to get the hang of it so don't be too hard on yourself. And I *had* been fishing before."

Erin seemed to mentally be going over her instructions, then she raised her hand and with a flick of her wrist, sent the line sailing out into the middle of the creek. Melanie clapped.

"Damn. Perfect on the first try."

Erin grinned as she watched the line float past them. "How far should I let it go?"

"If it's too far and you get a hit, you'll never be able to bring the fish in. I'd say no more than thirty, maybe forty feet downstream."

Erin reeled the line in, then tossed it back again, making another near perfect cast.

"You sure you haven't fished before?"

Erin shrugged. "Mechanical engineer."

"Oh, I see. Do you help design your houses then?"

"No. We've got a firm for that. Of course, clients can bring in their own design plans. We're a custom home builder. We can do anything." Erin reeled in the line again. "We're in talks to purchase some property in Waller County, close to Katy." She smiled. "I know that means nothing to you. It's northwest of Houston. Suburbs. We want to design—and build—a community." She cast out again. "And I'm supposed to forget about work for three months, so don't let me talk about it."

"You love what you do. It's hard not to talk about it, I guess."

Erin paused, letting the line float farther downstream than before. "Do I love it?" she asked quietly, almost to herself.

Melanie watched her pull the line in again, then saw the tip of the rod bend.

"Okay, so something's happening," Erin said, her voice excited.

"Reel it in. Don't let the line get too taut. You're out kinda far."

Erin glanced at her quickly. "You want to take it? It's not like I know what I'm doing."

"You're doing fine. Bring him in slowly." The trout jumped out of the water, its sleek skin glistening in the sunlight. "Nice one. Don't lose him."

The words were barely out of her mouth when the fish jumped again, this time twisting off the line.

"Well, damn," Erin said, obviously disappointed. "I could almost taste him."

Melanie laughed. "Yeah, that's usually the case." She handed her the power bait. "I'll leave you to it. I've got a basket of green beans I need to put up."

"Put up?"

"Can."

"Ah. The pressure canner thing. Do you want me to help?"

"I've got my routine down pat. It doesn't take me long." She pointed to the creek. "You're in charge of dinner. Two or three good-sized ones should be enough."

She went to walk away, but Erin called her back.

"Mel?"

She turned, eyebrows raised.

"Thanks for this. You were right. Being outside in the sunshine…"

She smiled. "Yes. Does wonders for your mood. Fish for dinner is simply the bonus."

CHAPTER SIXTEEN

Erin was absolutely filthy by the time she trudged back to the house, the fish bag slung over her shoulder. The knees of her slacks were stained with dirt, the sides dirty where she'd wiped her hands, and both of her shoes were wet. She'd rolled the sleeves of her shirt up to her elbows and had pulled the shirttail out at her waist, using it to wipe at the blood on her hand where the hook had caught her. Filthy, yeah, and she was grinning like a kid as she opened the kitchen door.

Melanie was at the stove, stirring something in a pot. She looked at her expectantly.

"I caught dinner," she said proudly.

"Yay! Let me see."

She handed over the bag, watching as Melanie opened it. She'd been having such a good time, she didn't stop with three.

"Four! Wow, they're nice. We'll have a feast tonight."

"That was fun. I could have stayed out for hours."

Melanie nodded. "Fishing is addicting. And relaxing. What is that quote attributed to Thoreau?"

Erin shook her head. "I have no idea."

"Some men fish all their lives, not knowing that it's not the fish they are really after…or something like that." She smiled at her. "I'm glad you enjoyed it." She handed the bag back to her. "Trout are easy to clean, by the way."

Erin's eyes widened. "Clean? You want me to…to…"

Melanie laughed. "Hey, you're the one who wanted to eat trout."

Erin took a deep breath. "Okay. Yes, I was. Show me what to do."

It was rather simple to clean the fish. Disgusting, but simple. Melanie had left her, saying she was going to the garden to get tomatoes and peppers for their lunch. She had to admit, she hadn't eaten this much food since…well, ever. Breakfast usually consisted of coffee, nothing more, nothing less. And lunch? A sandwich at a local deli, if she could squeeze in the time or the occasional business lunch. Dinner? Yeah, she was usually starving by then. And when Sarah came into her life, they'd cooked at home often. At first, at least. Until she'd started working more and more.

She stared out the kitchen window, seeing Melanie moving about in the garden. She'd met Sarah at a backyard barbeque—a friend of a friend of a friend. She'd been so lively, so flirty, laughing and teasing as if she'd known Erin for years. Erin fell a little bit in love that very day. Even toward the end, even when Erin could feel Sarah slipping away, she'd still been fun. Her friends loved Sarah. Everyone loved Sarah.

Well, except for Joyce and her family. What could they see that no one else could? She took a deep breath, seeing Melanie heading back toward the house, pausing to bend over and… pet a chicken? Melanie's hair fell around her face and as she straightened, she brushed it away. It was just long enough for a ponytail, which is how she normally wore it when she was outside working. When it hung loose, like now, she could see the different layers, the part on the side hidden as the breeze tossed her bangs about.

She continued to stare, seeing Sarah's face outside the window now, her bright blond hair long and silky. Her family could see through the act, she supposed. Sarah had a way about her. Erin couldn't refuse her anything. Yeah, she changed for her. It hadn't been hard, really. Sarah had pushed, guided, molded her into the person she was today. A person no one liked or wanted to be around, apparently. Even Sarah.

She looked down into the sink, seeing the four fish she'd cleaned. Well, no, not the person she was *today*. Not this very day.

"All done?"

Erin turned to Melanie, finding her holding two large tomatoes and a fistful of long peppers.

She motioned to her hand. "What kind are those?"

"Banana peppers. The spicy kind, not the sweet." She came beside her at the sink, gently nudging her aside with her hip. "I have the sweet ones too, but I'm making tacos." She put the veggies on the counter and inspected the fish. "Good job."

"I didn't know what to do with that," she said, pointing to the blob of fish guts.

"I have a spot out back, along the dry creek. The raccoons will clean it up tonight."

"Do the raccoons mess with the chickens or anything?"

"Oh, yeah, sure. If they could get into the coop, they'd kill them. But I've got it secure." She motioned out the window. "You might have noticed that I don't open the fenced yard until mid-morning, after the threat of predators fades." Then she smiled. "Or maybe not. I forgot you slept through the first five days."

"I'm really sorry about that. I—"

"No need to apologize. You obviously needed the rest. And like I said, if you're tired, take a nap. There are no rules." Then she grinned. "Other than Stella's rules, of course."

"Do you ever nap?"

"God, no. I've got too much to do. Especially during the summer when the garden is producing."

"Do you think…well, could you find the time to take me shopping?" She pointed at her pants. "You were right. I got these plenty dirty."

"I'll make time. We can go tomorrow, if you want." Melanie placed the fish into a plastic bag and handed it to her. "Fridge. And if you want to change before lunch, you have time. I still have to make the tortillas."

"You make your own tortillas?" she asked with amazement.

"It's not hard. I used to buy them and freeze them, taking them out as I needed, but when Angela moved here, about a year after me, she taught me how to make them. She even goes so far as to use a rolling pin, but I find it much easier with a tortilla press."

"No wonder they were so good."

"Go clean up. You can help me press them if you like."

Erin did as instructed, wondering at her sudden interest in cooking…and eating. Had she really been starving all these months? As she stared at herself in the mirror—naked—yes, she noted, she *had* been starving. Her breasts had shrunk to next to nothing. Not that she'd ever been well-endowed. She hadn't worn a bra in more years than she could remember. Who could tell? And her ribs? She could count nearly every one of them. She ran her hand over them now, feeling a bit more flesh than before. How much weight *had* she lost? And just how much had she gained back since she'd been here?

She stepped into the tiny shower, soaping herself quickly. She felt good, she noted. Relaxed. Dare she say content? She'd resolved herself to three months in exile. Once she'd accepted that, it seemed, she'd lost the will to fight the inevitable. And she'd escaped Rachel's house of horrors. She smiled, remembering that first dinner Rachel had fed her. God, that had been awful. And her head had been about to explode by morning. Now? No, her headaches had all but subsided. A couple—or three—cups of coffee each morning seemed to do the trick.

She'd lucked into Melanie, she decided. After hearing both Stella and Melanie describe the others, she'd probably have run screaming into the night by now had she been placed with someone else. Melanie was nice. She was normal. She was cute. Attractive. Why was she living out here with these...these misfits?

As she dried herself off, she wondered about their conversation last night. She'd been involved with someone...a man. The look in Melanie's eyes indicated she didn't want to discuss it any more than they had. She was curious, of course. Stella made it clear that everyone here was a lesbian, except for two, those both in their sixties. Melanie could have lied to Stella, she supposed, pretending to be lesbian so she could move out here. But why? If Stella now allowed any woman to move out here, why would she need to pretend she was a gay?

She shook her head. No. Melanie wasn't a straight woman, she could see that. Then again, she'd been out here, living alone for how long? Seven years? She supposed she wasn't a gay woman either. She nearly rolled her eyes. Since when was having sex a criteria for that label? After Sarah had left her, she hadn't even considered having sex with someone else in...what? Six, eight months? Even then, it was half-hearted. They never stayed around long. Of course, she wasn't really around either, was she? No. She was working. Keeping busy. Keeping her mind occupied to keep from wondering how long it would take her to get over the breakup.

She sometimes wondered if it wasn't so much a broken heart she was trying to get over or a bruised ego. Yes, when Sarah had first told her, she'd been shocked. Shocked about Sarah's affair, that is, not shocked that they'd drifted apart. She had felt that coming on for months. Despite that, she had no clue that Sarah had taken a lover two years prior. She remembered that day vividly—Sarah holding nothing back. The look in her eyes, the tone of her voice...it was a bit boastful. And condescending. And yes, arrogant. Perhaps Joyce had been right all along. Sarah *had* used her.

She remembered how empty she felt when Sarah had walked out. She thought she would shrivel up and die right then and there. There'd been no tears, though. She'd been too angry. Sarah had actually *cheated* on her. For two whole years and she'd had no clue.

She looked at herself in the mirror, giving a humorless smile to her reflection. She'd had a broken heart, sure. She'd loved Sarah. But she'd be lying if she said her ego hadn't taken a major hit too. Six wasted years. No. Seven and a half now. These last eighteen months had nearly killed her. If Joyce and her father hadn't intervened, how long would she have gone on like she was? She'd already hit rock bottom, hadn't she? There wasn't much farther to fall.

"Hey…you okay in there?"

Melanie's voice brought her out of her musings, and she stuck her head out of the bathroom, looking at the closed bedroom door.

"Yeah. Be right out."

"Okay. Lunch is ready."

CHAPTER SEVENTEEN

Melanie put the rocker in motion and closed her eyes, a smile curling up her lips as she pictured Erin's face as she ate fresh trout for the first time. Melanie had fixed all four, baking two and frying two. She'd had a feeling that Erin would devour them and she had. That's not to say that she didn't get her share. It reminded her of how long it had been since she'd taken the time for fishing.

She cupped the mug of tea, savoring the fragrance of it before taking a sip. She looked up into the nighttime sky, the sliver of moon hanging above the bluff to the west. It wasn't bright enough to be disruptive and the sky was still filled with stars. There were no clouds marring the sight and they were too far away from towns of any size for them to pollute the darkness.

It had been a nice couple of days, she noted. Different. Different from when she normally hosted guests. They were around for mealtimes but certainly not around to help with meal prep. And she'd never had a single one muck the goat stall before. Different. She would even go so far as to say she'd enjoyed Erin's company. Who would have thought that possible after the first few days? First five days, actually. She'd been dreading the three-month sentence as much as Erin had been, no doubt. Today, though—it had been nice. Nice to share time with someone her own age, for one. Nice to...

The loud, shrill howl behind the shed literally made her jump. But then she smiled.

"There you are," she murmured. "I've missed you."

Their howls turned to barks and yips, the chorus sounding like there were ten or twelve when she knew it was most likely only the two of them—Goldie and Rick. No doubt the chickens and goats were awakened by the howls, and no doubt, too, Bandito would be patrolling the area, running the coyotes off in short order.

"What the hell was that?"

She turned, finding Erin standing by the door. She pushed it open, walking out onto the porch. She was wearing nothing more than a T-shirt and undies.

The pair started singing again, their chorus echoing against the bluff, making it sound louder than it was.

"Wolves?"

"No. Coyotes."

"A pack? Should we be worried?"

"Probably just the two of them. A pair. They come frequently. Goldie and Rick."

Erin walked beside her rocker. "You've named them? The coyotes?"

"Yes. I tend to do that."

Then Erin stared at her. "Coffee?"

Melanie shook her head. "Tea, decaf." She arched an eyebrow. "Would you like a cup?"

"A glass of wine would be nice."

Melanie nodded. "Yeah...rules and all."

"That would be an easy rule to break. What's the real reason?"

"Does there have to be a reason?" She motioned to the chair. "Would you like to join me? I'll make you a cup."

"Will I be interrupting your quiet time?"

"No." She got up. "Would you like honey? Or sugar?"

"Honestly, I've never had hot tea before. You choose."

Erin followed her inside and went into her bedroom while Melanie filled another cup with hot water. Erin came back out wearing pants, but her feet were still bare. They took their tea back outside to the porch.

"It's nice out here. Cool. Still."

Melanie smiled when the coyotes started up again.

"Was still," Erin corrected. "They sound so close."

"Behind the shed. Bandito will chase them to the creek."

"He roams?"

"Yes. Never far."

"Aren't you afraid something will…I don't know, get him?"

"Donkeys are pretty fierce. A lot of ranchers keep donkeys with their herds for protection from predators. Especially for sheep and goats. He's quite intimidating when he puts his head down and charges."

Before long, the coyotes moved away, their chorus dwindling to nothing but a few barks now.

"And they're off to go hunting."

"You sit out here every night?"

"Pretty much, yes."

"Your quiet time? To reflect on the day?"

She nodded. "Yes. Sometimes I do. Other times, I sit and think of nothing. Just watch the sky, listen to the night. It's a good way to…to relax. No stress."

"And have you been stressed?"

"Not in the last few days. Earlier, yes."

"Because I was here?"

"Because you were here, but you weren't *really* here. You weren't talking. You were—"

"Hiding in my room," Erin finished for her. "Yes, I was. I was lonely and depressed and really, really tired." She turned to look at her. "I can only apologize so many times."

"I wasn't seeking another apology. I mean, you're the paying customer here. If you want to sleep all day, that's your business.

If you want to participate in chores, that's your choice. If you want to run naked along the creek, feel free," she added with a smile.

Erin laughed. "That would be a first for me. Though I have run naked around my pool before. Would that count?"

"I'm just saying, don't feel like you need to apologize for something you do. Or don't do."

"What brings most people here? I'm assuming they're not like me." She sipped from her tea. "This is very good."

"Thank you. And no, they come for different reasons than you. Most come for the solitude. Most of our guests come by themselves. Some enjoy the interactions with their hosts, others don't. Some go off at sunrise and don't come back until dusk. Last summer, I hosted a young woman. She had graduated college but wasn't enthused about her job offers. She stayed three days. She hiked up the bluff in the dark each morning to watch the sunrise. She'd stay out until noon, when she'd come back for lunch. Then she'd go out across the creek and climb the bluff there. She'd stay until the sunset colors had faded, then she'd come back at dusk."

"Every day?"

"Yes. She was meditating. Looking within herself, hoping to find a path to take, I guess."

"And?"

"By the time she left, she was at peace. She told me she knew which job she was going to take." She set the rocker in motion. "Some come for reasons like that...to *find* themselves, as they say. And there are the few who look at this as a vacation. They hike and play in the creek and take photos and collect rocks and stuff. For a few years, we had an artist come each summer. She was in her seventies and always requested to stay with Stella. I think she came five years in a row, maybe six. She stopped coming and Stella didn't know why." She paused, remembering how Stella had cried when the package had come. "A painting was delivered one day last summer. It was of Stella, out in her garden." She turned to look at Erin. "The woman had died. She'd been ill and hadn't told Stella. She'd left instructions to have the painting sent upon her death. There was a lovely note and…"

"And?"

"And it was all so romantic. I picture these two women, in their seventies, gently flirting with each other for one week a year, for five or six years. I think they both fell a little bit in love. In fact, I'm sure of it."

"Has Stella ever lived with someone?"

"Yes. She and her lover started this place. But it wasn't for her, it turned out. She missed the city, missed the amenities. She stayed almost ten years. Stella was heartbroken, to hear her tell it."

"What about you?"

"What about me?"

Erin started rocking beside her, and Melanie wondered if she'd reconsidered asking the question. Melanie knew what she was asking, of course.

"You always lived here alone?"

"Yes."

Erin turned to her. "Why?"

Melanie shrugged. "Why not?"

She met her gaze, almost daring her to ask more. Erin didn't look away and in the dim light of the porch, she could see the questions drifting around in her eyes. Then Erin finally did look away, taking a quick glance skyward as she drank her tea.

"The sky is amazing. I've lived in Houston my whole life. I never knew there were so many stars."

Melanie relaxed, knowing there would be no more questions tonight. But Erin's curiosity was obviously piqued. She'd known that when she'd mentioned Adam. It had slipped out. She'd never shared anything about her personal life with any of her guests. As far as she knew, Stella was the only one who knew about her childhood, but Melanie had not told her about Adam…or what had happened. When she'd first moved, the ladies had been curious—nosy—but she'd managed to get by with vague answers and a little fibbing now and then.

But Erin would be here for three months. They got along well enough. They talked. Actually, she could see them becoming friends. And friends talked. And friends asked questions.

Yes. But not tonight.

CHAPTER EIGHTEEN

Erin stared up at the huge letters on the store, then turned to Melanie. "Walmart? I'm going clothes shopping at Walmart?"

Melanie nudged her arm playfully as they walked in. "Don't be so snobbish. They have jeans. They have shorts. They have T-shirts. They have shoes." Then she stopped. "Although, maybe we should go to a sports store for your shoes. You need a good pair of hiking boots too. And if you plan to get into the creek, you'll need something for that. I wear sandals."

"Like swimming?"

"Like playing. There aren't any deep pools to really swim in. I've found a few spots that are chest deep, not much more. Big enough to splash around. Then there's the hot springs, but that's more soaking than swimming."

"Wow. You're full of surprises, aren't you? I wouldn't mind soaking in a hot spring. That would be relaxing."

Melanie led her to the clothes section, finding the racks of jeans. "Unfortunately, it's a tough hike to get there." She glanced at her. "But if you want to go, I'll take you. I wouldn't mind taking a break from work." She studied her, then held up a pair. "What size? Four?"

"Four? Come on. I wear at least an eight."

"Maybe in another life. You're very thin, Erin." Melanie stared at her. "Although, you look much better. Healthier, that's for sure."

"I know I looked like crap when I got here. I felt like crap too. And yes, I have gained some weight back." She took the size four jeans and held them up to her waist. They did seem like the right size. She shook her head anyway. "Six. Let's go with a six. The way I'm eating, I'll grow out of the four in no time."

"Okay. I'll let you shop in peace then. I've got a few things I need." Melanie squeezed her arm as she walked away. "I'll meet you back over here."

Erin watched her go, her eyes lighting on her tan legs. Then she smiled and nodded. "Oh, yeah. I'm supposed to buy shorts too." Her gaze never wavered, though, until Melanie was out of sight.

I like her, she thought. She was...easy. Easy to be around, easy to talk to. Easy to look at, she added with another smile. It had been a while since she'd made a new friend. It had been a while since she'd had a friend, period. The old ones had disappeared, it seemed. Disappeared with Sarah. No. She was the one who had disappeared, not them. They'd finally stopped calling, stopped coming around. She'd hardly noticed, really.

She turned her attention to the jeans in her hand, then looked back at the shelves that lined a wall. There were black ones, dark blue, faded blue, and *really* faded blue. Some were fancier than others and she dismissed those. She needed something suitable for a farm, not a night out on the town. She found a style that worked, then took one of each color. She was about to toss them into her cart, then decided she should probably try them on. As expected, they were too large. The size four would have probably fit perfectly, but as she'd said, the way she was eating, she would grow into them.

Her basket was filled with four jeans, three pairs of hiking shorts, some comfortable cotton shorts, an assortment of

T-shirts and tanks, and even a couple of pullovers. All she needed was socks and shoes and she'd be set.

She was about to head out to see if she could find Melanie when she saw the other woman approach. She smiled when she saw her and Melanie did the same.

"Success?"

Erin nodded, motioning to her cart. Melanie inspected the clothes, holding some up to her and nodding.

"Good choices. I think this will get you through summer." She met her gaze. "When does your jail sentence end?"

"September ninth."

"The days will still be warm. And if the nighttime temps drop, I'll let you borrow a sweatshirt." She smiled again. "Come on. Let's get out of here."

"What about shoes?"

"Yeah…we'll go somewhere else."

Erin pushed her cart along with Melanie's, spying what she had inside hers. Staples, mainly. Flour, sugar, a box of whole wheat pasta, a large bag of brown rice, and two huge bags of dried beans. A few toiletry items—shaving cream and shower gel. There were also three blocks of tofu and several boxes of mushrooms.

"What do you have planned for the mushrooms?"

"You like them?"

Erin nodded. "Particularly sautéed in butter and placed on top of a medium rare steak."

Melanie smiled at her. "I'll allow fish in my kitchen. That's as close as you'll get to a steak. But the tomatoes are coming in. I thought I'd make a sauce for spaghetti. I like to can some each summer, enough to make it through the winter without having to buy any." She arched an eyebrow. "You like spaghetti, right?"

"And meatballs?"

"Yes, actually." Another smile. "Lentil meatballs."

"Not gonna complain. You're an excellent cook. Besides, I could be stuck with Rachel and her beans. Anything could beat that."

"Nobody lasts with Rachel, although you were probably the quickest to run. Stella really should stop placing guests with her, but Rachel enjoys the company more than anyone, I think."

"She tried to get me to knit. I was about to stab her with the needles."

Melanie laughed outright. "Oh, poor Rachel. No, I don't think she could have handled you."

"And you can?"

"Of course." Then she nudged her arm. "After shoes, you want to get lunch?"

Erin grinned. "Lunch? Like a burger or something?"

"If that's what you want. You're not at the ranch and you're not a vegetarian, so yes...if you want a greasy cow burger or chicken or whatever...have at it." Then she winked. "We just won't tell Stella."

Later, though, as she sat across from Melanie, she almost wished she'd gotten the veggie burger. Melanie's bun was exploding with spinach and lettuce, tomatoes and cucumbers and curly sprouts. But, as she bit into her own—hot, juicy, *real* meat—burger, she couldn't contain a moan.

"That good, huh?"

Erin wiped the corner of her mouth and nodded. "Excellent. And to think I was envious of yours. This is like a gourmet burger."

"I'll take your word for it."

"You're not even tempted when you get off the ranch?"

"Tempted to eat meat? No. Not anymore. It's been over seven years. I'd probably get sick if I ate something like that. If this had been the first couple months, I would have already beaten you up and stuffed you under the table while I had my way with your burger."

Erin laughed. "Yeah, well...you could have *tried* to take my burger," she said as she took another bite. Then she winked. "But you would not have succeeded."

"So you say."

They stared at each other, smiling. Erin was the first to look away from the smiling eyes...eyes that were not quite green, yet not quite blue.

"Thank you."

"For lunch?"

"For everything, really. For taking me in, feeding me, making me get outside and do something. For today." She met her eyes again. "I…I thought this was going to be a very long, very lonely three months. Honestly, I didn't think I could make it. Not with my sanity intact anyway."

"Well, truthfully, I was dreading it as much as you were. I'm used to being by myself, alone…you know, the hermit thing." Then she smiled. "I never imagined I would find myself becoming friends with you."

"Yes. Joyce reminded me that I no longer had any friends. I think I had forgotten what it was like to have someone to talk to, be with…laugh with. Normal stuff that didn't involve the office. I don't guess I've laughed much—if at all—in the last eighteen months. So thank you for that too."

Melanie looked at her for a beat longer, then nodded. "You're welcome."

Erin went back to her burger. "So—about the hot springs. Or the creek. Can we go?"

"Sure. If you help me with some of my chores, then I can spare an afternoon."

"Deal. Because I did buy a swimsuit, just in case."

Melanie met her gaze again, a slow smile forming. "A swimsuit can be used for the creek, if you want."

Erin arched an eyebrow. "Oh?"

"Hot springs are meant to be enjoyed naked." Melanie reached over and stole a fry from her plate. "I actually enjoy them both naked. I don't own a suit."

Erin was shocked when she got a mental picture of that. She'd seen Melanie in shorts and a tank as she'd worked in her garden. It didn't take much to imagine her *without* the shorts and tank.

What really shocked her the most, though, was that it wasn't Sarah's face and body she pictured. That was a first. The handful of women she'd slept with in the last eighteen months—including Jessica, the last one she'd attempted to date—it was always Sarah she was in bed with, never them.

She met Melanie's gaze, but her blueish green eyes were a bit guarded. A smile was still playing around her lips, however.

"A hermit...and yet an exhibitionist. Who would have thought?" she teased.

Melanie simply smiled at her as she stole another fry from her plate.

CHAPTER NINETEEN

"Are you sure?"

She went up onto the porch, beckoning Erin to follow. "You said you wanted to get your hair cut."

"Yeah. I do. But…" Erin lowered her voice. "Does she know what she's doing?"

Melanie patted her arm reassuringly. "Dianne owned her own shop in her previous life. She cuts everyone's hair here, including mine." She tucked her hair behind her ears. "In fact, it's time for me too. I usually cut it short every summer, then let it grow the rest of the year. It's about to drive me crazy. I'm at least a month past due."

She knocked on the door. "Dianne? It's Mel," she called loudly, knocking again.

The screen door opened and Dianne peeked out, her smile nearly beaming as she looked past her to Erin.

"You must be our guest. How nice of you to bring her around, Mel." Dianne made a show of puffing and straightening her hair, which still had a trace of auburn color to it.

"Yes. This is Erin," Melanie introduced. "Sorry to come unannounced, but…"

Dianne waved her apology away. "I don't have a phone. What should you do? Send a smoke signal?"

Melanie saw the amused expression on Erin's face, and she smiled at her, then turned back to Dianne. "Erin wants a haircut. So do I. Do you have time?"

"Oh, my goodness! Yes, of course! I've just come in from the garden. I try to get my chores out of the way before it gets too hot, you know." She opened the door wider. "Come in, come in."

"Thank you for doing this on such short notice," Erin said as she followed Melanie inside.

"Oh, of course. I take care of everyone out here." Dianne led them into the kitchen. "Sit, sit. I'll put coffee on."

"Don't go to any trouble," Melanie said quickly, knowing it would fall on deaf ears. Dianne, like most of the others, enjoyed company. Besides coffee, she knew that Dianne would push food on them as well.

"I must have known you were coming," Dianne said, ignoring her comment as she busied herself with the coffeemaker. "I baked a zucchini cake just this morning."

"Zucchini *cake*?" Erin whispered questioningly to her.

"Yes. It's very good. I was actually going to bake one too."

"Are your zucchini as thick as mine?" Dianne asked her. "Bumper crop this year. I have no idea what I'll do with them all."

"Yes. We're eating squash for practically every meal. Erin is probably sick of it."

"Not yet," Erin interjected.

"Oh, well…we must eat what our gardens provide, mustn't we." Dianne placed three cups on the table. "Have you adjusted to being here, Erin? I heard Rachel ran you off rather quickly."

Melanie smiled as Erin had an embarrassed look on her face.

"She…well, I can't decide if it was the threat of knitting or the beans and broccoli she served for breakfast."

Dianne laughed. "Oh, poor Rachel. I hope I never get to where our guests run from me." She poured coffee into each cup, then pushed over an ancient sugar bowl. "I have some cream if you like. I know Mel likes hers black."

"None for me, thanks."

The zucchini cake came out next and they spent the next twenty minutes or so making idle chitchat while they ate. She didn't know if Erin was getting restless or not, but she sure was. She declined a second cup of coffee.

"I've got to get back into my garden this afternoon," she said. "And we shouldn't take up any more of your time."

Dianne didn't seem offended and she turned her attention to Erin. "So how are you wanting your hair, Erin? A trim or something more drastic?"

Erin fingered her hair now, which Melanie noted was looking so much better—alive—than when she first met her.

"I'm thinking drastic." Then she looked at Melanie as if for confirmation. "A change. Being out here is an emotional, mental change for me. I think I need a physical change too. Don't you think?"

"Too drastic might be a shock for you. Is this how you've had it for a while?"

"I haven't really bothered with it…in a year and a half or so."

"I see." Meaning, since Sarah had left her. She reached out a hand now, touching Erin's hair. It was thicker than she'd thought. It had looked so thin, so lifeless, dull and dingy. Now? Now it had a healthy shine to it; it was soft, silky. Then she dropped her hand, realizing she had no right to be touching her like that. "Drastic is good."

"Let me get my things. We'll do it on the back porch. Show her, Mel. I'll be right back."

Erin stood up when Dianne left. "That cake was really good. I'm not going to complain too much if you make one of those."

Melanie was smiling as she led Erin to the back porch. It was such a change—a pleasant change—to cook for someone. Someone who enjoyed eating. She wouldn't have suspected that about Erin. Not after their first meeting. She turned, studying her. She'd been here over three weeks already. She'd obviously gained some weight, which was badly needed. Her face was no longer gaunt, her skin no longer pale. Her eyes had lost the cloudiness from the first few days. The hazel eyes were bright, nearly twinkling now. She was amazed at the transformation.

"What?"

Should she apologize for staring? "You look good."

"Oh, yeah? Compared to what? Me on death's door?"

"Why?"

"Why what?"

"Why did you do it?"

"Let myself go like I did?" Erin turned away from her. "I don't know, really. Several things. I blamed it on a broken heart, bruised ego. I was hurt, lonely… Lost. The only constant in my life was the job and I made that my sole focus. I ran—and hid—from what had become my reality."

"You must have been terribly in love with her."

Erin met her gaze. "I must have been, right?"

Melanie could see the doubt in her eyes. Yes, she supposed after eighteen months, doubt would creep in.

The back door opened and Dianne came out with her kit. "Sit in the tall chair there, Erin."

Melanie pulled out another chair to sit and watch. Erin had a bit of an apprehensive look on her face as Dianne flung an old, faded, cloth cape around her and tied it at her neck.

"Do you want a mirror?"

"No. Better not."

"Okay. I'm going to start trimming. You tell me when to stop. Then I'll get it all shaped up for you." She looked at Melanie. "This is so exciting! Everyone always gets the same old thing. And you, Mel, you look so cute with your hair shorter. I don't know why you won't let me keep it up for you all year instead of just summer."

Melanie knew why, of course. It wasn't something she fussed with and having to sit through a haircut every five weeks or so was too much trouble. But she said what she'd said last year.

"Maybe I'll come by more often."

"Heard that before," Dianne muttered as she snipped off about two inches of Erin's hair.

For the most part, Erin kept her eyes closed and Melanie wondered what she was thinking. She also wondered how Erin normally looked...prior to Sarah leaving. She'd been so thin, so frail looking before, she hadn't really noticed her attractiveness. She imagined when she was healthy—normal—she was quite striking. Her hazel eyes were dark with just a hint of green in them. As she stared, those eyes opened, meeting hers. A quick smile, then Erin closed them again.

Melanie was shocked that Dianne kept cutting and Erin had yet to stop her. Another two inches and she'd be over her ear. The back was already above her neckline. She glanced at the pile of hair on the porch around the chair, wondering if maybe this was cleansing for Erin. She looked up, seeing Dianne flick her gaze at her then back to Erin.

"Should I keep going, dear?"

Erin kept her eyes closed. "Mel can decide."

Melanie's eyes widened. "Me? But..."

"Drastic," Erin reminded her.

Melanie got up, moving in front of her, close enough that her thighs brushed Erin's knees. She ran her fingers through Erin's hair, brushing it back. It was all one length and needed some layering done but...

"Over the ears," she said. "Then layered some on top."

"Yes, I think so," Dianne agreed. "She's quite pretty this way. Handsome," Dianne said with a fluttering of her eyelashes. At that, Erin's eyes popped open.

Melanie met them and smiled, letting her hand fall away. "Yes. Handsome."

* * *

Erin rubbed her hand over her hair once again. Never in her life, not even in college, had she worn her hair this short. She had yet to look in a mirror, but both Melanie and Dianne had insisted it looked "wonderful" on her. If it looked anything like Melanie's neatly trimmed hair, she'd be pleased. Erin had to agree with Dianne. Mel looked gorgeous with short hair. It was a fresh, sporty cut and it suited her. But Erin knew why she only got it cut once a year. It was quite the ordeal and knowing Melanie as she did now—and her professed claim that she was a hermit—she would imagine this was a bit too much for her to endure. The coffee, the visiting, the haircut, and more visiting.

"You're fidgeting. Look in the mirror already," Melanie said, motioning to the visor above her head when they were heading back home.

"I'm afraid to," she admitted.

"It looks good," Melanie said. "Of course, I didn't know you before or how you are *supposed* to look, but this is a good look for you. Much better, in my opinion."

"Yours too. I like it like that. You should keep it."

"Do you?" Melanie bounced them along the crude road in her truck, turning along the creek that would take them back to her cabin. "It's definitely easier. And I don't know why I put it off…you know, getting more frequent haircuts."

"Don't you?"

Melanie smiled. "What? You think you know me already?"

Erin laughed. "Yeah, I do. Hermits don't like quite that much visiting."

When Melanie parked next to the cabin, between the two trees that she'd told Erin were piñon pines, the old white dog limped over. They hadn't seen him in nearly a week.

"I see Fred has made it back around." Melanie slammed the door, then bent over to pet his head. "Where have you been, boy?"

"So he roams from house to house?"

"Pretty much. I don't know why they were so adamant that I adopt him. Everyone takes care of him. I probably see him less than they do."

"Do others have pets?"

"Oh, a few. Angela has two cats. Rebecca has a little house dog. A few have outdoor dogs." She held open the door. "Come on. I want to see your reaction to your hair."

Erin followed her into the house and instead of going into her tiny bathroom, Melanie led her into her own bedroom. It was neat and tidy and airy, with three windows, all open. It was quite a bit larger than Erin's room. Big enough for both a dresser and a set of drawers and…

"A king bed?"

Melanie shrugged. "It's what I had when I moved."

She pushed open another door, revealing a large bathroom with a walk-in shower. It, too, was neat and tidy. Erin paused at the door, then stepped in, her eyes going to the mirror without much delay. And who in the hell was she looking at? Surely that wasn't her. The hair looked even shorter than it felt and she brought a hand to it now, fingers moving slowly above her ear.

"Well, it's drastic, all right."

Melanie stood beside her and they looked at their reflections in the mirror, their eyes meeting that way. Melanie smiled at her.

"I'm sure it's a shock to you, but it looks really, really good."

"A shock, yes. I don't…" She shook her head. "I don't recognize myself."

"Give it a few days." Melanie touched her own hair, the part on the side still in disarray from the wind. She straightened it. "This is how I prefer to keep mine. In fact, I wouldn't mind it to be as short as yours."

"Only because you wouldn't have to go back as often," Erin teased. Then her smile faded. "Why don't you like people?"

"I never said I didn't like people."

"Then why the hermit thing?"

Melanie looked away from her gaze in the mirror, touching Erin's shoulders and turning her, nearly pushing her out of the bathroom.

"I believe you promised to help me in the garden this afternoon in exchange for some playtime in the creek tomorrow. Instead of lunch, I thought we could do an early dinner. I'm too full of cake and coffee to think about lunch."

"Just tell me it's none of my business."

"Okay. It's none of your business. There. Now go change into something suitable for the garden." She motioned toward her bedroom door. "We have compost to move today."

Erin looked at the shorts she had on. One of the new pairs of hiking shorts she'd bought. "Suitable?"

"Jeans. You'll be on your knees."

Erin stood in the doorway of the bedroom, watching as Melanie went into her bathroom and quietly closed the door. She wondered what demons Melanie was fighting. Now that she had her wits about her, now that she wasn't wallowing in self-pity, she could see the sadness in Mel's eyes, could see the wall she'd built around herself. What was she trying to keep out?

Who was she trying to keep out?

CHAPTER TWENTY

Melanie was used to being by herself, used to making this trip upstream alone—usually on her bike and not on foot, like today—and she was used to stripping off her clothes, completely uninhibited. None of the others ever came up this way so she didn't concern herself with modesty. In fact, even in her previous life, she was never shy about her body.

Yet now, as she and Erin stood beside the creek, a half-mile or so up from her cabin, she was feeling self-conscious. No one had seen her naked in over seven years. Actually, eight, she supposed. She remembered the dark-haired woman she'd met at the bar, remembered thinking "why the hell not?" when that woman had propositioned her. She couldn't remember her name, but she could see her face plainly. It was the last time she'd been touched. The last time she'd been intimate with anyone. The last time she *tried* to be intimate, she corrected. She hadn't actually been able to go through with it.

Since Adam's death, she hadn't been able to…to connect with anyone. It had been more than a year later before she'd been comfortable enough to even consider being with someone. It had been a disaster. Her therapist encouraged her to try again. And she had. A few times. And that night at the bar was the last try. At the time, she had decided it was her punishment for Adam's death. She was to go through life alone, without love. Love? No. She wasn't looking for love. She was simply looking for some human contact, some comfort, some release.

It never came. She finally gave up looking for it.

She glanced over at Erin, who was wearing the new swimsuit she'd bought, a rather plain, black one-piece. She had on a pair of her hiking shorts over it and the new sandals. No shirt. It emphasized how thin she still was, but Erin didn't seem to care. Melanie noted that her pale skin was finally getting some color back, thanks to her time being outside and helping in the garden.

"We picked a great day for this," Erin said. "It's hot. The hottest day yet, I think."

"Yes. Summer is upon us. The monsoon season will start soon."

"What is that?"

"Not monsoon in the traditional sense, but for here, it means it rains nearly every day, usually in the afternoon, then it clears up by evening most days. Occasionally we'll have an all-nighter. That'll be the pattern into August. If we're lucky, it'll last into September. After that, we're pretty much dry and rain-free until next year." She smiled at her. "As you can tell, I don't mind the rain. And it certainly helps cool things down."

"Is the water cold? I mean, when I was fishing I didn't really notice it too much."

"It's a mountain stream so...yes. But that, too, is relative." She bent down and ran her hand through it. "It feels like it always feels." She stood up and placed her hand on top of Erin's arm. "Cool, not cold."

"It'll feel good."

Erin unbuttoned her shorts and stepped out of them. Again, Melanie was conscious of how thin she was. This time, Erin seemed to read her thoughts.

"I know. I could probably stand to gain twenty pounds." She

ran her hand up her chest. "My breasts have all but disappeared."

Melanie followed her hands with her eyes, nearly blushing as Erin's hands rested on her breasts. She quickly shifted her gaze lower. "You...you used to be a runner?"

Erin raised her eyebrows. "Why do you say that?"

"You don't have any fat on your legs, but your muscle is still defined."

"I'm surprised. I haven't even been on my treadmill in..."

"Eighteen months," she finished for her.

Erin sighed and leaned her head back, looking into the blue sky overhead. "I stopped...living. I stopped doing everything I enjoyed. I cut off my friends...*our* friends. I retreated into my own little shell and worked until I collapsed." She looked back at her. "As much as I hated my father—and Joyce—for making me do this, I feel so...so *good*. And that word seems far too mild to use. Every day I feel better. Stronger."

"Every day you look better. And stronger."

"I...I don't think about her much. She doesn't cross my mind much at all anymore, in fact."

"Are you still in love with her?"

"Oh, honestly, I don't even know that we were still in love toward the end. I was working so much and she'd obviously lost interest. At the time, when she told me she was leaving, yes, I would have said I was still in love with her. Surely. I mean, why suffer all of this," she said, motioning to herself, "if it wasn't love?"

Melanie didn't say anything, giving Erin the opportunity to voice her thoughts without Mel injecting her own feelings on the matter.

"I think back now," Erin said, turning to look at her. "Now, meaning now that I've been here and I'm not doped up on caffeine and booze. I can see things a little more clearly now. The last year, at least, we weren't really happy. If we'd go out, sure. Sarah was fun. Life of the party, in fact. Then sure, we looked happy. But at home? Alone? I always seemed to be in my office and she...she was in front of the TV or on her laptop." She shrugged. "There wasn't a whole lot of intimacy toward the end. I imagine it was hard for her, to sleep with me, when she had a lover across the country who she wanted to be with."

"Did she have a job?"

"No. I made enough to support us and we liked to vacation, to be able to take off when we wanted. She quit her job that first year we were together. Why? Are you suggesting she was bored?"

"I know I'd be."

Erin smiled at her. "Would you? Or would you have found something to do?"

Melanie laughed. "Would I have a garden and chickens and goats if I didn't have to? I guess I could get by with less. I could stock up at the grocery store instead of growing my own, I suppose. But I told you, it's relaxing. It's therapy. I mean, don't get me wrong, it's hard work and sometimes I do tire of it, but the rewards I get from it outweigh anything else." She held her hand up. "I didn't mean to shift the subject to me."

"It's okay. Like I said, I don't think about her that much anymore. No sense in talking about her." Then Erin smiled. "You really don't have a swimsuit?"

"I really don't." She pointed at her teasingly. "And the proper thing for you to do would be to turn your back while I undress."

"No way." Erin was still smiling as she walked into the creek, the water up to her knees. "A little cold, but not bad."

"Do you see the deeper hole in the middle? That'll be above your waist. This is one of the spots I come to. There is another deep pool a little farther up. It's deeper than this but not very wide."

She watched as Erin moved toward the middle, the water creeping above her thighs now. The creek was flowing lazily, gurgling and rippling over the rocks, the sound mixing with the breeze. Once the rains came, the creek would swell, the water more fierce than it was now.

She tossed her backpack down beside Erin's discarded shorts. She was apprehensive about stripping, but she firmly pushed it away. This was her creek, her place. This was her routine—stripping naked on the edge. And long after Erin left, this would still be her creek and her routine. No need to feel embarrassed about it now, no matter how long it had been since someone had seen her naked.

So, without looking in Erin's direction, she pulled her tank off and tossed it down. Her breasts were small—too small to be considered sexy or alluring, she supposed. And too small for her to bother with a bra. Her shorts followed and without much ceremony—and without looking at Erin she walked into the water, moving directly to the deeper hole. She sunk down up to her neck, ignoring the coolness of the water. She finally dared to glance at Erin, who was blatantly staring, her mouth parted slightly. The crystal clear mountain water hid nothing.

"You...you," Erin said, swallowing. "You have a really nice body." Then she smiled. "You must do this often. Your tan..."

Melanie smiled and tilted her head back into the water, wetting her hair. "On particularly hot days, I garden without a shirt on."

Erin laughed. "So you really are an exhibitionist."

"The benefit of living out here away from everyone, yes. It's freeing to be shirtless."

Erin moved into deeper water too, then ducked under, soaking her face and hair. She came up, wiping it away with both hands. "I think I really love the cut. No one back home would recognize me."

"I like it too. And your face isn't quite so thin anymore. Isn't it amazing how quickly your body can heal when you nourish it properly?"

"Yes. Body and mind. And I've been sleeping like a rock. That's a first for me."

"I think sleeping with the windows open helps. I love it cool and breezy and dark."

"Was it hard for you to adjust when you moved out here?"

"Oh, yeah. At first, it was too quiet. As you know, living in the city, there are always noises of some kind at all hours of the day and night. And the first time the coyotes came close...well, it scared the shit out of me," she said with a laugh.

They were quiet for a moment and she listened to the

chatter of a group of chickadees in the piñon pines, foraging for pine nuts, most likely.

"What are they?"

"Chickadees. Cute little birds."

Erin ran her hand slowly under the water. "And the hummingbirds? I really love watching them."

"Those are black-chinned hummingbirds. During the fall migration, I'll get different species coming through—broad-tailed, for one. I usually put up three feeders then."

"And what are those large black and white birds that I see around the chickens?"

"Magpies, looking to steal corn."

"You've really embraced living out here, haven't you?" Then Erin smiled. "I guess you have, it's been seven years." She tilted her head thoughtfully. "Have you ever wanted to leave?"

"Ever? Or do you mean recently? Because at first, yes, I thought often about leaving." She held her hand up sideways against the current, watching it spill over. "I had sold my house in Phoenix for almost three times what I paid for it. I used that money to build the cabin, dig a well—which cost a small fortune—and bring electricity out. I didn't use all of it, thankfully, and was able to have a nice savings account and even invest some. My little cabin was quite reasonable to build." She moved into shallower water and found a rock to sit on, the water splashing just below her breasts. "I sold my car and bought the truck, used. By the time I had the shed built, the chicken coop, the fence…Well, I'd spent way too much money to walk away. That's not to say I didn't think about it."

She knew the more she talked, the more questions Erin would have. The question she asked now, however, wasn't the one she was expecting.

"You were involved with a man?"

Underneath the water, Melanie wrapped her arms around her knees, wondering at the question. Wondering how she should answer it.

"Yes."

"So…you're not gay?"

Melanie met her gaze. "Yes, I am." She could see the confusion in Erin's eyes, could see more questions forming.

"So you were with this guy when you realized you were gay? I mean, a lot of women do that, I guess."

"No. I knew I was gay at a young age." She blew out a quick breath. Did she really want to talk about this? "He—Adam—was the son of my last foster parents. I met him when I had just turned sixteen. We became fast friends. Close. Brother and sister close." She drew her knees up even higher, resting her feet on the rock she was sitting on. She leaned her cheek against her knee, picturing his sweet face, his dark eyes. "He was convinced he was in love with me. I didn't tell him I was gay. He kept saying that we would be good together, that we'd be happy… as a couple. I told him I didn't feel that way about him, but he seemed so sure of it, so sure that I could fall in love with him. I was eighteen when he first told me. Nineteen when he first kissed me. Every time I told him no, I could see the hurt in his eyes. I didn't want to keep hurting him, so when I was twenty, we became more than friends. I thought maybe—eventually—I could love him that way. We moved in together shortly after that, and we were a couple, like he wanted."

"You're here now so obviously that didn't work out."

Melanie dropped her knees and submerged into the deep pool, as if hiding from Erin would stop the questions. As if hiding from her would stop the memories from pouring back in. When she surfaced, she slicked her wet hair back from her face, noting the shortness of it.

She looked at Erin then, trying to decide how much to tell her. "I…I was much like your Sarah. I met a woman. I was twenty-three at the time. We had an affair for over two years. I couldn't bear to tell Adam. I couldn't break his heart like that. He truly, deeply loved me. And yes, I loved him. But I was never *in* love with him. Not ever. And he knew. He'd stopped asking me if I loved him."

"And this other woman? Were you in love with her?"

"More lust than love. She gave me what was missing with Adam, that's all. Physically, she gave me what I needed. I wasn't in love with her, no."

"She's obviously not around either."

"No. That...that ended." She held her hand up when Erin would have asked another question. "That whole story, that time in my life...To talk about that, I'll require a very dark night."

"I'm sorry. I have no right to pry."

"No, you don't." Then she smiled, softening her words. "But friends pry, don't they?"

CHAPTER TWENTY-ONE

Erin was pleasantly tired and pleasantly full. Tired from their hike and the play day in the water and full from the dinner Melanie had whipped up. She was quite enjoying the vegetarian meals that Mel threw together, almost without much thought. Vegetables, of course. Always two, sometimes three varieties. Potatoes or rice. Beans or the occasional tofu. There was even something Mel called soy curls that had a rather chicken-like consistency. Simple meals yet full of flavor. Tonight's meal was a combination of leftovers in the fridge along with some squash she'd cut into strips and grilled.

"If you're in the mood for trout again, feel free to fish any day," Melanie offered.

"I'm too full to think about fish right now."

"Too full for a cup of tea?"

Erin eyed her, wondering at the request. Was Melanie inviting her to join her on the porch this evening? As if seeing the question in her mind, Melanie nodded. "If you want to…to talk."

Ah. So Melanie was ready to tell her life's story. After today, after she'd ended that vein of conversation so quickly, she had thought it would be days—or even weeks—before she'd want to broach it again. Ending the conversation hadn't put a damper on their outing, though. They'd lounged in the water, tossing rocks about as they chatted. Chatted like friends. Melanie was very comfortable in her nakedness and Erin—after a while— adjusted to being in the water with a nude woman. Erin found herself telling Melanie anecdotes from her childhood, her teenage years...even college. And Mel, too, shared some things, although her words had a tinge of sadness to them. She'd been lonely growing up, she'd told her, making friends only sporadically until she'd gotten older and gotten into a more stable environment.

Erin looked at her now, taking the last plate from her to dry. Mel was in shorts, a navy T-shirt. No bra. Again, comfortable. Erin finally nodded, seeing the anticipation in her eyes...blue tonight. She'd learned Melanie's eyes changed color, often matching the shade of the shirt she wore. As those eyes held hers, she wondered how many people she'd shared her story with. Mel looked almost eager to talk.

"Sure. I'd love a cup of tea," she said finally. "It's a nice evening. Maybe Goldie and Rick will come by for a song."

Melanie smiled. "You're secretly afraid of them, aren't you?"

"Yeah," she admitted with a laugh.

After they'd put the dinner dishes up and tidied the kitchen, Melanie took down two cups and filled them from the kettle she'd had heating on the stove. Erin opened the cabinet where she kept her tea bags and pulled out a box, one she'd seen Mel use before.

"This okay? Chamomile and vanilla?"

"Yes."

They took their seats in the rockers and she remained quiet as she took a sip of the hot tea that had been sweetened with a drizzle of honey. The moon was already sliding in the western sky, larger than half-full tonight. She supposed a full moon would be upon them before too long. Even now, it was bright enough to dim the stars, but she didn't mind. She found she enjoyed watching the night sky. If she lived here permanently, she might be inclined to get a telescope.

"That's Mars," Melanie said quietly, pointing to a bright star hovering just over the bluff to the east. "It has a little touch of red color."

"Are you a stargazer?"

"Amateur at best. I have a few books and sky charts. And I get daily emails from a website that is devoted to starwatching."

Erin smiled. "Ah. A website? What's that?"

Melanie laughed. "I'm sorry. I suppose I could give you the password, if you still want it."

"Oh, I don't know. Like you said, it is kinda freeing not to have all that. Besides, I only used it for work, really. There aren't friends to keep up with."

"Facebook?"

"God, no. I never got into that, thankfully." She raised an eyebrow. "You?"

"No. And before you ask, no, there aren't any long-lost friends that I still keep in touch with. When I moved here, I left all of that behind. Intentionally. The ladies out here, Stella, they've become my extended family. I wouldn't say I'm friends with any of them other than in passing. Perhaps Angela. She's closer to my age although still twenty years older. But she and I have become the caregivers. Most of them are still very independent, but there are some things they can't do—like operate a chainsaw, for instance."

"You can?"

"Of course. If I want to keep a fire going during the winter, I have to cut my own wood."

"Surely you don't cut wood for everybody, do you?"

"No, no. Most of them heat with propane now. Those who don't buy wood and have it delivered. I suppose one day I'll do the same, convert my wood stove to propane. But now, while I'm still able, I enjoy it." She waved out at the vastness. "We have seven hundred acres. There are always dead-standing trees to cut. In early fall, when it's cool, I like to go out. I love being out in the forest like that. Angela goes with me sometimes. She doesn't have a truck, so I haul hers back for her."

Erin was quiet for a moment, then turned to her. "Why don't you have friends to keep up with?"

Melanie let out a quiet sigh. "I never really had a lot of friends to begin with. I would sometimes try to surround myself with people to combat loneliness, but I realized that didn't really help. Being lonely had absolutely nothing to do with being alone. I've learned that living out here."

Erin said nothing, waiting. After a while, Melanie stopped the motion of her rocker. She took a drink of her tea, then turned to Erin.

"Adam caught me with Courtney, the woman I was having the affair with. He was supposed to be away, for work. He came back a day early. We were...in bed. He'd stood outside the bedroom—listening as we made love."

"Damn," she whispered.

"Yeah. He said he knew right then that I...that I had never really been *into* him like I was her." Melanie started rocking again. "He wasn't really all that angry. In shock, more so, I think. Courtney, of course, left. I wanted to talk about it with him. I wanted to explain. But he...he didn't want to. There was no yelling and screaming. We had a few words, that was it. It was quite civilized."

"How old were you?"

"Um...twenty-five. About to turn twenty-six, actually. Three days," she finished in a whisper. Another deep breath. "Adam was crushed. He wouldn't talk to me about it. And then, on my twenty-sixth birthday, he...he killed himself." The rocker stopped abruptly. "He shot himself. In our bedroom. On our bed. I found him when I came home from work."

"Oh my God," Erin whispered. She didn't know what she was expecting, but that wasn't it. Melanie's words were quiet, calm, but she could hear the emotion in her voice. She didn't know what to say to her. Didn't know if she should say anything at all.

"He didn't leave me a note. He didn't need to. He left something for his parents, though. They blamed me, rightfully so. And I did too. He apparently told them enough so that they knew what had happened." Melanie leaned her head back, her eyes closed for a moment. "I was a mess after that. Adam and his family, they were really all I had. And they were gone. And I couldn't reconcile the fact that it was all my fault. Grief counseling, therapy—that helped some, but I still couldn't get past it. I had nightmares...when I slept," she added. "I was on medication for depression. I couldn't sleep without a pill. I started drinking a lot. Wine first. Then vodka. Gin. I lost a ton of weight." She looked over at her. "When I first saw you, I recognized myself in you. Yet your eyes—while you looked lost—weren't filled with despair like mine had been."

Erin shook her head. "No." She took a deep breath. "Go on. Tell me the rest."

"After three years of therapy, I was dependent upon meds to get me through each day, each night. Dependent upon them to keep my job, keep my sanity. And then my mother started coming around again. Long story short, she broke into my house one day—she and this guy she was living with—and stole everything of value and my medications." She blew out a breath. "A week later, she came back, asking for more drugs. And I looked at her and I saw myself. I saw myself becoming what she was...not able to function without drugs or alcohol. I was becoming my mother. I was so close to that line."

Melanie startled Erin by standing. She moved to the edge of the porch and leaned against the railing, her eyes looking skyward.

"I...I was lost, Erin. Completely. I was a stranger in the mirror. I knew I had to do something. I had to get away, I just didn't know where or how. Would moving to a new city, new job, change anything? My therapist didn't think so. She was afraid for me to be alone, actually."

Erin raised her eyebrows. "Because?"

"Because I had talked to her about suicide."

Erin's breath caught. Melanie seemed so strong, so in control, so...together. She would have never guessed that thought had crossed her mind. But again, she said nothing, waiting for Melanie to finish.

"It was another six months, though, before...well, before I'd finally had enough. I came home from work and found my mother leaning against my door, passed out. I thought she was dead. I remember looking at her, wondering if I could muster any tears for her. Turns out her boyfriend dumped her there after they'd scored a hit and she'd collapsed." She turned back around, facing her. "So that was it. That was my slap in the face. I saw myself lying there, slumped against the door. Not my mother, but me. And I knew then that I didn't want to die. I was lost—and stuck—in this...this vortex that I'd created and I didn't know any way out. The only thing I could think of was to run away. My plan was to get away for a couple of years, live off my savings or get a part-time job or something. Anything."

"Where did you work?"

"Law firm. I was a paralegal." She smiled. "I hated my job, actually. The work, I hated, not the job," she corrected. "One of the attorneys thought of me as a daughter and he tended to favor me. He was there for me during all of that, he stood by me, even when I missed a lot of work. When I told him what I wanted to do, when I'd found Stella and this place, he helped me sell my house, helped me with some investments when I had cash left over." She moved back into the rocker with a sigh. "He was really the only one who I would have wanted to keep in touch with. But I made a clean break. I was thirty. I'd spent four years existing on medications and booze and therapy and I wasn't getting any better. I was getting worse. So I made a clean break."

"You came out here to heal?"

"Yes. Instead of medication, I did meditation and yoga. And honestly, I think the diet helped too. Probably the most. Everything was healthy. Everything was peaceful. Now...the garden is therapy. I don't look at it as work."

"Does Stella know about all that?"

Melanie shook her head. "No. She knows about my mother, about my childhood, but not about Adam, no."

"Why did you do it? I mean, if you weren't in love with him, why?"

"I felt...safe with him and I was afraid he'd leave. He was familiar. He was family. Being a foster child...he was my family." She shrugged. "All those things. All those selfish things." Melanie looked at her in the shadows of the porch. "It's a guilt I'll always carry. Adam was such a sweet, gentle boy, and he grew into the same kind of man. And I...I ruined him." Her voice turned into a whisper again. "I killed him as surely as if I'd pulled the trigger myself."

Again, she got up abruptly, keeping her back to Erin. She could hear the tears that Melanie was trying to hide and she didn't know if she should offer some comfort or if it would be rebuffed.

Is that why Melanie was out here, living alone, in solitude? As penance? Punishment for her deeds? Perhaps trying to make atonement for Adam's death somehow? She'd obviously reconciled what had happened. She appeared strong, in control. Erin had a hard time picturing her being depressed, being dependent upon prescription drugs to get through each day. Melanie seemed so healthy, both physically and mentally.

But not right now, though. She wasn't strong. She wasn't in control. Erin got up, going to her. When she would have reached out to touch her, Melanie turned.

"I'm sorry, Erin. It's been so long, yet it still seems so fresh sometimes."

"You don't have to apologize to me." Erin took the cup from her fingers and set it down, then tugged her closer into a hug. She felt Melanie stiffen, felt her try to pull away, but Erin wouldn't let her escape. After what seemed like minutes, she felt Melanie's hands touch her, felt arms circle her waist. She closed her eyes, offering what comfort she could as she heard quiet tears against her neck.

It occurred to her then that this was probably the first time in seven long years that Melanie had had someone hold her. Comfort her. Touch her. Seven years without intimacy? Without another's touch? She closed her eyes, pulling Melanie even tighter, bringing their bodies into contact. She rubbed her hands across Mel's back, hoping to ease her pain somewhat. She had no right to be doing this, of course. She had invaded Melanie's space without asking. But Mel seemed to sink against her and Erin continued to hold her, letting Melanie take from her what she wanted—needed.

Melanie pulled away rather quickly, though, wiping at her eyes before turning away. "I'm sorry," she said again. "I'm your host. You're the guest. You shouldn't have to—"

"I'm not a guest, Mel. Don't apologize."

Melanie went to the steps, still holding on to the railing. "I…I need a minute. Don't wait up."

Erin nodded, knowing she'd just been dismissed. She stood there, watching as Melanie walked out into the night, watching until the darkness swallowed her. She picked up their cups and made her way back inside.

Melanie was used to being alone, used to providing her own comfort, she told herself. She looked out onto the empty porch one more time, then headed into her bedroom, debating whether to close the door or not. After a moment's hesitation, she closed it, not wanting to invade Melanie's privacy any more than she already had.

CHAPTER TWENTY-TWO

It had been a very long time since Melanie had not been up before dawn. But this morning, she was feeling sluggish and instead of getting up, she rolled over and closed her eyes, sinking back into nothingness. She'd had a difficult time getting to sleep last night. So much so that after tossing and turning about in her bed she gave up and went back out to the porch, wrapping herself in one of the three afghans Rachel had knitted for her. She must have sat out for an hour or more, her thoughts bouncing around between past and present and everything in between.

She still didn't know what had compelled her to share her story with Erin, other than... Well, she hadn't had a friend in so long, it felt good to share something with someone. That part of her life, as painful as it was, had only been recounted to her therapist. Even when she'd gone to grief counseling—one-on-one and with the group—she'd left out major parts, especially her affair with Courtney.

Erin had been so sweet last night. And the hug? God, she hadn't known how to react to that. She hadn't had a hug in—well, not since Adam died. It had felt odd to have someone touch her, hold her. Odd, yes, but yet it had felt oh, so good. Erin was stronger—sturdier—than she appeared, and she had wanted to simply go limp in her arms, hoping Erin would hold her up as she burrowed against her. But she could do no such thing. How inappropriate would that have been? She was the host. Erin was the guest. She had no right to expect comfort from Erin. Stella would be appalled.

What would Erin say to her today? Would she bring it up? Would she have more questions? Friends always had questions, didn't they? Or maybe she'd pretend they hadn't had such a serious talk and keep everything light, normal between them. She hoped that was the case. She needed to leave the past where it belonged—locked up tight. Always in the back of her mind, yes. Always. But there was no need to bring it out front. It served no purpose other than to compound her guilt. She'd learned to live with the guilt. It was just there. It always would be, hovering around her. No matter how much she wished things were different, she couldn't undo the past. She couldn't undo her relationship with Adam. She couldn't undo the affair with Courtney. She couldn't bring Adam back to life.

She could only live with her guilt. So much so that it had become a part of her, a part that she sometimes forgot about.

Sometimes.

But then it reared its ugly head, reminding her that it was still hanging around…waiting to pounce.

* * *

Erin stood quietly in the kitchen, wondering if she should start breakfast. Actually, she was wondering if she should open Mel's bedroom door and check on her. She was always—*always*—up by dawn. Even in those first days, when she'd stayed in her room, she could hear Melanie in the kitchen at ungodly hours of the morning.

But this morning? No. All was quiet. She'd gotten out of bed at the first light of dawn, going out to the kitchen. Melanie's door remained closed. After a moment's indecision, she started coffee, then went back to her room to shower. After she'd dressed, there was still no sound from the other bedroom.

She glanced out the kitchen window, seeing the sun creeping over the bluff already. She could hear the chickens clamoring in their coop, ready to be let out for the day. With one more glance at Melanie's door, she poured a cup of coffee and took it with her.

It was a still, cool morning and the sky was a brilliant blue. She heard—or felt—a buzzing of wings, and she turned toward the hummingbird feeder, watching as some early customers vied for position. She heard the now familiar calls of the magpies as they danced along the top of the fence, hopping away from her as she headed to the shed. A hoarser call was heard and she glanced up, seeing two ravens soar past. Behind the shed, she heard Bandito braying, welcoming the new day.

She paused, smiling, noting how good it felt to be up and about this early. No wonder Melanie started her day at dawn. There was so much to see and hear as the world awakened around her.

She went into the fenced yard and opened the door to the coop. The chickens nearly ran her over in their haste to get outside. Much clucking ensued as they shuffled around her feet, looking for food. Before going to let the goats out, she went into the shed and got the bucket of hen scratch and tossed it out, laughing as the chickens fought for the treat. She sipped her coffee and watched them for a moment, then went to the goat's stall and opened it. Carly and the twins came running out, the young twins kicking up their heels as they chased after the chickens.

Another new day has begun, she thought. And she felt as happy as the twins appeared to be. As she'd told Melanie, "good" seemed to be too tame a word to use for what she felt. She felt... reborn, almost. She felt different, new... As new as the day that was just blooming. She certainly wasn't the same person who'd come here a month ago. She wondered, after three months, who she'd be. Would she be her old self...before Sarah? Or would she be even different from that? Would this three-month experience change her completely?

"Time will tell," she murmured to herself.

With one last smile at the chickens and goats, she went back toward the cabin. When she got inside, however, the bedroom door was still closed. At what point should she worry? She knew it had been late when Mel had come inside last night. Melanie had still been on the porch when she'd finally fallen asleep— she'd heard her in the rocking chair.

So she'd start breakfast, she supposed. She'd watched— helped—enough to know how to get the spicy, fried potatoes going. She rummaged in the fridge for onions and peppers, then pulled out the cast iron skillet that Melanie always used. After a drizzle of olive oil, she had the onions and peppers browning as she cut the potatoes. She got the eggs ready to scramble and took the green sauce from the fridge, but then remembered the tortillas.

She shook her head. She didn't think she could pull that off. But she'd watched nearly every morning. She knew how to make them. Still...

"Smells good."

She turned, relief on her face at the sight of Melanie. Her hair was in disarray, her eyes were puffy—from crying?—and she was standing there in nothing more than a short T-shirt and black underwear. As she rubbed her eyes with both hands, Erin smiled, thinking she'd never seen anyone look quite so adorable before.

"Hey. Yeah. So...I don't know how to make tortillas."

"Yes, you do," Mel said around a yawn. "I'll supervise while you make them. Let me get dressed. But I need to tend to the chickens first."

"Oh, I already did."

"You did?" Then Melanie smiled. "Thank you, Erin."

"Well, they were about to break the door down. Thought I'd better let them out. And the goats too."

Melanie touched her arm, patting it quickly as she went back to her bedroom. "You're pretty good for cheap labor," she teased. "I think I'll keep you."

Erin let out a breath. Okay, so she seemed perfectly fine—normal—this morning. Other than sleeping two hours longer than usual, that is.

CHAPTER TWENTY-THREE

Melanie was feeling exceptionally lazy. How long had it been since she'd taken the time to read? As her eyes flicked up, watching as Erin tossed the fishing line into the creek, she knew she was getting little reading done. She was sitting against a ponderosa pine, her legs stretched out, ankles crossed—fighting sleep. She yawned again, finally putting the book down.

Erin seemed content and in no hurry to leave. She'd caught two trout already but thought two more would make it a "feast" so Melanie had waved her on. She was comfortable enough where she was. And comfortable was what Erin looked. She was wearing hiking shorts and sandals, her feet wet from standing in the water as she fished. Her hair was windblown but short enough not to be a bother to her. Even as she concentrated on her fishing, there was a smile on her face. It was such a transformation, Melanie had a hard time remembering how she'd been those first few days. Now? Now she was healthy, she was smiling. She looked happy. She looked content. She looked like a different person.

She smiled then, thinking back to their breakfast and Erin's attempt to make fresh tortillas. They were a little thick and even with the press, their shape was anything but round, but Erin had been so pleased with herself, Melanie had eaten two with their potatoes and eggs as she heaped praise on them. As she'd warned Erin then, if they were *too* good, she'd be in charge of making them from now on.

"You know, Stella hasn't been around this week," Erin said, breaking the silence.

"No, she hasn't. But the potluck dinner is tomorrow." She paused. "Do you want to go with me?"

Erin looked over at her, eyebrows raised. "Do guests usually go to them?"

"No." Then she shrugged. "Only the ladies—the tribe, as Stella likes to call us. But you're not a normal guest. I don't think she or anyone else would mind. In fact, they'd probably love for you to come."

Erin paused, her head tilted thoughtfully. "Do you want me to go?"

Their eyes met and Melanie nodded. "Yes," she said simply.

"Okay. I'll go." Erin cast out again, then turned to her. "Are you bored sitting over there while I fish?"

Melanie shook her head. "No. Just watching you."

Erin wiggled her eyebrows teasingly. "And just what is it that you're watching?"

Melanie laughed, letting her gaze drop to Erin's hips, her legs, then back up again. Erin had turned her attention back to the water, but there was a satisfied smile on her face.

* * *

Erin eyed the last piece of fish, then looked up at Melanie who was smiling at her.

"Take it already."

"Are you sure?" She'd only caught three, not the four she was hoping for. "We can share."

"No, take it. I'm full."

Erin snatched it up with a grin. "I'm going to get fat living with you. In case you haven't noticed, I've gained weight."

"I have noticed. You look good."

Erin flicked her eyes up. "You think so?"

"Yes. Nice. Healthy. You were rail thin, Erin. Frail, almost."

"Frail? That's a word I wouldn't have ever used to describe me." She looked at Mel thoughtfully. "Mentally, at least. I suppose physically...Yeah, in the last year or so, I had become—geez—*frail*. How sad is that?"

"Loss, pain. It does things to us," Melanie said, her voice quiet. "Without us really even knowing it." She looked up at her then. "Until it's too late."

Erin met her gaze, noting that the blue eyes were still a bit shadowed this evening. "Are you sorry you told me your story?"

Mel looked away, staring off behind her. "I...I'm not sure, really. I haven't told anyone, other than my therapist. What compelled me to tell you...I don't know."

"Sometimes it feels good to say things out loud."

Melanie shrugged. "These things I feel—think—they've been a part of me for so long, I don't know that saying them out loud has any bearing. It's not like they're going to go away."

"You mean your guilt?"

"Yes. My guilt. It hides sometimes. Sometimes for weeks. And then sometimes it jumps right out at me, waving its hands wildly in front of my face. Reminding me that it's still there. That it's not going to go away...no matter how much I wish it would."

"Why did you tell me?"

Melanie rested her chin in her palm, looking across the table at her. "Honestly, I don't know. I've kept it hidden from everyone out here. You...I felt almost compelled to tell you. I'm not sure why." She leaned back, crossing her arms against her. "Maybe like you said...It's good to say things out loud. Get them off your chest."

Erin nodded. "Temporarily?"

"Yes. And don't get me wrong, when I think about Adam, I don't *always* think about that day. I had known him since I was sixteen. He died on my twenty-sixth birthday, so there were ten years that were mostly good. I felt safe with him. I finally had a family. His parents were so good to me." She paused. "Until, of course…"

"Did you ever try to reconcile things with them?"

Melanie shook her head. "No. There was nothing to say. He was their only child. In their eyes, I killed him." She shook her head again. "There was nothing I could have said that would change that."

No, Erin supposed there wasn't. But that was ten, eleven years ago. That seemed like an awfully long time to hang on to guilt. Hang on to it tight enough that it still choked you at times. And last night, Melanie had been nearly strangled by it.

Their eyes met across the table, those blue ones looking tired and clouded. Erin much preferred the bright, twinkling ones she'd come to know.

"I can clean up from dinner," she offered.

"Thank you. If you don't mind, I'm going to grab a shower and…get to bed early."

Erin's eyebrows shot up. There was still a touch of daylight filtering in through the windows. But who was she to comment on it? Those first few days, hadn't she escaped to her room after dinner too? As Melanie walked past her, she paused, touching her shoulder and squeezing gently.

"I'll be better tomorrow, Erin. I promise."

"Okay."

"And thank you for cleaning up dinner. Thank you for *catching* dinner."

She smiled at her as Mel's hand still lingered on her shoulder. "You're welcome."

Melanie's hand slipped away then, but she turned back around before going into her room. "Feel free to use the TV if you want."

"Okay."

But after she'd put away the leftover veggies and washed the dishes, she wasn't in the mood for TV. Instead, she opened the cabinet and took out a mug. She went about the business of making tea, surprised at how much she'd grown to like it. She took the hot cup outside, but instead of sinking down into one of the rockers, she leaned against the porch railing, her gaze going up to the sky. To the west, there were still the remnants of the sunset streaking across the rocks, hanging on for a few more seconds. To the east, it was already dark. The moon was climbing higher, hiding behind drifting clouds. Stars were starting to show themselves and her eyes moved over them absently, her thoughts still on Melanie...and those guilt-ridden blue eyes.

CHAPTER TWENTY-FOUR

"Oh, so there's Fred. I was beginning to worry."

Melanie smiled at Erin. "You were beginning to worry?" She patted the old dog's head. "I told you, he makes the rounds."

"How old is he?"

"Old. Fifteen or more, I think. He disappeared last winter and no one had seen him for ten days or so. We thought he'd gone off to die. Then he showed back up one day at Vivian's place. A little thin but no worse for wear." She sighed. "I don't imagine he'll make it much longer, though. He hardly eats a thing anymore."

She walked on up the steps, but Erin stopped her with a hand on her arm before they went into Stella's house. Melanie looked at her questioningly.

"What should I say to Rachel?"

Melanie smiled at her. "Rachel is not going to corner you and demand an explanation for you running out on her."

"But—I feel bad. I mean, I was rude to her. Very rude."

"Then she was probably glad to be rid of you," she teased. "Come on. Be your usual charming self. They'll love you."

Erin arched an eyebrow. "Am I charming?"

Melanie paused, wondering at her choice of words. Did she find Erin charming? Yes. This morning, for instance, she'd been completely charmed as she'd spied Erin petting and talking to the twins when she'd gone out to open their stall. Melanie had stood at the kitchen window, breakfast forgotten, as she watched her. Before coming back inside, Erin had paused to watch the hummingbird feeder, then she'd looked toward the bluff where the sun had risen, a smile on her face as she came back inside.

Melanie looked at her now, meeting Erin's teasing eyes. "Yes, you're charming. And nice. Had you asked me that the first week, though..."

Erin held her hand up. "I know, I know. I was insufferable." Again, a teasing smile. "How can I make it up to you?"

"Breakfast in bed," she said without thinking. "I didn't mean *that*," she said as she swatted playfully at Erin's arm. She knew she was blushing, but she couldn't seem to stop it. "I mean—it would be nice to be served breakfast in bed...just once."

Erin was grinning as she held the door open for her. "Just once, huh?"

Melanie stopped. "If you served me breakfast in bed, that means you'd also have to tend to the chickens and goats, seeing as I'd still be under the covers."

"I tend to them some mornings as it is, but I don't think you could stand it. You'd be missing your coffee time on the porch at dawn."

"True."

"How about a massage?"

"A massage?" Melanie repeated, blinking at her stupidly.

"I give great massages."

"You do?"

"Uh-huh." Their eyes met again and Erin gave her a quick wink. "It's been a while though. I may be out of practice. It may take me an hour or so to get back in the swing."

"An hour-long massage? God, I'd be useless after that." She laughed. "When can we do it?"

"Any time you want. It's a full-body massage, by the way," Erin said with a saucy grin, then walked inside, quickly being swallowed up by the group of gray-haired ladies as they surrounded her all at once. Melanie shook her head, wondering how in the world they'd gone from charming to breakfast in bed to a full-body massage, of all things.

"Dianne told us she'd cut your hair," Stella was saying to Erin. "It looks so good on you, dear." Stella then glanced her way, almost as an afterthought. "You too, Mel."

Before Melanie could reply, Stella had linked arms with Erin and was leading her away. Melanie took her dish into the kitchen—another squash casserole—and found a spot for it on the table.

"She's cute," Angela said as she bumped her arm. "I mean… *cute*."

Melanie nodded. "Yes, she is."

"Is she single?"

"As a matter of fact, yes."

"Oh, lucky you," Angela teased. "I wish it had been my turn to host next. We all knew Rachel wouldn't be able to keep her. I heard she ran the very next morning." She leaned closer. "Stella said she was in really bad shape, but she looks good to me. *Really* good."

"A month…yeah, she's improved tenfold." She heard laughter from the living room and went back out, finding Erin crammed on the sofa with four ladies. The look on Erin's face was a cross between amused and frightened. Erin looked up, finding her watching. Their eyes met and they exchanged a smile—a secret, almost intimate smile. Then Stella walked through their line of sight, breaking the contact.

"Oh, Mel, I must say, the change in Erin is remarkable. Not only the hair—which looks lovely on her—but her whole *self*," Stella said, waving her arms dramatically. "You've worked wonders on her. She's like a completely different person."

"I'm not sure it's anything I've done," she protested. "She's eating healthy, she's getting outside in the sunshine and doing a little exercise. She's eliminated the stress in her life. She caught up on sleep." She shrugged. "I had little to do with it."

"Well, her sister called me again. Two evenings ago, I think it was. I hadn't seen Erin so I didn't know what to report, other than—as far as I knew—she hadn't run away. Dianne tells me that you took her into Silver City for some shopping."

"Yes, I did. A week or so ago."

Stella leaned closer. "Did she try something?"

Melanie raised her eyebrows. "Try something? Like sneak off to buy a bus ticket out of town?"

"It's just that her sister...well, she seems shocked that Erin is still here. In fact, when I spoke with her, she asked me if I was *sure* she hadn't left. I very nearly drove out to your place right then and there to check on her."

"You know I would let you know if anything happened. She's fine. I would go so far as to say that I think she's enjoying herself. It is sort of like a vacation for her. Now...after another month of this, she may get bored and be ready to leave, but I think she'll last the full three months."

"Maybe you should suggest that she call her sister then. She can use my phone, of course. Maybe that would put her sister's mind at ease."

"Okay. I'll do that."

Later, however, when she suggested that to Erin, she shook her head.

"I don't think so, Mel."

"She's apparently worried about you."

"She's probably feeling guilty that she and my father forced me into this, that's all." Erin pointed at the table. "Look at all these dishes. Everything looks great." She leaned closer. "Which one did Rachel bring?"

Melanie pointed to a pot with a lid on it. "There. Beans."

"Stay clear," Erin warned with exaggerated wide eyes. "Lots of squash too. I think I'll just stick with ours."

Melanie smiled at her use of "ours" and indeed, Erin had helped prepare the casserole. "Are you sure you don't want to call?" she persisted.

Erin turned to her. "I feel good. I feel...sort of detached from that life. If I talk to her, I'm going to ask about my projects, then I'll start worrying about my projects." She shoved her hands into the pockets of her jeans. "I needed this break, obviously. I don't want to think about my real life anytime soon." Then she winked at her. "I'm having fun hanging out with you, sneaking off to go fishing and naked swimming. Cleaning up goat shit," she added with a laugh.

Melanie smiled at her. "Okay, then. I'll tell Stella. Is there a message you want to pass on should your sister call again?"

"Yeah. Tell her to stop worrying and I'll see her in September."

Whatever apprehension Erin may have felt when they'd gotten to the party had apparently disappeared. She wasn't shy about loading her plate and she chatted with the ladies around her. Stella's table was used as a buffet and everyone took their food into the living room, finding any available spot to sit. When Valerie would have pulled Erin down beside her, Erin declined.

"Gonna sit with Mel," she said, moving over to the loveseat with Melanie. "You don't mind, do you?"

"Of course not." Then she leaned closer. "Although they'll start to gossip about us."

Erin nodded. "I know. I was already asked if I was still sleeping in the spare room or not."

Melanie's eyes widened. "Oh my God! *Who* asked that?"

Erin's gaze moved across the room. "There. In the yellow dress."

Melanie sighed. "Rebecca. She always questions me, wondering why I'd move out here alone, at my age. The week before you got here, I was at her place, cutting some limbs in her garden, and she said I was too young to live my life alone." She smiled, remembering the conversation. "She said I'd turn into a bitter old woman if I didn't find some love soon." She laughed quietly. "She suggested a mail-order bride."

Erin laughed. "Guess she's not familiar with online dating."

Melanie took a bite of their casserole, pleased with how it turned out. She turned to Erin. "I...I'd actually thought about it." She smiled. "Online dating. Not the mail-order bride."

"Why haven't you?"

She looked around, seeing a few eyes on them. "We can talk later," she whispered. "How's the food?"

"I like this meatloaf stuff."

"I think that's Angela's. It's made with lentils and oats. She's a good cook. She gave me the lentil meatball recipe."

"I took some of the other squash, but I like ours best. And these potatoes are sinful," Erin added as she scooped up a cheesy forkful. "Maybe we should try making these too."

"We're trying to cut back on cheese, remember? And if you keep eating like this, we'll be shopping for new clothes again."

CHAPTER TWENTY-FIVE

"I'm stuffed."

"I guess so. You had two pieces of pie *and* chocolate cake."

Erin sat down in the rocker, her hands resting on her full belly. "That chocolate cake was really good. I wanted to steal a piece to bring home."

"That was Stella's. She loves to bake."

"I noticed you didn't eat any."

"I'm not big on dessert. Not that kind anyway. When the strawberries are in, I like a pie or cobbler. And we'll have peaches very soon. I have a recipe for peach ice cream, if you're interested."

"Homemade ice cream? Count me in." She turned to look at her. "So tell me."

"Tell you what? The recipe?"

Erin smiled. "No. Online dating."

Mel waved her question away. "Oh, that. Just something I considered a few years ago." She took a deep breath, then blew it out. "I get lonely sometimes, as I've said. And so I thought, maybe I should give it a try." She waved her hand again. "But no. We're so remote out here, who would come?" She smiled. "I'm talking normal people. I'm sure *someone* would come, but I'd at least want them to be sane."

"So you didn't try?"

"No. Besides, I'm not sure I could…Well, since Adam, I haven't been able…Well—"

"You haven't been with anyone since your affair—when you were twenty-six?"

Melanie nodded. "I mean, I tried…Only I couldn't actually ever go through with it. My therapist encouraged me to keep trying but…it became humiliating, really."

"Mel! You've been alone all this time? When I hugged you the other night…?"

"Yes. The last time someone hugged me—I guess it was Adam or Courtney. When I was twenty-five, about to turn twenty-six."

Erin turned in the rocker, facing her. "My God, Mel. You're—?"

"Thirty-seven." Melanie stood up quickly. "I'm used to it, Erin. It's nothing to be concerned about." She walked off the steps. "I'm going to make sure the chickens are locked up."

It was an excuse, of course. They'd put the chickens and goats up when they'd come home, right at dusk.

"I get lonely sometimes."

The thought of Melanie being lonely—so lonely that she'd considered inviting a complete stranger out here to her bed—was heartrending. She'd done the same thing, though, hadn't she? After Sarah left, after she'd gotten over the shock of it all—six or eight months—hadn't she fallen into bed with near strangers? Some hung around long enough to lose the stranger tag—like Jessica. Six or eight months—the loneliness had eaten at her. She couldn't imagine going ten or eleven *years* without someone.

No wonder Melanie had stiffened when she'd hugged her. Another's touch was probably so foreign to her now, it must have felt unnatural. But she'd given in, hadn't she? Mel had clung tightly to her, if only for the few moments she allowed herself.

Erin pushed out of the chair, pausing to look out into the darkness, wondering what Mel was doing. Was she inside the shed, perhaps standing in the goats' stall, talking to them? Was she leaning against the hay bales, crying? Or was she walking out behind the shed, where Bandito roamed?

Her eyes would be sad, she knew. A little clouded over. Teary. But she would push her loneliness and guilt away, tuck it back into the place where she hid it, wherever that place was. And tomorrow, over breakfast, her blue eyes would be bright again. She'd be smiling.

Erin made a silent vow right then that she wouldn't bring up Mel's past again, wouldn't encourage her to talk, to bring memories to the surface. No. She wanted Melanie to be happy and smiling, not sad and crying.

No, not sad. That would be her mission, she decided. Making—and keeping—Melanie happy.

CHAPTER TWENTY-SIX

"Are you sure? It's quite a hike," Melanie warned.

"We've been working all morning. It's gotten kind of cloudy and cool. Doesn't a soak in the hot springs sound like fun?"

Melanie looked at Erin's face, wondering at her exuberance today. Last night, after she'd come in, Erin had already been in her room, although her bedroom door was open, not closed. Mel had paused, calling a quick "good night" to her as she'd moved into her own room. For some reason, she'd left her door open as well.

Erin's piddling about in the kitchen this morning had woken her, a good half hour earlier than usual. She'd stared at the ceiling, the smell of coffee and breakfast wafting about. She'd ruined Erin's surprise, however, when she got up to help. She'd missed out on her very first breakfast served in bed.

She met Erin's gaze now, a smile on her lips. "What about lunch?" She knew it must be close to noon by now.

"We can make a quick burrito or something." Erin moved closer. "Come on. Please? Show me the hot springs."

Melanie, of course, could not turn down those pleading eyes even though they'd picked a huge basket of green beans that needed to be canned. As Erin had said, the sky had clouded over, it was rather cool—a prelude to the summer rains that would start any day now. "Okay. Let's do the hot springs." Then she grinned. "No clothes allowed, remember."

Erin laughed. "Of course I remember." Then she wiggled her eyebrows. "Can't wait!"

* * *

Melanie hadn't lied about the hike being a bit difficult. The rocks turned to boulders as they climbed steadily up the creek past the area where they'd gotten in the water that day. On the opposite side, the mountain had crept closer, making this look more like a rocky canyon than a fertile creek valley. On the side they hiked on, in between the boulders, were large pine trees— ponderosa, Mel had called them. A large, blueish bird landed on a limb up ahead of them, its voice scolding.

"Piñon jay," Melanie said before she could ask. "We see Steller's jays sometimes too—their blue is a little more brilliant with a black crest—but they usually stay up higher on the mountain. We can hike up sometime, if you like."

"Seven hundred acres…How much of it is up there?" she asked, motioning to the high mountain across from them.

"Probably half of it, I'd guess. The property line is on the other side of the bluff, to the west of the cabin, so we get all of the creek, right up until it dumps into the Gila River." Melanie turned to look at her. "I almost settled there by the river instead of back here."

"What changed your mind?"

"Privacy," she said with a smile. "It's flatter there, less rocky. But it's right by the road. Too easy for someone to pop over to visit. Back here? As you know, the road to my cabin is rather rough. It's rare that anyone other than Stella comes around."

"Thus you get to garden topless," Erin said with a grin. "I've yet to witness that, though."

"There's not much to look at, is there?" Melanie asked, pointing at her chest. "My breasts are the same size they were when I was in middle school, I think."

"Well, I wouldn't say there's nothing to look at, Mel," she said with a wink. Yes, Mel had small breasts, but they weren't nonexistent, like her own. Although since she'd gained weight, she wasn't quite as embarrassed by them. Her glance landed on Mel's breasts now as the tank top she wore was stretched tight as she climbed over a rock. When they'd gone swimming, she hadn't wanted to stare—much—but Mel's breasts were very firm, her nipples dark as they too had been touched by the sun.

She followed Melanie up the rocks, using her hands to balance as they made their way across a boulder the size of a small car. She was out of breath when they stopped, and she bent over, resting her palms on her knees.

"Damn. I'm out of shape."

"It's easier going back down, but not by much."

She stood up straight. "So this is it?"

The creek wasn't as wide up here, twenty feet across, if that. The pool they were standing near was deeper than where they'd gotten in downstream. This looked deep enough to actually swim in.

"It's a nice pool here," Melanie said. "In the winter, you can see the steam coming off the water. I usually come up a couple of times during the colder months to soak."

Without much fanfare, Mel stripped her shirt off, seemingly unconcerned with her nakedness as her shorts followed. Erin watched her unabashedly as Mel casually walked into the water.

"Glorious," she said with a smile as she sunk down, submerging in the springs. When her head popped up again, she slicked the hair back from her face. She raised her eyebrows. "You coming in?"

Erin nodded. She wished she could be as nonchalant about stripping as Mel had been. Then she reminded herself she wasn't as sickly thin as she'd been a month ago. In fact, she was getting damn near close to normal.

"Are you shy?"

Erin smiled and pulled her shirt over her head. "Not really."
Neither was Melanie as she openly stared at her. Erin met
her gaze questioningly.

"I haven't seen a woman naked in…well, in a very long time."

"Sorry you're stuck with me then."

"Why sorry? You have a very nice body. Not so thin any
longer."

"Sickly thin is what I was just thinking," Erin admitted as
she took her shorts off. She was aware of Melanie still watching
her as she maneuvered over the rocks and into the water. "Oh,
yeah…This is great. Well worth the hike."

"Not sickly, no. Nice."

Erin glanced at her, seeing a rather shy, sweet smile on Mel's
face. "Nice? Well, as you said, it's been a rather *long* time since
you've seen someone. Your judgment may be skewed."

"What is it? You don't like to be considered nice-looking?
Attractive?"

Erin ducked under the water, hiding for a second from Mel's
gaze. Was she attractive? People used to say so, didn't they? But
that was before. Sarah had changed her, yes. Her hairstyle, her
clothes, her demeanor. And then, of course, after Sarah, she'd
totally gone to hell. Was she back yet?

Her hair was short enough that it didn't fall into her eyes,
but she wiped at it anyway. Mel was still watching her, still
expecting an answer.

"I don't feel attractive, no," she admitted.

"But you are." Melanie moved a little closer, but not too
close. "On the outside, anyway. You seem to have healed quite
nicely." Mel studied her for a long moment, then when she
spoke, her voice was very quiet. "Does your heart still ache for
her? Do you still feel lonely without her?"

Did it? Did she?

"I don't know anymore. As I said, I don't really think about
her much." She met Melanie's gaze. "Not since I've been here,
anyway. Back home, she was always there. At the house, she was
always there—because she *wasn't* there. At work, when I pushed,
when I got crazy with everyone, it was because I could still hear

her in my ear, telling me to do better, telling me to work more. To make more money." She splashed at the water. "That's not fair, really. I did all of that willingly. It wasn't all her. I liked the money too."

"You still defend her. Is that your way of defending *your* actions?"

Erin tilted her head. "Are we having a therapy session?"

Melanie waved her question away. "Of course not. I've simply sat through too many of them, I guess. I know what questions to ask."

Erin nodded. "Joyce blamed Sarah for all of this, blamed her for what I turned into. And yes, I defended her, even the last day when Joyce was bringing me out here. Maybe you're right. If I blamed Sarah for everything, then how weak must I have been? And weak is something I would never use to describe myself." She took a deep breath, taking an honest look inside herself. "But I was weak, I guess. I had no defense for her."

"You were in love...I guess there was no defense."

"She was flirty and fun and pretty—and I felt like an adolescent with a huge crush. We moved in together very quickly. Too quickly, Joyce would say," she added with a smile.

"I get the feeling your sister didn't care for her much."

"Not at all, actually. I should have trusted her intuition, I guess, but I wouldn't listen." She shrugged. "The first two years were good, happy. The next two? By then, I was working a lot and we started to drift. I couldn't see it then, but I can see it now. Obviously she drifted more than me." She heard the bitterness in her voice and wished it wasn't still there...not after all this time.

"So you had no clue that she had a lover?"

"None."

Melanie nodded. "When you're not as emotionally invested as your partner, I think it's easier to hide it. Or maybe you don't have to hide it at all."

Erin met her gaze but didn't comment. She was talking about Adam, she supposed, but Erin didn't want to be the one to bring him up.

"The fact that I had a lover didn't change my actions with Adam at all. I wasn't ever in love with him so it wasn't like I had to all of a sudden pretend that I was." She held her hand up. "And I can tell by the look on your face that you're afraid I'll go into that dark place again. I won't. At least not today. I'm...I'm feeling okay about things today."

"I don't like it when you go to your dark place," she admitted. "It's scary. You're not yourself."

"I know. I'm sorry. Sometimes..."

"So maybe we shouldn't talk about it."

Melanie nodded. "You're probably right. I've gone all these years without saying it out loud to someone. Now, well, I guess it's on my mind more."

Erin looked at her thoughtfully. "So you're saying maybe that's not necessarily a bad thing? That it's on your mind, I mean."

Melanie smiled at her. "Seeing as how I've had to retreat to that dark place a couple of times now, I'm not sure it's a *good* thing either." She dipped lower in the water, almost up to her ears. "One thing that has sent me reeling is that my guilt isn't quite as profound as it was—as it should be. And I didn't realize that until last night. I hadn't ever really examined it again...It was just always there, lurking, if you will. I always assumed it was the same, but it wasn't."

"Ah. So lack of guilt has you feeling guilty now. It's been ten years, hasn't it? Is that something you think you should carry with you forever?"

"It's been eleven years and yes, I thought I would—*should*— carry that with me. My punishment. My penance." Melanie splashed water at her. "Isn't that what you were doing? Your own self-punishment? Because you thought you had failed Sarah?"

"Failed her?"

"She found someone else. Someone you perceived to be *better* than you."

Erin smiled. "You've got this therapist act down pretty good."

"So it's true? My guess is you never even met the woman."

"No, I didn't. There was no need to. She was 'wonderful and smart and pretty and witty' and I, apparently, was no longer any of those things."

Melanie nodded. "Self-loathing is a scary thing, isn't it? The most destructive thing we can do to ourselves, I think."

"Are you saying I hated myself so much that I wanted to die? Because that's not true. I never once thought that."

"Subconsciously, perhaps? Erin, what do you think would have happened to you had you continued on the path you were taking?"

Erin leaned her head back into the warm water, looking into the darkening sky as she thought back over the last year or so. Of course what she'd been doing was self-destructive. She knew that. But it wasn't like she didn't care about herself...didn't care what happened to her. Was it? She lifted her head, looking at Melanie across the rippling water. Her eyes were more green than blue today. Yet they were bright, alert—and compassionate.

"I was beyond exhausted. I think I was afraid to sleep... Afraid I wouldn't wake up. So no, I didn't want to die. I just didn't know how to get my life back."

"I know. I didn't want to die either...At least I don't think so. I wanted to sleep. I didn't want to be awake—awake with my guilt and the truth. And I was taking more and more pills to keep myself asleep longer and longer. You were drinking massive amounts of caffeine to keep you awake longer and longer. We were each heading toward the same end, I'm afraid."

"How were you able to snap out of it so easily? I mean, you said your mother showed up..."

"I didn't mean for it to sound like it was easy, Erin, because it wasn't. I would come home from work each day, pop a few pills, and crawl into bed. That was my routine. I functioned at work much like a robot—or a zombie. I'm not sure what it was, but finding my mother there, against the door and thinking she was dead...something just clicked. Like I said, I saw myself there, not my mother. For a minute there, I thought I was having an out-of-body experience; it was so real to me."

"You think if Joyce—my father—hadn't intervened..."

"I don't know. Maybe something would have clicked for you too. Does it matter so much now?"

"No. I don't feel like I'm that person anymore. I feel…in control again."

"Good."

"And you?"

Melanie smiled. "Most days I'm in control, yes. But that person I was? No. She doesn't have a hold on me any longer."

It went without saying that Melanie's guilt still had a hold of her. Although it was a different kind of guilt, as of late. Erin wondered, if she wasn't here, if Mel hadn't opened up to her, would her guilt—the original guilt—still be lurking about? Probably. As Mel had said, since she'd never talked about it— examined it—she'd had no reason to suspect that the guilt had started to slip away…or at least change.

Erin bobbed in the water, her hands resting on a rock in shallower water. Eleven wasted years. That must seem like a lifetime to Melanie. The eighteen months she'd wallowed in her own self-pity now seemed like it had lasted twice that.

"Erin?"

"Hmm?"

"Thank you for…listening. Talking. Sharing. It's been really nice having you around."

"You're welcome."

She kept her own thank-you to herself as Melanie held her arms out to her side, gliding under the water like a nymph. She surfaced farther away, the bubbling flow of the creek just under her breasts. Erin stared as water droplets raced down her skin— her breasts—clinging to her nipples before sliding away. She raised her gaze, finding Melanie watching her. Should she be ashamed for having stared?

"We should head back soon. I hear thunder off to the west."

Erin pulled her gaze from Melanie, thinking… No, she had no right to stare. Melanie's body, while slender and firm, looked soft and feminine. She was obviously comfortable in her nakedness, comfortable in her skin. Erin mentally shook herself, then looked past Melanie, down the slope of the canyon that the creek took. It widened as it went, a valley forming as it flowed past the cabin and Mel's homestead. She looked back at her.

"Have you ever thought about floating down the creek instead of hiking back down?"

Melanie laughed. "You're not looking forward to that hike, huh?"

"No."

"Well, I actually have thought about floating down." Melanie moved toward the bank. "Too many rocks. Too shallow in spots. I think it would be more trouble than hiking down." Then she grinned. "Probably more fun, though."

CHAPTER TWENTY-SEVEN

They didn't make it back to the cabin before the rain hit. Oh, a good long sprint would have done it, but instead, Melanie led them into the shed and they ducked inside. The chickens and goats had already taken cover and she moved past the chicken coop to the goats' stall, rubbing Nora on the nose. Rosie was sticking her face between the slats that separated their stall from the rest of the shed. She was apparently looking for Erin as her big eyes darted around.

"That hit quick."

Melanie glanced at Erin, who was running her hands over her damp hair. "Yes. This early in the summer, it usually stops just as quickly too." She moved to the stack of square hay bales and sat down as the rain pelted the roof.

"Why do you call this 'the shed' and not 'the barn,'" Erin asked. She moved closer, leaning against the goats' stall.

"I don't know. It started out as a shed, I guess. The chickens and goats came later, so it's been added on to twice. I guess it is more barn than shed now."

Erin reached out, touching her fingers to Rosie's nose, smiling as the young goat's tail wiggled. "So the twins are not really good for anything, are they?"

"After they were born, I was supposed to continue milking Carly, to keep her lactating. But I don't really like milk and it was too much trouble to make cheese and yogurt, so I gave it up. So no, they are pets only. They keep the weeds down, that's about it."

"And your rosebushes trimmed."

"True. And they provide manure for the garden."

Erin wrinkled up her nose. "Yeah—my favorite job, mucking the stall," she said with a laugh. "That was pretty mean of you."

"Yeah, it was."

A loud clap of thunder seemed to rattle the shed and the goats huddled farther away from the door as rain blew inside. The chickens—all twelve of them—were already up on their roost.

"It's gotten colder."

She nodded. "These early afternoon storms usually don't linger long. The sun will be back out and it'll warm up again."

Erin sat down beside her on the hay bale. "Is this the beginning?"

"Of the summer rains? Probably. It's time. We're into July already."

"So every afternoon, these storms pop up?"

"Yes, most days. And sometimes it'll rain all night long. Those are my favorite nights, as long as it's not a thunderstorm," she said, smiling at Erin. "The best sleeping. You'll love it."

"Hard to believe I've been here over a month already."

"I know." She crossed her arms and leaned back. "Are you homesick yet?"

"Surprisingly, no. The first few days, I was feeling sort of... well, not homesick, really. Kinda lost, I guess."

"Out of your element, I believe is what you said."

"Yes. I was feeling incredibly lonely, like a lost soul...Like I didn't belong anywhere. Not there, not here. Like I was suspended in time, drifting about, not knowing where to land.

Not knowing if I *should* land at all." Erin leaned back too, next to her. "I'm comfortable now. Here. With you." Erin looked at her questioningly. "And you? Are you used to me being around yet?" Then she smiled. "Or ready for me to leave already?"

It was dark and shadowy in the shed, the heavy clouds blocking out the sun. The rain pattered on the roof and thunder rumbled, the kind of thunder that starts deep in the clouds and rolls out slowly, bouncing along the bluff behind the cabin.

Was she ready for Erin to leave? Long weekends were normally her max with guests. When she hosted someone for a week, by the fourth day she was antsy, ready for her peace and quiet to return—ready to resume her solitary life.

Now? This time? She met Erin's gaze in the shadows, eyes that were familiar to her now. Her presence was familiar too. There were no uncomfortable silences between them. It felt normal, natural for Erin to be here now.

"I'm not ready for you to leave, no."

She didn't intend for the words to be spoken so quietly, so intimately, like a secret was being passed between them. The air felt charged suddenly and she drew in a quick breath as Erin's eyes never wavered. Then she couldn't breathe at all as those eyes came closer. She should have turned away. She should have stopped her.

But no, her gaze dropped to the lips that were only inches away from her own. The tiny moan was out even before Erin's mouth touched hers. It was the gentlest of kisses, quiet and soft. Erin pulled back only far enough to look into her eyes again— trying to read them, she supposed. Melanie couldn't imagine what she saw there. Her own thoughts were nothing but a jumbled mess. Erin moved closer again, her hands cupping her face, pulling her closer, her mouth touching hers once more. Melanie's eyes closed and her mouth opened, accepting the kiss, moving against Erin's lips, feeling the barest touch of tongue. The jolt she felt from that hit her directly between her thighs, and she sprang to her feet, pushing away from Erin.

"No," she said hoarsely. She was breathing hard, far too hard from a simple kiss. She shook her head. "No. I...I don't need your pity, Erin."

Erin stood up too. "Pity? Where did that come from?"

Melanie walked away from her. "I...You don't have to feel sorry for me."

Erin frowned. "What are you talking about?"

She turned back to her then. "I...I haven't been kissed—touched—in so long, I hardly remember it." She shook her head again. "I don't need your pity."

"Oh, Mel. It's not pity." Erin came closer. "I like you. You're attractive. I wanted to kiss you." She held her hands up. "But I'm sorry. You obviously didn't want that too. But believe me, it had nothing to do with pity."

Didn't it? Why else would Erin kiss her? She took a step away, only then realizing that the rain had stopped, that the sun was shining again. The chickens hopped off their roost, going back into their yard. The twins were already out playing. Only Carly remained, standing half in, half out of the stall, as if not knowing if it was safe to go out yet.

Melanie felt the same. Part of her wanted to run. Part of her wanted to stay. But Erin was the one to move, the one to walk away. Melanie stared at the wall of the shed, hearing the door open and then close behind her. She wrapped her arms around herself and closed her eyes.

What a sweet kiss it had been.

CHAPTER TWENTY-EIGHT

Dinner had been a relatively quiet affair, their conversation guarded, measured…careful. It was her fault, she knew. Erin had simply followed her lead. She leaned against the bar now, arms folded, her gaze on Erin, who was on the sofa watching TV.

She needed to apologize. She needed to explain. But what would she say? That the kiss scared her more than anything? That she wasn't prepared for it? That she'd forgotten what it felt like to be kissed? That she'd gotten such a rush from that simple kiss, she'd thought…

She closed her eyes then, remembering the jolt that had shook her. Scared her. She opened them again, staring at Erin, wondering what she should say to her. Erin turned then, as if feeling Melanie watching. She took a deep breath, then made herself move, walking slowly into the living room, her eyes still locked with Erin's.

She stood beside the sofa and Erin touched the remote, muting the TV. Melanie opened her mouth to speak, again not knowing what to say. Not knowing how to explain but knowing she needed to. Erin's eyes were gentle on her and she wondered if an apology was even necessary. Yes...she decided it was. She stepped in front of her. The whispered words that left her mouth, however, stunned her. They had nothing to do with an apology.

"Will you kiss me again?"

They spilled out before she could stop them, before she even knew that she was thinking them. Her eyes widened, wanting to take them back. But Erin stood, her gaze never leaving hers.

"Is that what you want?"

Melanie felt tears sting her eyes and she blinked them away. "It's...it's been so long," she said, her voice cracking with emotion. "I've been so lonely." She wiped at a tear that escaped her eyes. "I didn't really know how lonely I'd been until you kissed me."

Erin reached out and wiped a tear away. "Please don't cry."

Melanie nodded even as she felt more tears escape. "I'm trying not to," she managed between trembling lips.

Erin's arms went around her then, pulling her to her. It felt odd to be this close to someone and she nearly stiffened, just as she'd done the first time Erin had hugged her. Having someone touch her, having arms hold her, was so foreign to her now, she felt as if someone else were standing here, not her. But Erin pulled her in, their bodies touching—their breasts, their stomachs, their hips, their thighs. Her arms finally moved, snaking around Erin's waist. She clung to her then, burying her face against Erin's neck.

After a few deep breaths, she made herself relax. She became aware of being in someone's arms, aware of warm breath against her face, aware of soft hands on her back, moving gently. She raised her head then, aware of a mouth close to hers. She didn't dare move, though. She didn't dare initiate a kiss between them.

She didn't have to. The lips that touched hers were incredibly soft, and her eyes closed as she let Erin do what she may. She tried to remember the last time someone had kissed her. The woman at the bar? Had they kissed? Surely, they had. But all she remembered were hands touching her—a stranger's hands. She had so desperately wanted to go through with it, to be able to be intimate with someone without the weight of guilt choking her. That night was no different than the other times she'd tried. She'd been humiliated by her lack of arousal—once again—and had pushed the woman off her.

She felt different now as Erin deepened the kiss. She felt the hitch in her breath, felt her heart hammering away in her chest, felt the tightness between her thighs...and heard the low moan that escaped when Erin's tongue gently, subtly, touched her lower lip.

Then she heard an answering moan, heard Erin's breathing change. What were they doing? This was no longer the gentle, placid kiss she'd expected. Their bodies were pressed together impossibly close...and she longed to get closer. Another moan as Erin's tongue slipped past her lips; without thinking, she felt her hips arch, felt herself push against Erin.

She should stop... She should apologize... She had no right to take such liberties... But she could do none of those things. Erin's hands moved up her back, then into her hair, holding her close as their kiss deepened further, tongues and lips moving crazily—passionately. Surely the soft whimpers weren't hers... Were they?

By the time Erin slowed, easing out of the kiss, Melanie felt like she'd run a marathon. She was literally gasping for breath when Erin's mouth left hers. Embarrassed, she loosened her hold, trying to step away, but Erin held her close.

"Don't," Erin whispered.

"Don't?"

"Don't run from me. Don't try to hide."

"Erin—"

"It's okay, Mel. There's nothing wrong with kissing."

"I...I..."

"Do you want to do it again? Do you want to do more?"

"Oh...*God*. I...I can't."

Erin let her pull out of her arms, but she kept hold of her hands. She looked at her with raised eyebrows, and Melanie wasn't sure what Erin expected her to say.

"I...I freeze up. I can't...I can't ever go through with it. It's humiliating. I haven't been able to get aroused like—"

"Maybe it'll be different this time. I'm not a stranger."

Melanie searched her eyes. "Why, Erin? Why do you want to be with me? Just to end my drought? Just for—"

"God...Are you still thinking I'm taking pity on you? That kiss—I'm not that good of an actress." Erin gave her hand a squeeze. "Neither are you," she whispered.

Melanie held her gaze. No, she wasn't. And she was pleased to see that there was no pity there either. Desire, yes. That surprised her. She certainly wasn't used to seeing *that* in someone's eyes. But she took a step away and Erin dropped her hands. She didn't know what to say, what to do. So, she would do what Erin asked her not to.

She would run and hide.

At least for tonight. At least until she could wrap her mind around what was happening...around what Erin was offering her.

Because right now—the fear was too much. But fear of what? What was she *really* afraid of?

She'd told Erin she'd been lost. And she had. Lost in grief, lost in booze, lost in the many, many pills she swallowed each day. She'd told her she'd moved out here to find herself again. That was the truth. But had she really found herself?

She'd pushed the guilt away...most days. She was clean and sober and healthy. Her mind was sharp, her feelings no longer raw. But who was she? Was she the woman who ambled along on her solitary walks, her mind focused on her surroundings so intently that old memories didn't dare intrude? Was she the woman who spent hours and hours and *hours* in her garden, tending steadfastly to the vegetables in the guise of providing food? In reality, she knew it was simply a distraction—a mental and physical diversion—to keep her guilty memories buried deep where they belonged, lying dormant somewhere in that dark place where she hoped they'd stay. She could say her garden was therapy and she supposed it was. She'd healed. On the surface, she'd healed.

Underneath those layers she'd piled on, however, her scars were still inflamed, still painful. Still angry.

So what was she afraid of? Was she afraid that if she let Erin in, let her touch her, kiss her, make love to her…was she afraid those scars would open and bleed again? Or was she afraid that she *wouldn't* freeze up this time? Was she afraid that she'd actually be able to be intimate with someone without Adam's ghost scolding her from the corner of the room?

Was she afraid that if she made love with Erin, those scars might mend and heal? Then what would she have? Erin would leave. What would she have then? Those scars—as painful as they were—were like old friends. If she healed, if Erin took those scars with her…then what would she have?

She'd have her freedom, that's what she'd have.

Free of guilt, free of pain. Free to live her life again.

But she'd be alone. Still. Nothing would have really changed. She'd still be alone.

CHAPTER TWENTY-NINE

Erin stood on the porch, cupping the steaming mug of coffee between her hands. It was barely after four, but she'd given up on sleep. She'd been tossing and turning most of the night, fearing how things would be between them now. She'd changed the dynamics—the kiss in the shed. But she didn't feel responsible for last night. Not solely, anyway.

She was attracted to Melanie, that was obvious. She was cute, nice, pleasant. She was likeable. She was easy to be around. She was confident, sure of herself… Strong.

Yet she was vulnerable and uncertain. Afraid.

And no matter how much the look in Mel's eyes made Erin want to wrap her up in her arms and protect her from all those thoughts that brought on her guilt and insecurities, she could do no such thing if Mel wouldn't allow it. She wanted to do more than hold her and protect her, though. Didn't she?

The kiss had been nice…out in the shed, it had been nice. It had been a very long time since she'd kissed someone for the simple pleasure of it. Her and Sarah's first kiss had been heated, frantic, and they'd been naked five seconds after it. Since Sarah left, any kissing she did on dates was done with one thing in mind—getting them into bed.

She smiled a bit wryly as she took a sip of the hot coffee. Jessica had been the last date she'd been on. She stayed around a month or so. How long ago had that been? Like Joyce had suspected, she hadn't even realized that Jessica was no longer there. What an ass she must have been. Even though she had no feelings for Jessica—truth was, she barely recalled the woman— she probably owed her an apology.

She leaned against the railing of the porch, her gaze going to the east where the sky was still dark. There was no sign of the impending sunrise, no sounds to indicate that a new day would be upon them soon. No sounds of the night either. Had the nighttime creatures already scurried off to their daytime hiding places? Were the owls still out hunting for their last meal of the night?

She tilted her head as she continued to stare out at nothing. It was a nice kiss—out in the shed. And last night? Nice, yes, but something more. More heated, more intimate. She'd sensed they were going too fast and she'd slowed things down. Why had Melanie been afraid of it then?

Well, it could be the fact that she hasn't kissed anyone in seven or eight years. That timeframe nearly made her head spin. Could someone really go that long without *any* kind of physical contact? A hug? A pat on the back? Something? Had she had *nothing*?

It was too sad to think about, really. The person she had come to know was sweet and passionate and affectionate. She sipped from her coffee, thinking of the times Mel had touched her arm, patted her shoulder... The times she'd seen her petting the twins or even a chicken. And the times she'd fondled old Fred's ears when he happened to come around. Was that how she survived? Making contact with the animals since there was no human around?

"You're up early."

Erin nearly dropped her cup and she juggled it, sloshing what was left of the coffee onto her hands.

"Sorry. Didn't mean to startle you out there."

She heard the smile in Mel's voice and she turned around, seeing her standing on the other side of the screen door. She was still in her sleep shirt, but her legs were covered by a pair of sweats.

"Couldn't sleep," Erin murmured. "You're up rather early as well."

"Yes."

She said nothing else and Erin watched her go into the kitchen, presumably for her own cup of coffee. She let out a quick sigh, then went inside. Melanie was pouring a cup and she raised her eyebrows questioningly at her. Erin nodded and set her cup down beside Mel's. She rinsed off her hands quickly, watching as Mel took both cups to the bar and sat down.

So, Mel wanted to talk. In this early morning hour, it was still black as night out…and Mel wanted to talk. With another—this time quiet—sigh, she joined her. She didn't know where to start, though.

"I should…I should apologize." That was always a good start, she thought. Apologize and get it over with.

"No. You don't owe me an apology," Melanie countered. "I owe you one, if anything." She held the cup between both hands. "I've been sending you mixed signals." Mel turned slightly, meeting her gaze. "I'm feeling a bit…out of sorts, I guess."

She nodded. "I've disrupted your routine. Taken you out of your comfort zone."

"Definitely."

"I wish I could take it all back, Mel. I don't want things to be strained between us. Uncomfortable. It's my fault and I—"

"Erin, please don't apologize." She stared into her cup of coffee for a long moment. "I like you. And…I'm attracted to you." She looked up then, meeting her gaze fully. "I haven't been intimate with anyone—truly intimate—since Courtney, since the night Adam caught us." She looked back into her cup of coffee. "The other attempts were—well, as I said, humiliating."

"And painful?" Erin guessed. "Emotionally painful, I mean."

Melanie nodded. "Yes. The guilt was suffocating and…all I could see was Adam on our bed, the blood, the gun." She closed her eyes. "The last time, I guess it had been four years since he died, the image wasn't quite as fresh, as raw, but it was there. And the woman—I have no idea what her name was—had no clue what was going on with me. She must have thought I was a nutcase, I guess." Melanie looked at her then. "And I was, I suppose."

"So last night? When we were kissing, was Adam there with us? Did you see him? Had I disappeared?" Erin wasn't certain what she expected to see in Melanie's eyes, but sadness wasn't it. It wasn't grief, no. It was something else. Despair?

"No. Adam wasn't there," Mel said quietly. "I think…I think that frightened me." She shook her head. "No. I *know* it frightened me. I keep my guilt in check, for the most part. Buried, at least. Hidden, out of sight." She took a sip of her coffee. "When we kissed and there was no sign of Adam or my guilt—" She met her gaze again. "I felt a bit lost again. Alone." She shook her head. "I know that makes no sense."

"It's been so many years, Mel. Maybe—whether you wanted it to or not—your guilt has slipped away."

"Yes. Maybe it has. Or maybe it's just hiding, waiting to spring out at me again."

"Ah, I see. If we're together—intimate—then you're afraid it'll come back full force."

"Yes. And when you leave, I'm afraid I'll have to start all over again."

Erin nodded. "I understand." She reached over and took Melanie's hand, squeezing it tightly, then relaxing her hold a bit. "So let me apologize again and we won't talk about it. It's over and done with."

Melanie arched an eyebrow. "Pretend it never happened?"

"Exactly. Pretend it never happened." She offered a quick smile. "Back to normal for us."

CHAPTER THIRTY

Melanie pushed the straw hat up and wiped her brow, taking the time to glance up into the sky. It was a hot day, but the clouds were building in the west. She figured they had an hour before the rain started.

"My back is killing me. You're a slave driver."

She laughed. "My basket is twice as full as yours. Don't start with me."

"You have experience doing this." Erin stood up straight and rubbed the small of her back. "Who knew picking green beans was so much work?"

"Are you trying to get out of the canning process later?"

"Yeah." Erin grinned at her. "It's blistering hot. How about a dip in the creek? We can do the pressure canning thing tonight."

She shook her head. "No time."

She motioned to the sky, watching as Erin glanced to the west. The smile Erin had been flashing disappeared when she recognized the rain clouds coming. Yeah, a dip in the creek did sound refreshing. And if she was alone, she might dash off for a quick swim, just to cool off. But she thought it better not to even suggest it. Because they'd go to the creek, they'd both strip naked...and after what had happened the other day, she'd just as soon not put them in that position again. Because they were pretending the kisses never happened.

She couldn't avoid the creek forever, though. They'd been managing quite well the last few days. There was no awkwardness between them, even though she knew it was only because of great effort on both their parts. They'd teased and laughed and chatted like always. Things had been normal. Because they were pretending the kisses never happened.

On the surface, things were normal. It was what lurked beneath the surface that scared her. Still.

"You weren't kidding when you said it rains every afternoon."

"It won't rain *every* day. And sometimes the rains won't come until later...three or four. Plenty of time for a swim."

"Or maybe we should plan to go at noon, before the rains come."

"Or we could do that."

Erin laughed. "You're afraid to go swimming with me, aren't you?"

"I most certainly am not!"

Erin came closer, her eyes dancing with merriment. "You, my friend, are lying through your teeth! But...we can use the rain as an excuse, if you want to. Be warned, though. We're not going to spend the rest of the summer avoiding the creek. Because *I* can control myself around you, whether you're naked or not." She grinned wickedly at her. "You, apparently, are afraid that you can't."

She sauntered off, back to the row of green beans she'd been picking. Mel was left to stare at her, noting the tan, shapely legs that had replaced the thin, pale ones Erin had first sported. Erin had changed in so many ways. Certainly physically—her hair, her weight, her appearance. But her personality had changed too. The quiet, serious, withdrawn woman had been replaced with a vibrant, talkative, teasing, and playful one.

And she enjoyed being around her. She enjoyed her company and she enjoyed her presence. Whether they were cooking together and chatting or watching TV and sitting quietly, or even on the porch not speaking at all…she enjoyed Erin being there with her.

She turned her attention back to her own row of beans when she heard thunder rumble behind the bluff. Yeah, she enjoyed Erin. And yeah, she'd lied.

She *was* afraid to go swimming with her.

* * *

"I'm not sick of squash or green beans," Erin said as she stabbed beans with her fork. "Why do you keep asking if I am?"

"Because I'm trying to be a gracious host."

"So if I said I *was* sick of them, what would be the alternative?"

"Broccoli or cauliflower. I have both in the freezer from the spring harvest."

"And when do we dig potatoes?"

Mel smiled at her. "That's the third time you've asked."

"I'm looking forward to it. Because these are fabulous," she said, biting into a wedge. Mel had dug around one of the potato plants, picking out three nice-sized potatoes for their dinner. They'd been the best tasting ones she'd ever eaten.

"Most people don't even know what a real potato tastes like. Those you buy in the store have been refrigerated. It totally changes the taste. Even the ones we've been eating, they're from the fall harvest. You can tell they're no longer as fresh once you taste these."

"In case you haven't noticed, I'm finding all of this totally fascinating. Eating in season, canning, the whole garden thing. It's so different than what I imagined." Then she shook her head. "Actually, I don't think I ever did really imagine it. You just go to the store, hit the produce aisle, and get what you want. It never really occurred to me how things were grown, I guess."

"I'm sure most people are like that. I know I was."

"So you eat what the garden is producing until it stops. Then what?"

"What? You want a seasonal tour?"

She motioned to her plate. "Tonight, for instance. We've got pinto beans, which are so much better than Rachel's. We've got potatoes, squash, and green beans." She moved the green beans around. "And some onions and peppers here." She scooped up a forkful of beans. "Never in a million years would I have thought I'd enjoy eating like this. You're an excellent cook."

"Thank you, but it's all pretty simple fare."

"What do you do during the winter?"

"I still have some things in the garden. Carrots do really well, winter and spring. Spinach, lettuce, kale, collards. Cabbage. I usually make soups during the winter months. And I eat the veggies I either froze or canned. Now that I've got my routine down, it isn't difficult at all."

"Why no tofu? I mean, we've had it...what? Twice? Three times? And those soy curl things...Those were good."

"Like Rachel, beans are a staple for me. And even though I can buy tofu any time of year, I usually only eat it during the summer, for some reason. I love a good stir-fry. I'll need to make one for us soon. And yes, I'll do the soy curls again."

"Pasta?" she asked hopefully.

"We can. I usually use rice, but pasta is a good change."

She took a swallow of water before stabbing another potato with her fork. Surprisingly, she no longer missed having some sort of meat with their meals. At first, it seemed like something was lacking. But now? Now she filled her plate with either potatoes or the seasoned rice Mel made. Then she added a huge helping of beans and covered what was left of the plate with veggies. There was no room to even consider where a piece of chicken might fit.

"You look good."

She looked up, meeting Mel's gaze. "Thanks to you."

"Not all me."

"Mostly. You, the food. Being out here, away from...my life."

"Do you miss it yet? Your life?"

Did she? Honestly, she rarely thought about it. Mel had been keeping her so busy and perhaps that was the plan. She really didn't have time to contemplate...*things*. How were her projects? Did her father have them running on schedule? Had they had rain? Thunderstorms? A tropical system and flooding? What about her house? Were the yard guys coming as planned?

Did the cleaning lady still come by once a week? Was her pool being cleaned? She hadn't given it a thought. Joyce was supposed to "check on things" and she assumed she had. She hadn't thought about it, no, but did she miss it?

"I don't know, really. I don't think about it." She shrugged. "I'm just here...until I'm not."

"You don't have a secret calendar in your room that you mark off each day with a giant X?" she teased.

She smiled at her. "The first few days...yeah, I thought about building one on my laptop. Now? I don't even know where my laptop is."

Melanie stood up and took their plates to the sink. "If you want the password, just say the word."

"I haven't missed being online. I don't see you use it much either."

Melanie held up a cup. "Feel like tea?"

"Sure."

"I don't use it much, no. Check the weather, that sort of thing. When I first moved out here, I'd read newspapers, trying to keep up with what was going on out there," she said with a wave of her hand. "It was mostly depressing and I found I had a much better outlook on life if I wasn't exposed to all that. Politics, mass shootings, protests." She shook her head. "My life is so much more peaceful without it."

Erin nodded. At first, that was something she missed. Being connected, knowing what was going on. In her old life, when she got ready for work, she'd have the news on. Her commute to the office—talk radio. She was informed. She knew what was going on in the world. She was also usually angry, anxious, worried about the state of the nation, worried about the stock market. Now? Like everything else, it was out of sight, out of mind. Peaceful, yes. But unlike Melanie, she couldn't hide away from the real world out here forever. She'd have to go back to it.

Eventually.

She took her cup of tea that Melanie offered her and followed her out to the porch. The air was still cool and damp from the earlier rain. Today's showers had passed rather quickly, but they were a little more intense. Mel had warned her that some afternoons and evenings, the storms would be severe, with lots of lightning and even hail. Those were the storms she dreaded, she'd said, as they could wipe out her garden if they were severe enough.

She sat down beside her, putting the rocker in motion. There was a breeze this evening and the piñon pine at the corner was rustling, its fragrance drifting about as the branches brushed the cabin walls. And even though she was expecting them, the first loud howls of the coyotes made her jump.

"I don't know if I'll ever get used to that."

"I love it," Melanie said quietly. "Some people equate the sound with loneliness. To me, it's quite the opposite."

"You mean, it's more lonely when Goldie and Rick aren't around?"

"Yes. It's so quiet then. At night. I sometimes feel like I'm the only person left in the world."

Melanie's words weren't much more than a whisper, and Erin turned her head slowly, watching her. The porch light was off, like they usually had it when they were out. The inside lights cast enough of a glow to allow her to see Mel's features. As more yips and howls sounded, a smile formed on Melanie's lips. In the muted light, Erin was certain she'd never seen a more beautiful woman. Mel turned to look at her then, the soft smile now for her.

"I'm glad you're here, Erin."

She stared into her eyes, trying to read them. "Me too."

The words didn't surprise her. She *was* glad she was there. The three-month prison sentence she'd been dreading was nearly half over and she now felt like the days were speeding by too fast. She was still amazed at how much she'd changed in such a short time. Not only physically. That was easy to see. But mentally, emotionally—she felt a peace within her that had been missing for so long. Missing? Was it ever there to begin with? Like this?

It was a quiet peace that she could almost feel surrounding her, comforting her. Protecting her. Protection from what, though?

Herself, maybe.

They sat there in silence, their rockers moving in near unison as the coyotes moved away, their song disappearing in the wind, the night swallowing it up, making her question if they'd even been there at all.

CHAPTER THIRTY-ONE

"Hurry!"

Erin was laughing as she struggled to carry the five-gallon bucket full of potatoes. "Why am I doing all the heavy lifting?"

"Because *you* wanted to dig some potatoes. Not me."

Mel ran ahead of her, the cold wet rain pelting them mercilessly. She opened the door to the shed, letting Erin go in ahead of her. Erin dropped the bucket, then plopped down on the hay bale, catching her breath.

"That came out of nowhere."

Mel brushed her damp hair back from her face and nodded. "I know. I thought we had plenty of time."

"That was fun though. What'd we get?"

"That's probably more than twenty pounds." She smiled at her. "You're pretty handy."

"You think I'm a keeper, huh?"

Mel grinned at her. "Definitely. You've become quite adept at many things."

"Like making tortillas?" A boom of thunder shook the shed and Erin's eyes flew to hers. "That sounded close."

She nodded. "You have thunderstorms in Houston, don't you?"

"Sure. We have our share of severe weather—tornado warnings and such. I don't pay much attention, I guess. Our office suite is on the eleventh floor of a high rise—"

"Wow. You must have a nice view of storms up that high."

"I don't know. Not sure I've actually watched one before."

Mel tilted her head, studying her. She could see that, she supposed. She had to remind herself that the Erin she knew out here wasn't the same person she'd be back in the city. She wouldn't be on her knees, digging in the earth, squealing with delight when she brought up a potato, her hands covered in dirt. And she wouldn't be traipsing off to the creek, walking in up to her knees to clean off. And she wouldn't be walking with chickens and goats, talking to them as if they understood—much like she herself did.

"You're wondering how I could miss seeing a thunderstorm, aren't you?"

Melanie shook her thoughts away, nodding at Erin. "They're so powerful. Nature at its best. Out here, with the bluff behind us and the mountains out there," she motioned with her hand. "They're wild...spectacular."

"Scary."

She nodded with a smile. "Yes. Especially if you're caught outside in one."

A double boom shook them, its sound echoing against the bluff, then trailing off down the creek. The chickens clucked nervously on their roost and the twins pressed closer to the wooden railings that separated their stall from the shed. Erin reached out and rubbed Rosie's nose. Melanie smiled as Erin whispered reassuringly to her.

Erin turned then, her dark eyes still gentle—warm—from cooing at Rosie. Her hair was damp and standing on end from where her fingers had brushed through it. She had dirt on her cheek. Without thinking, Melanie moved closer, reaching out to brush the smear from Erin's face. Her thumb rubbed gently against her skin. The dirt smudge was gone, yet her fingers remained. Her gaze fixed on Erin's, and she realized that Erin was holding her breath, afraid—maybe—that she would spoil the moment by making even the slightest movement.

Melanie's gaze dropped to Erin's mouth. Again, without conscious thought, she traced her thumb along the bottom of her lip. Even though Erin remained still, Mel could see her pulse beating rapidly in her neck. Their eyes met again and she swore she felt an energy between them—a charge in the air. She heard a bolt of lightning sizzle across the creek, its flash illuminating the darkening sky. The subsequent rumble barely registered as she bent down, lowering her mouth to meet Erin's.

When their lips met, she felt her heart flutter in her chest, felt her stomach flip nervously, heard the tiny moan she couldn't contain. Instead of deepening the kiss, which is what she wanted to do, she pulled back with a quick shake of her head.

"I'm sorry, Erin. I have no right—"

"Mel...stop." Erin stood up, standing in front of her. Standing too close. "Quit thinking so much."

"That's just it. I'm not thinking. Not rationally, anyway. We agreed—"

"We agreed to not talk about it, to pretend it didn't happen... to ignore it." Erin touched her hand, rubbing her fingers across the back of it. "We've done that. It's not what either of us really want, though. Is it?"

"Oh, Erin. We can't want *this*, can we? Kisses stolen in a smelly barn?"

Erin smiled at her. "Yeah...there must be something about this shed that makes us kiss."

She finally took a step away from Erin, away from her touch. "I'm sorry. Again—I obviously don't know what I want."

"Mel, you *do* know what you want."

"Okay. Yes. But I don't *want* to want it." She smiled slightly. "You were sitting there, all damp from the rain, cooing at Rosie and...and—"

"You wanted to kiss me?"

"Yes, I wanted to kiss you."

"And so you did. That's how it should be. There shouldn't be all these rules and restrictions. We're two adult women, both single." She shrugged. "We shouldn't have to fight this, Mel. Like I said earlier, stop thinking so much." Erin moved away from her, back to where she'd dropped the bucket of potatoes. "So what do we do with these babies? You have someplace where you store them?"

Melanie stared at her, surprised at her change of subject. But it was good, she supposed. She *was* thinking too much. She should simply let it go, let things fall where they may. She should stop trying to control things. She should let it be. So, she took a deep breath and blew it out quickly, then offered a smile.

"Through the door there. It's like a small closet."

"Why haven't I noticed this before?"

"I guess because I haven't asked you to come out and get onions for me. I harvested them last October. I moved what was left of last fall's potatoes into the house. There's nothing in there but onions right now and a few carrots that are left from fall."

Erin opened the door and the pungent smell of onions hit them. Erin grinned.

"Oh, wow. That actually smells really great."

There were six wire racks on the three big walls, two racks hung on each. A smaller wire rack was next to the door. The room had been a corner of the original shed, but since she didn't have a cellar, she needed someplace dark and cool to store her veggies after spring and summer harvest. This corner faced north and was shaded by a piñon pine. High windows with screens let in cool air, enough for the vegetables to keep over the hot summer months. The fall harvest even overwintered in here, with her only having to cover the racks on the coldest of nights.

"I put the potatoes on this side," she said, motioning to the inside wall opposite the onions. "If they're too close together, the onions will make the potatoes sprout."

Erin went about unloading the potatoes, placing them carefully on the wire rack. "What else do you keep in here?"

"Carrots go in the wooden crates there. I cover them with dirt. I leave them in the garden as long as I can and pull them when I need them, but there comes a point where they need to come out of the ground or they'll get woody."

"Woody?"

She smiled. "It's a term gardeners use. Once they start sprouting and make seeds, they lose their flavor quickly. So then I pull them all at once, chop the green off and store them in here. I put up—pressure can—maybe ten or twelve pints, though. Winter squash keeps well too. Butternut and acorn squash are the two I normally plant. I'll harvest them in October. They'll keep through the winter."

"So there's no carrots in the garden now?"

"There's a row from the late spring planting. I'll leave those in the ground as long as I can. I'll plant the fall garden in a couple of weeks—into the first week in August. That's when I plant broccoli and cauliflower and cabbage—things like that. And I'll plant another round of kale and spinach.

"Wow. That all makes my head spin."

"I know. It's a lot of variety, but I don't overdo the volume. I'm one person. I can only eat so much."

Erin stood back, surveying her work. Then she smiled. "We're going to have some of these for dinner, right?"

"Of course. Pick three or four."

The sun was shining again when they went back out, and the goats and chickens were already in their run. She and Erin stood in the sunshine, looking at each other. The air was still cool from the rain, the ground damp. It had been a short-lived storm, more noise than rain. She looked to the west, seeing more clouds building. They already looked dark and ominous.

"More rain?"

She nodded. "I should probably check the forecast. We might be in for a stormy night." She headed toward the cabin, then stopped. "Do you mind bringing Bandito up? He's probably under the lean-to on the other side of the shed. That's where he normally takes cover when storms pop up."

"Gonna put him in tonight?"

"I'll check the weather first. If it's a lengthy storm, I usually put him in with the goats. He hates it, but it makes me feel better."

CHAPTER THIRTY-TWO

It was one of those nights that she dreaded, when the storm settled on top of her, the blackness of night hiding its power. As was her habit, she moved from window to window, looking out into the darkness as the rain pelted the panes. She normally hated these nighttime storms. Hated being alone during them, really. She'd even pulled old Fred inside one night under the guise of giving him shelter when he'd been perfectly content lying on the old blanket on the porch.

But tonight?

She wasn't alone tonight. Having another person there seemed to settle her nerves a bit. Erin was in the kitchen, peering out the window that looked out toward the shed. She was obviously concerned. She'd gone out twice before the storm hit to make sure the chickens and goats were secure.

"They'll be fine."

Erin turned, looking a bit embarrassed. "Yeah. Not their first storm." Then she smiled. "But it's mine."

"Are you scared?"

"A little, yeah. You can't see a damn thing outside." A boom of thunder moved Erin away from the window. "Don't know why I never noticed storms when I was stuck in a high-rise."

"I'm having a hard time picturing you in an office setting," she said as she took out two mugs for their tea. "Power suits?"

Erin leaned against the bar and nodded. "Mostly. Before Sarah, I lived in jeans and work boots and spent as much time out at the construction sites as I did the office."

"Yes. I can see that. Why the change?"

"I guess I didn't fit the image that Sarah wanted."

Melanie paused in her task, wondering what Erin's emotional state had been back then. The woman she knew now, she couldn't see her giving in to the demands of someone else. At least not on such a personal level as the way she dressed.

"What?"

Melanie placed the tea bags in each cup. "I'm trying to picture someone telling you how to dress and you going along with it. None of my business, of course."

"The changes that Sarah made—or suggested—were made so subtly, so slight, that I don't think I really noticed how different I was becoming. Joyce noticed." Erin shook her head. "I was willing to change, I guess, to make her happy. Keep her happy."

"That's funny and sad, isn't it? People do that all the time, I suppose. Change to be someone they're not to please someone else. I did it to an extent too."

"I don't think you changed for Adam. Not really. You pretended to change. Big difference."

"Did you think Sarah wouldn't love you if you stayed the same? I mean, she must have fallen in love with you before the change."

"I don't know anymore. Was she ever really in love with me?" Erin stared at her. "Or was she pretending?"

"Are you trying to make comparisons with me and Adam? That was a completely different situation," she said a bit snappishly. *Wasn't it?* The teakettle started whistling, but when she reached for it, Erin beat her to it.

"Sorry. No. I wasn't making comparisons, Mel." Erin poured the boiling water into each cup. "As you said, completely different. What I meant was, maybe it was easier to pretend to love me than to live her life. She had a job, but she wasn't going anywhere there and it didn't pay all that much. I was selfish and wanted her around more, so I pushed her to quit. I made enough money to support us." She put the teakettle back. "I made it easy for her. I gave her everything she wanted." A flash of lightning again caused her to move away from the window. "She pretended to love me, pretended she was happy…until she couldn't anymore. Until she met someone who she could honestly love."

Erin shrugged and Mel noted that her eyes were mostly filled with regret, not sadness. She reached out, touching Erin's hand. "You can't say for sure that she never loved you, Erin. You spent six years together. She must have loved you."

Erin turned her hand over and let their fingers entwine. "I think I knew. I didn't want it to be true. All those hurtful things she said to me when she was leaving…At first, I thought it was just her anger talking, but really, I think that's how she truly felt. Joyce had been right all along." Erin lifted her gaze from their joined hands. "She used me. And I let her. What a pathetic fool I was."

"Oh, Erin. You weren't a fool. When you love someone, there's—"

"There's no need to offer up some defense for me, Mel. No need. I was stupidly blind. I take the blame."

"Sweetie…I'm sorry."

Her arms were around Erin's shoulders before she knew what she was doing and she pulled Erin to her tightly. It wasn't lost on her how fiercely Erin clung to her.

"She used me," Erin whispered hoarsely. "The truth of that hurts more than I thought it would."

Erin pulled away a little, but neither of them released their hold. Erin was too close, her lips too near. The situation called for a kiss, didn't it? The jumbled thoughts dancing around in her brain were all clamoring to be heard at once, effectively doing the opposite—she heard none of them. Much as the storm raging outside faded into the background, so did her objections. She no longer knew the reason she'd tried so hard to keep Erin at a distance.

She saw something different in Erin's eyes this evening. A mixture of things, to be sure. There seemed to be something akin to desperation there, something she'd not been expecting and certainly nothing she'd seen before, not even that very first day. It tugged at her heart now, and she moved the few inches necessary to touch her lips to Erin's. She felt Erin's hands clutch at her shirt and she let the kiss deepen, ignoring whatever concerns were still lingering about. Erin didn't have to say the words. She could feel it in her kiss.

Erin needed her.

Erin needed her like this. Tonight. When her mouth opened, letting Erin inside, the physical rush she got from Erin's tongue brushing her own told her that *she* needed this too. The storm outside couldn't compete with the one now beginning to rage inside. She let her emotions go unchecked, moving even closer to Erin, letting their bodies touch where they may. She could no longer fight this...she no longer wanted to fight this.

CHAPTER THIRTY-THREE

She'd led Erin into her bedroom without a word spoken between them. She'd undressed Erin, putting a finger to her lips when she would have spoken. She didn't want to talk. She didn't even want to think. The fact that they were about to make love, the fact that she was going about it in such a methodical way nearly made her pause, but she pushed the apprehension aside, determined not to let it guide her tonight.

The truth was, she wasn't sure she even remembered *how* to make love. That was at the root of her fears more than anything else. Lack of arousal wasn't an issue this time, but still, eleven years was a long time. What if—

She had no time to wonder, though. Erin's kiss quashed the doubts that were trying to surface and, with eyes closed, she let her hands drop to Erin's waist, uttering the softest of moans as Erin's lips traveled along her throat, her neck, nibbling lightly. She didn't protest when Erin's fingers pushed her shirt aside. She knew where the fingers would go, but she gasped anyway when they touched her nipples. She felt them harden under Erin's touch and another moan slipped out.

She had no thoughts of stopping, no more fears. She'd brought Erin to her bedroom with the intention of making love to her, with the intent to chase away the misery—the despair—she'd seen in her eyes. Yet here she was, her own eyes closed, her chest heaving as she drew quick breaths. Erin was the one chasing away demons, not her.

Erin ducked her head, her tongue replacing her fingertips. Warm breath skipped across her skin, drawing goose bumps in its wake. Her moan was louder now as Erin's mouth closed around a nipple. In the back of her mind, she knew the storm outside was losing steam, but inside, the storm was just beginning.

* * *

Erin ran her hands lightly across Melanie's skin, amazed at the softness. How long had it been since she'd touched someone like this? She was amazed, too, at the confident look in Mel's eyes. She expected her insecurities to show, at the very least. But no, Melanie seemed as self-assured as ever when she'd drawn her down to the bed with her. She was actually the one feeling a bit nervous. And why not? She was about to make love to a woman who had been celibate for eleven years. Of course she was nervous.

Melanie smiled against her lips. "I know what you're thinking."

"Do you now?"

"It feels nice...your skin on mine. Everything feels nice."

Erin leaned up, finding Melanie's eyes in the shadows, the room lit only by a candle and the residual flashes of lightning outside the window. Yes, those blue eyes did have a bit of wonder in them. Was she thinking back to the last time—all those years ago—that she'd tried to be intimate with someone? Or maybe she was thinking about Courtney, the woman Adam had caught her with. Or was she not thinking about any of that at all?

What about her? The few women she'd been with since Sarah left were nobodies. She hardly recalled names much less faces. Even the last one...Jessica. She had come and gone without much fanfare. Even so, each and every one of them had shared the bed with Sarah too. Sarah was never too far away.

Tonight? No. She could hardly picture Sarah's face. It was Melanie lying naked with her, Melanie whose legs were wrapped around her own, Melanie whose hands were sliding up her bare back, pulling her down for another kiss.

Whereas she and Sarah had been rather boisterous in bed—rarely taking it slow, rarely taking the time for soft caresses, gentle kisses, or whispered words—things were more measured with Melanie. There was no rush, no hurry. The slow pace seemed to have a calming effect on her as her touch became more sure, more deliberate.

She pulled away from Melanie's mouth, moving to her breasts again. She covered one nipple and Melanie arched up, her low moan sending chills across her skin. She used her knee to spread her thighs and Mel's hips rose to meet hers. She could feel her arousal against her leg, and she moved back for another kiss, her tongue wrapping slowly around Mel's, their quick breaths mingling as they kissed.

She finally left Mel's mouth, moving lazily down her body, nibbling across her stomach and hips. Melanie's hands were urging her downward and Erin's eyes slid closed with a contented moan as she buried herself in Mel's wetness.

CHAPTER THIRTY-FOUR

Melanie held her hands out to her side, balancing on one of the large rocks along the previously dry Mule Creek. The storm hadn't produced enough rain to fill it, but she'd wanted to check.

"Sorry your first real storm had to come with severe weather warnings. Not enough rain to make much of a difference, though."

"How often are they severe?"

"Flash flood warnings are normal in July and August, during monsoon. Hail can occur with any storm, which is what mostly scares me—the garden, you know. Lightning, of course, but everyone knows to take cover."

"Tornadoes?"

She shook her head. "Tornadoes are very rare. I think the entire state averages ten a year. That's not something I ever worry about."

Erin came up behind her on the rock, grasping her waist. "So this is Mule Creek, huh?"

Melanie turned into Erin's arms, smiling as they kissed. "Uh-huh. Need more rain to get it flowing good."

Erin smiled too. "Have you thanked me for breakfast in bed?"

"Several times." She hopped over to the next rock. "We could make that a habit, if you like." She turned, meeting Erin's gaze.

"The breakfast in bed part or the sleeping in the same bed part?"

"Both."

A slow smile formed on Erin's face. A relieved smile. Had she been expecting something else? Had she assumed things would go back to the way they'd been between them? She admitted she'd had a moment of doubt that morning when she'd awakened to find Erin still in her bed, to find herself still tangled in Erin's arms. But only a moment. The night had been too special to ruin it with doubts and fears.

She'd watched Erin sleep for a good half hour, reliving the night in her mind. She'd been shocked, actually, that Adam's ghost hadn't made an appearance. Not even once. She'd expected his presence to be hovering over her while Erin made love to her. That wasn't the case at all. She'd been able to empty her mind of all the uncertainties, all the fear. It was only she and Erin, no one else. Not Adam. Not the nameless women she'd been unable to feel anything with. She and Erin. Mutually giving and taking what they both needed. She'd been so relieved that Adam wasn't there, she hadn't wanted to stop. As she'd whispered to Erin last night, she had a lot of years to make up for.

It occurred to her that it was the first time she'd slept with someone who she would consider a friend. Other than Adam, that is. What she and Courtney shared was never friendship. And while she and Adam were friends—best friends, in fact—there was never any physical heat between them. Adam had to have felt that too.

It also occurred to her that it was the first time she'd been intimate with someone in a relaxed state. When she was a teenager, just coming of age, there was always the fear of getting caught—rushing through the act which such haste, she hardly recalled it afterward. With Adam, she was never relaxed. There was the fear that he'd know that she wasn't as aroused as she should be, know that she was pretending. And of course, with Courtney, there was nothing at all relaxing about it. She was cheating on Adam, a fact that weighed on her then and still followed her to this day. She cheated on Adam. He caught her. He committed suicide. Her fault. End of story.

"Hey."

She blinked several times, bringing herself back to the here and now.

"Where'd you go? Your smile disappeared."

Should she force one? No. She and Erin were now lovers, yes, but she and Erin were friends. They'd talked about everything. No need to hide things now.

"I'm feeling guilty all of a sudden," she admitted.

Erin's expression softened. "I expected it sooner than now, I guess."

She looked past Erin to the muddy red creek, watching as the runoff carried away the small sticks and twigs that had littered the dry bed. The first few rains would clean it. When the monsoon hit, when the heavy rains came, the little creek would flow clean and clear, winding around the back of the bluff, past the cabin and shed where it would eventually empty into Eagle Creek.

"I didn't think of Adam…last night, I mean, when we were… Well, I—"

"You have a life, Mel. You can't let him dictate how you live it."

"Can't I? I killed him."

"No, Mel. That was his choice."

"Brought on by my actions."

Erin came closer and grasped her shoulders, forcing her to look at her. "Don't you think there was something else to it? Could there have been? Mel, if everyone did what he did…"

"What about you? You were cheated on by someone you loved."

"I didn't put a goddamn gun to my head."

"No, but you stopped taking care of yourself, you stopped caring. You very well could have met the same fate."

"And how stupid of me would that have been?" She dropped her arms and took a step away. "Now? I feel like an idiot. I let her take eighteen months of my life. For what? The only good thing to come of it was that I came out here, I met you. I feel normal again." She met her gaze and held it. "If everyone killed themselves because they were cheated on...My God, the world would be an empty place, wouldn't it?"

"It's not that easy to brush away, Erin."

"It's been eleven years. How long do you hold on to it? How long before you forgive yourself?"

She bit her lip. "I don't know that I can forgive myself."

Erin came closer again, reaching up to touch her cheek. "What you did—your affair—you can't undo that, Mel. No matter how hard you try, you can't undo it."

"I know. If I could..."

"Don't do what-ifs, Mel. That'll do nothing but drive you crazy."

Melanie let out a deep breath, then took Erin's hand. "You're right. I shouldn't do what-ifs and rehashing it won't change anything either. Let's finish our walk."

A few steps later, Erin bumped her shoulder. "Are you sorry?"

"Sorry we slept together? Not at all. Are you?"

"No." Then she grinned. "It seemed overdue."

Melanie laughed. "Yes, maybe so. Just thinking about making love with you terrified me. I was so afraid I'd freeze up or cry or not remember *how*. But last night...It seemed to all happen naturally. So no, I'm not sorry. Relieved, really."

"Not remember how?" Another playful bump to her shoulder. "Like riding a bike."

She stopped walking and so did Erin. "I've always had a hard time reaching...Well, what I'm trying to say is that orgasms didn't come easy. Ever. Last night, everything seemed so effortless. Natural." She shrugged. "I never had any doubt that I'd climax."

Erin leaned closer and kissed her. "Well, I could say it's because I'm so skilled, but it's probably because—after eleven years—your body was ready to explode."

Melanie pulled her closer for another kiss. "We could say that, I guess. We'll need to experiment further to be sure."

Erin smiled against her lips. "I'm all for that."

CHAPTER THIRTY-FIVE

Erin felt Melanie watching her, and she turned around, pausing in her chore of mucking the goats' stall. She wiped the sweat from her brow and grinned.

"Never thought I'd be doing this topless."

"I told you, gardening topless is awesome."

"And it'll make it so much easier when we get in the creek later."

Mel took the wheelbarrow and headed toward the compost pile. "Are we getting in the creek?" she asked over her shoulder.

"We are." She followed, the shovel balanced over her shoulder. "In fact, I'm ready right now. It's hot as hell out here today."

Melanie surprised her by stopping. She looked up into the clear sky, shielding her eyes from the sun. "You're right. It is hot. Let's go cool off."

They held hands as they walked to the creek. Erin thought it was sweet, and she tried to remember a time when she and Sarah had walked together and held hands. She couldn't think of any.

"You're getting so tan."

She nodded. "I am. Going around topless helps."

"You have a nice body. And I'll be honest, I would not have said that even a month ago."

She patted her stomach. "I'm glad you don't have a scale in the house. I'd be almost afraid to weigh myself."

"When you get to a healthy weight, you'll stop gaining."

"Not if I keep eating the way I am."

"You're eating good food, though. Well, we could stand to cut down on cheese, that's for sure. And probably olive oil. Other than those two things, you're eating whole, healthy foods. Look at me. I never count calories or mind my portions. I eat when I'm hungry, I stop when I'm comfortably full, and I don't eat again until I'm hungry. I never gain weight."

"It's easy out here. There aren't fast food junk options at every corner or pizza delivery or things like that."

"I would never go back to eating that way. It makes me cringe to think of all the crap I used to eat. In fact, I think I'm going to seriously give up cheese. I talk about it, but I never actually *do* it. There's absolutely nothing healthy about it. It's pure fat."

"And eggs?"

"God, no! Are you crazy!"

Erin stood back as Melanie dropped her shorts and glided into the creek, unmindful of the rocks. She found the deep pool and sank down, dipping her head back, then sinking to the bottom. The clear water hid nothing and Erin stared, thinking back to that first morning in bed. Mel had been almost shy, covering herself with the sheet when the light of day invaded the bedroom. Shy after making love. Yet out here, or in the garden, she was completely comfortable in her nakedness. Maybe because she was in her element, it was familiar. Being naked in bed with another woman? She obviously hadn't adjusted yet, even though they'd shared the same bed for the last several nights.

"You coming in or are you just going to stare?"

She smiled at her. "It's a nice view."

Mel splashed water in her direction. "You're too easy."

She tossed her shorts on top of Mel's then headed—a bit more carefully than Mel had—into the creek. She held her hands out to balance herself, then before sinking into the water, she bent her head back and looked into the deep blue sky, relishing the feel of the hot sun on her face. After a few seconds, she turned, this time finding Melanie watching *her*. She moved into deeper water, not nearly as gracefully as she'd planned; she slipped on a rock at the last moment. She caught herself before going under, then ducked under anyway. The water didn't seem as cold as the last time.

"Nice."

Melanie was smiling as she came closer, then she pulled her into a kiss. "I kinda like sharing my creek with you."

"It's so peaceful here. Close your eyes and all you hear is water and birds. No traffic, no buzz."

"Did you have a long commute?"

"The last three years, yes. We moved our office to the downtown area. Parking is a bitch and I hate that I pushed so hard for it. Of course, the hours I worked, there wasn't much traffic to fight. Still, it was a half-hour drive, even at my odd hours."

"Why did you push to move?"

"Why do you think?"

"Ah. Sarah?"

"Yeah. And it totally makes no sense where we are. Sure, it's in a fancy building and we even have a view of Minute Maid Park. That's baseball—the Astros. And we have a lot more amenities than the old building." She shook her head. "For our clientele and where most of our projects are, it's not convenient in the least. When our lease is up, I think I'm going to push to move us back." She rolled her eyes. "They'll think I'm crazy, of course."

"Sarah wasn't impressed with your old building, I take it?"

"I'm realizing that Sarah wasn't impressed with a lot of things. You were right. It's sad how much had to change—me included—to make her happy. Even then, it wasn't enough for her." She held her hand up. "I don't want to talk about Sarah. It's too pretty a day."

"Yes. It'll have to be a quick soak, though." She pointed toward the west. "Clouds are already building. I believe you have some mucking to finish."

She shook her finger at her. "I believe you're taking advantage of me."

Melanie gave her a rather saucy look. "I believe you're being compensated quite well."

She laughed, then drew Mel to her. Their eyes met and Mel's were as relaxed as her own must be. "I like you a lot."

"That's good. I like you a lot too." Then Mel grinned. "We must. We've been doing all sorts of naughty things together."

"Well, you're certainly sleeping later than normal."

"I know. I'm sure the—" She tilted her head, listening. Then her expression changed. "Oh, crap! We've got to hurry!"

"What?"

Melanie pulled her out of the water. "Stella's coming."

As Erin watched Melanie try tug her shorts on over her wet legs, it finally dawned on her. They were both topless. She struggled into her own shorts, finally hearing the faint sound of Stella's old truck.

"How did you even hear that?"

Melanie took her hand and they ran back toward the garden. They stopped past the shed, where they'd left the wheelbarrow. Melanie covered her mouth as she started laughing.

"Where did we leave our shirts? They're not on the garden fence."

"I don't know. If I recall, you took mine off me. Where did you toss it?"

Melanie's eyes lit up. "On the hay bale."

They both ran at the same time, stumbling into the shed—and out of sight—just as Stella's truck appeared. Melanie was giggling uncontrollably as she tossed a T-shirt at Erin. Erin found herself laughing too when she realized they had put on each other's shirts.

"Yoo-hoo! Girls? Mel? Erin?"

Melanie took a deep breath, a grin still on her face. "I have *never* been this close to getting caught before!"

"You look good in my shirt. Better out of it, but—"

"Shh! Come on."

Stella was heading toward the garden when they came out of the shed. Erin noticed that Melanie was still trying to keep the smile off her face.

"Stella, over here."

Stella turned, nodding. "There you two are. At this hour, I knew you had to be outside. We'll have rain before too long."

"Yes, trying to finish up the stalls before it starts. Want to get the compost stirred before it rains." Mel put her hands on her hips. "What brings you around this late in the afternoon?"

"Oh, I know, dear. I meant to come out this morning, but I got sidetracked. Then Vivian had a few of us over for lunch and of course we stayed longer than we should, drinking coffee and chatting." Her attention left Mel and moved to her. "My goodness, Erin, you are looking fit as a fiddle."

"Thank you. I feel good too."

"Well, I've been remiss in coming around to check on you. I apologize for that."

"No need to check on me."

"I feel it's my duty. Especially since you have such a long stay. I hope Mel isn't forcing you to work for your dinner." Her tone was teasing, but Erin suspected she meant the question literally.

"I've quite enjoyed my time here on the farm. She's not forcing me to do anything."

"Good, good. Well, I thought I must come out. Your sister called again last evening. I told her you were fine, but of course it's been a while since I've checked on you. She really would like for you to call her. I told her I would pass on the message. You're certainly welcome to use my phone at the house."

A bark from the back of the truck brought their attention around and Fred stuck his head over the side.

"Why do you have Fred back there?" Mel asked as she walked over to rub his head. "We haven't seen him in a week or more."

"No, he seems to have camped out at my house. Or he sneaks over to Dianne's. She's got more eggs than she knows what to do with. She fries him up a couple for his dinner."

"So you're leaving me, huh?" Mel said to the dog.

"I think the trek way out here has just gotten to be too much for him," Stella said. "Thought I'd bring him by, though, in case you wanted me to leave him with you."

"No, no. That's fine. The last year or so, he hasn't stayed around more than a few days at a time anyway." Mel rubbed his head again, and Erin noticed a wistful look on her face before she turned back to Stella. "I've got some yellow squash. Do you need any?"

"Oh, no, dear. Everyone seems to have a surplus. Angela loaded me up yesterday and my own bush is still producing." She glanced toward the garden. "I see you haven't dug all your potatoes yet. I'll take some of those off your hands when you do."

"Of course."

"Well, I should get back. Don't want to get caught in the storm. The news said this one will bring more rain than the one the other night. That one was a doozy. I guess the lightning was bad up here too."

"Yes…that was quite a storm."

Stella turned to her. "And how did you fare, dear?"

Erin was positive a blush lit her face. "It was quite the storm, yes. I couldn't sleep, in fact. Mel stayed up with me." She finally glanced toward Melanie, who was again trying to keep a smile from her face. "What time did we finally get to sleep? Well after midnight, wasn't it?"

"I believe so."

"Well, you get used to it. My first summer here, I was deathly afraid. The lightning seemed to be hitting the treetops and the thunder bounced around so, you couldn't even tell if it was coming or going. Now? I go right back to sleep when the storms hit." She looked to the sky. "I do prefer the afternoon rains, though. Much more tame than those nighttime storms." Stella surprised her by giving her a hug. "Give some thought to calling your sister, dear. I'm afraid she thinks we've lost you or something."

Erin nodded. "You're probably right. I'll get Mel to run me over there tomorrow."

"Good, good. Come about nine. I've got some old bananas I've been saving for bread. I'll bake us up a loaf to go with our coffee." Stella turned to Melanie and hugged her too. "You're doing such a good job with our guest. She looks positively radiant. You both do."

It was Mel's turn to blush. "It's the food."

"And the sunshine," Erin added quickly, although she didn't know why. How bad would it be if Stella found out they were lovers? It wasn't really any of her business, was it?

Melanie didn't seem to relax, though, until Stella's truck was out of sight. "So, you look radiant, huh?"

Erin laughed. "Apparently we both do." She arched an eyebrow. "I take it you don't want Stella to find out why we look so radiant?"

Melanie shrugged. "As you said, we're both adults. Stella feels responsible, though, for your well-being. Just like she doesn't want me forcing you into work, she may think I've forced you into my bed."

A low rumble sounded off in the distance, signaling the approaching storm that would bring more needed rain. She smiled at Melanie, pausing to brush her still-damp hair from her forehead. "Wonder why she didn't comment on our wet hair."

"She probably thought it was from working. Speaking of which, we should probably get back to it." Mel picked up the wheelbarrow, then paused. "Remind me to check the weather later. If it's a strong storm like Stella said, we'll need to bring Bandito in again."

She followed after her toward the garden. "Are you going to miss Fred?"

"I suppose. I haven't thought about him much since you've been here. But when I'm alone, he's company." She smiled. "Not very talkative, but he listens well."

"Why don't you get a puppy?"

"Oh, I don't know. I've thought about it over the years, but it just never happened. Maybe now I will."

Yeah. What was it? Six more weeks? Seven? She'd lost track of the days...the weeks. She imagined Melanie would miss her company. She opened the garden gate, letting Mel push the wheelbarrow in. She stood at the gate, looking around the pristine garden, knowing she'd helped keep it that way. She actually enjoyed pulling weeds. It was a mindless, therapeutic task. And picking vegetables was...well, fun. Eating them was fun too. She looked around, knowing her time here was slipping away.

"Too fast," she murmured.

Yes, time was slipping away, and damn, but she'd miss it here. She glanced over to where Mel was turning the compost pile with a pitchfork. She'd miss it here. And she'd certainly miss Melanie.

Funny how time changes one's perspective on things. Funny how time changed a lot of things.

Including her.

CHAPTER THIRTY-SIX

Erin jumped back from the window, wondering why she was standing there in the first place. "Okay, I don't mind saying it: that one scared me."

"Yes, it was close. It's nights like this that I wish I had curtains on all the windows." Melanie patted the spot beside her on the sofa. "Relax."

"There are curtains in the little spare bedroom. Why?"

"It offers a sense of privacy to my guests. There's not a soul out here and no one to see in. I didn't see the point of curtains or blinds. I'm usually up before the sun anyway, so that was never an issue."

Erin took her hand and folded their fingers together. "You're worried it might hail?"

"Yes. It could wipe me out."

"Then what?"

"Then I eat what's left in the freezer and hope I don't go through all of the canning I did." She smiled. "And I resort to buying produce in the grocery store. I could manage, but most of these ladies live on their Social Security checks. Any extra expenses—like unexpected grocery bills—would really be a hardship to them."

"What about the money Stella gets from her guests? She said something about having a general fund."

Melanie nodded. "It's used for repairs, mostly. And yearly taxes. Or like, for instance, when Rachel wanted to convert her heating to propane, when she couldn't manage the wood stove any longer. Things like that. There's never a huge amount of money and it goes quickly some years."

"So me staying here this long is adding a good chunk to it then."

"Yes. I think the next in line for repair is Vivian's roof."

"In line?"

"At the beginning of each year, everyone submits things they'd like done at their place. Stella ranks them."

"What about you?"

Melanie shook her head. "I manage okay on my own. So far. I imagine when I get to be their age, I'll be more inclined to accept money from the fund. If there is still one."

"Stella is what? Seventy-five? What happens when she's gone?"

"She says we're taken care of. In her will, I mean. I have no reason to doubt her."

"You're the youngest. Do you worry you'll be left here all alone?"

Melanie nodded. "The thought has crossed my mind, yes. No one has come since Angela and she came a year after me. Times have changed. It would take a unique circumstance for someone to want to move here."

"Why did Angela move here?"

"Her partner died. Long battle with cancer. There was a lot of family drama and a nasty dispute over the house and her belongings and stuff. I think she wanted to get away from all that and grieve in peace. She told me in confidence one time that she didn't know how long she'd stay. That was six years ago. She seems entrenched now." Melanie squeezed her hand. "Why all the questions? Something to take your mind off the storm?"

She tilted her head, then smiled. "It must have worked. The thunder and lightning seem to have moved past us."

"Is that it really?"

"No. I guess I wanted a picture of it all in my mind. Make sure you're going to be okay and all."

"You mean when you leave?"

Erin nodded. "Yeah. That." She squeezed Melanie's hand a little harder. "I didn't plan on getting quite so attached to the place. To you." Melanie surprised her by leaning her head against her shoulder.

"I know. Me, either. It's going to be quiet around here." Melanie turned her head, kissing her lightly on the cheek. "If it's all the same to you, I'd rather not talk about it yet. We still have time."

Erin leaned over, meeting her mouth. "I vote we go to bed early."

"Oh, yeah? Tired, are you?"

She deepened the kiss. "No."

CHAPTER THIRTY-SEVEN

Melanie leaned up on her elbow and rested her chin in her palm as she watched Erin sleep. The candle she'd lit earlier cast enough light for her to see Erin's features clearly. Her face was relaxed, her breathing even…her eyelids fluttered slightly as she dreamed. The storm had passed, but there was still enough breeze to lift the limbs of the piñon pine; they brushed against the wall by their heads.

She was feeling lonely—and loneliness was something she knew well—but this was a different kind of lonely. She'd spent seven years out here regretting her past, keeping her neighbors at arm's length, living a solitary life. She knew loneliness. She feared, though, that when Erin left, it would be altogether different. She feared she'd live not regretting her past but rather regretting what her future held for her. Or rather, what it didn't hold.

Nothing. Her future held nothing. Just like her past. There was only emptiness, both behind her and in front of her.

With Erin here, she got a glimpse of how it would be—could be—if she had a partner, a lover, someone to share her space, share her bed, share her life. She quite liked it.

She smiled and shook her head. Yeah—she liked having Erin in her bed. She'd been terrified at the prospect, but it had been unwarranted fear. Maybe she had healed after all. Maybe during the eleven years of hanging on to the guilt, clutching it to her like a baby might a favorite blanket, she'd grown stronger, without even knowing it. She'd clutched the blanket of guilt tightly, covering her head—hiding—in the darkest of hours.

What was she hiding from? At the beginning, she'd had such self-loathing, she hadn't felt she deserved to live, much less have any happiness in her life. She hated herself so much, she could hardly stand to look in a mirror. Unlike Adam, though, she didn't have the courage to take her own life. She would be lying if she said she hadn't thought about it…hadn't talked about it with her therapist.

She'd felt so strongly about getting away, moving out here, it was as if a higher power had been directing her. It became a compulsion. At the time, she knew she was running away from society, from her mother, from the sure fate that awaited her if she'd stayed. And maybe, way down deep, below the surface of reality, she'd hoped she could run away from her guilt and the awful memories that haunted her.

That had proven to be nothing more than false hope.

Or was it? Now—eleven years since Adam's death, seven years since she'd run away—where was her guilt? Was it still there? Or was it only the *memory* of her guilt that lingered?

She rolled onto her back and stared at the ceiling, watching the shadows dance in the candlelight. Why had Adam killed himself? She'd asked herself that question a thousand times and she always had an answer. Her fault. Could there have been more to it, though? Adam truly loved her, without doubt. Why would he have taken his life, knowing how badly it would hurt her? He wasn't a spiteful person, he wasn't vindictive. He was always kind, always loving.

Why had he killed himself?

How long was she going to take the blame?

Could she possibly let it go? *Had* she already let it go? Admittedly, she felt lighter somehow. The heavy weight of guilt wasn't crushing her. She attributed it to Erin, of course. That's the only thing that had changed in her life—Erin. Well, not the only thing. Erin was a presence here—as a friend, as a confidant...now a lover. That's a lot of change for someone used to living alone, *being* alone. Existing alone.

If someone had asked her if she was happy, her answer would have always been yes. Happy enough, that is. When she was younger, she kept waiting for happiness to find her—or for her to find it. It proved to be elusive on both ends. It wasn't until she was older that she realized that happiness came from within. She didn't need to rely on someone else to make her happy. Of course, those years after Adam's death, she'd forgotten all about happiness. She was so focused on her guilt, on her own pain, she was blind to everything else. Happiness and anything that resembled it—those had been secondary.

And now? Right now? Right this second?

She turned to look at Erin again. An involuntary smile formed and she let it come. No, she didn't need someone to make her happy. But it sure helped. It was fun to have someone around, someone to talk to, someone to cook with and eat with. Someone to laugh with. And someone to share her bed, someone to love, someone to touch. All those things brought her happiness. Right now.

What would happen when Erin left? Could the memories sustain her? The memories of Adam and his death sustained her for years. Could Erin's memory do the same?

She was surprised that her smile didn't fade altogether. She would miss Erin, yes, but she wouldn't allow that to define her. She wouldn't allow that to control her. Not after Adam. Not after eleven long years of feeling bound by chains. She wouldn't do it again.

Happiness came from within and it was the here and now. It wasn't her past and it wasn't her future. It was now.

And for now, she was choosing to be happy.

CHAPTER THIRTY-EIGHT

"You don't really want to talk to her, do you?"

Erin shook her head. "Not really, no. Part of it is, I don't want to think about work. The other part, though, it's cruel, I guess."

"Cruel?"

"Joyce feels guilty for bringing me out here, leaving me. And the longer I go without talking to her, the more her guilt intensifies."

"Ah."

"Yeah. Mean. So I need to talk to her, let her know I'm okay." She squeezed Melanie's hand. "Let her know I'm not still pissed at her."

Melanie grinned. "Were you pissed at her?"

"Big time. Both her and my dad."

They pulled up to a stop in front of Stella's house and Fred limped out to meet them. She bent down, petting his head. She'd never had a pet growing up. She didn't recall ever asking for one. As kids, they'd been kept plenty busy, running from one activity to another. When Sarah moved in with her, she brought Elle, the yappy little foo-foo dog along. It was her first time living with a pet and she figured it would be her last.

"I didn't realize how much he'd aged."

She glanced at Mel. "How old did you say he was? Fifteen?"

"I don't think anyone knows for sure. Fifteen is the best guess."

"Is that old?"

Mel nodded. "I think anything past twelve or thirteen is considered really old for a dog." She, too, leaned down to ruffle his head. "I do kinda miss him being around." She smiled at her. "At least he barks when company comes by."

"Like a warning when you're out gardening topless?"

Melanie laughed at that. "Can you picture the look on Stella's face had she found us in the creek?"

"Can you picture the look on *your* face had she caught us?" she teased.

Melanie met her gaze, her expression becoming more serious. "It's not that, Erin. I'm not trying to hide this—*us*—because I'm embarrassed or ashamed or anything like that. Frankly, it's not any of her business."

"She would disapprove?"

"She's old-school. I'm the host, you're the guest. She would frown upon it. And she'd have a hundred questions. And then the others would find out."

"And we'd become the talk of the town?"

"Exactly."

She nodded. "I understand. I know you protect your privacy, Mel. Like you said, it's no one's business."

Melanie squeezed her arm as they walked up the steps to Stella's door. "Thank you." Then she grinned as she rapped on Stella's door. "You're the best."

The words were said casually, teasingly, but still, they affected her. No one had ever said that to her before, not even teasingly. She returned Mel's smile, but before she could reply, Stella was already opening the door.

"Good morning, girls," she said with a wide smile. "Come in, come in. The coffee is freshly made and I've just pulled the banana bread out of the oven."

"Smells wonderful," she said, then turned to Mel. "Why haven't we made banana bread?"

"Because *we* ate all of the bananas. And I thought you liked the zucchini bread?"

"Oh, I do. Especially last week when you put chocolate chips in it."

"You put chocolate chips in yours?" Stella asked. "I've never heard of that."

Melanie looked at her accusingly, and Erin laughed. "We were experimenting," she said to Stella. "We also found a recipe to make chocolate zucchini bread. Next trip into town, we're going to get the stuff for that." She rubbed her belly. "Mel is determined to send me home in a fatted state, apparently."

"Oh, please. The chocolate is all your idea!"

"You'll have to tell me how that turns out. Chocolate is my weakness," Stella said as she led them into the kitchen.

"I loved that chocolate cake you made. That was rich and gooey."

"Glad you liked it, dear. If you come to the next dinner—less than two weeks away—I'll make it again for you. You'll need to take some home with you this time. Heaven knows I don't need to eat all that." Stella poured coffee into the three cups she already had out on her kitchen table. "I'll get this bread sliced up. Why don't you give your sister a call? The phone is in the den by my chair."

Yes, she supposed she should get it over with. She picked up one of the cups and took a sip, then put it back down. "Be right back."

"Take your coffee, dear. If I remember correctly, you are quite a bear without it."

Melanie laughed and so did she. "A bear? I think maybe it was Rachel's decaf—and her tasteless beans—that had me growling. I'm not a bear. Tell her, Mel."

"You're not a bear," she said with a smile, then turned to Stella. "She's not a bear. She's quite pleasant in the mornings, actually."

"Thank you. Don't start on the banana bread without me."

"Go already." Melanie waved her away. "I won't eat your bread."

She was still smiling when she went into Stella's small den. There was an ancient TV on an equally ancient stand tucked into one corner. A small sofa, not much bigger than a loveseat was against one wall. A large, comfy-looking brown chair with matching ottoman took center stage. There was a tall lamp behind it and an end table on the right side of the chair. Besides the phone—how often did that ring? she wondered—there was a pile of books, six of them, and a pair of reading glasses on the table.

Her smile faded as she stared at the phone. What time was it? Hell, what day was it? Should she try Joyce at the office? At least she knew that number. She had no clue what Joyce's cell number was. Her phone, like her laptop, was forgotten, somewhere in her bedroom. Her smile returned. A bedroom she no longer used, except to grab fresh clothes. She'd even been using Melanie's spacious shower instead of the tiny one in her room. Wonder what Joyce would think of that?

Like Melanie with Stella, she didn't fancy Joyce knowing about their relationship. It would bring questions, and she'd just as soon not have to answer them. And like Stella, it wasn't any of Joyce's business.

She went to pick up the phone when she saw a painting on the wall. It was of Stella, her short gray hair glistening in the sunshine, clad in knee-length blue shorts and a colorful blouse boasting sunflowers. There was a smile on her face as she surveyed her garden. This must be the painting Melanie was telling her about. She wondered if it was bittersweet for Stella to look at it. Did she remember the woman who gave it with fondness or sadness? Did she think of a lost love when she stared at it?

She let her gaze travel across the painting, landing on the rows of tomatoes, the bright red fruit a contrast to the vibrant green. There was a single sunflower blooming tall at the far edge of the garden, matching the flowers in Stella's blouse. She wondered if the sunflower was significant. It looked out of place in the garden. Maybe it was something private between the two women...a secret they shared.

She finally picked up the phone, smiling at the age of it. Only in her far distant memory could she recall her parents' phone being tethered by a cord. By the time she was old enough to use the phone, it was cordless.

She stood beside Stella's chair and dialed the office number. It was answered after two rings, the pleasant voice of Lacy, the receptionist, sounding in her ear. Erin cleared her throat before speaking.

"Good morning, Lacy. It's Erin...Erin Ryder. May I speak with Joyce, please?"

"Oh, Ms. Ryder! Good morning. Yes, ma'am. I'll put you right through."

Erin nodded, finally sitting down in Stella's chair. Lacy sounded surprised to hear from her. She wondered what the rumor was going around the office regarding her absence.

"Erin? My God...is that you?"

"Hi, Joyce."

"Are you okay? Why haven't you called me? I've been so worried."

She smiled at the urgency in her voice. Yeah, Joyce was feeling guilty for dumping her off here. "Because there's no cell service out here. None. Zero."

"But I've called Stella. She's—"

"She's got an ancient landline. I'm over at her house now."

"Where are you staying? Every time I call, she makes excuses as to why I can't talk to you. I was beginning to think—"

"That they'd locked me away in a dark dungeon?"

"Something like that. Are you okay?"

"Fine. You don't have to call and check on me. I think you're stressing Stella by calling. Apparently, she was under the assumption that this was a jail sentence and I would try to escape."

"I thought you would. Erin…I almost came out there to get you. I feel terrible about it. I had no right—Dad had no right—to force you into this. We—"

"Joyce, you did the right thing. I wasn't listening to reason, obviously. I *was* slowly killing myself." She paused. "I realize now how badly I needed this." She smiled as she glanced up at the painting again. "I probably wouldn't have picked this particular place at the time, but now that I'm here…I'm really glad you found it."

"You are? You're not still mad at me?"

"No."

"Good. Because I miss you being here. Dad misses you being here. I think he forgot how much work it was to juggle several projects at once. We shouldn't talk about work, though. Don't want you stressing over anything. It'll all still be here when you get back."

"You're right. I was going to ask how my projects were going but, you're right. I don't really want to think about it. I'm sure Dad is handling them fine."

Joyce laughed. "My God. What have they done to you? I thought you'd browbeat me to get status reports on each and every one of them!"

She realized she was still staring at the painting and she recognized how calm she felt, how peaceful. She really didn't want to know about her projects. At this particular moment, if truth be told, she didn't even *care* about them.

"Don't want to stress over them, as you said."

"Okay—so are they like some kind of a cult or something? Have you been brainwashed?"

Erin laughed at the seriousness of Joyce's words. "Yeah, I guess they are kind of a cult."

"Oh, my God. Erin, are you really okay out there? You sound kinda odd."

"I'm fine, sis. Got what? Six more weeks or so? I'll see you then…Out at the grocery store, under the pines. Call a couple of days before so you can set up a time with Stella."

"Does this mean I won't hear from you again?"

"Probably not."

"Erin, are you *sure* you're okay?"

"Quit worrying, Joyce. I'm fine. Great, actually. I'll see you in a few weeks."

"Should I give Dad a message or anything?"

"Tell him I'm fine." She stood up. "I need to go. There's some fresh-out-of-the-oven banana bread calling my name. See you in September."

She hung up without waiting for Joyce to reply. There wasn't really anything else to say, was there? She'd have plenty of time on the ride back to Albuquerque to fill her in on...on what? Where she'd stayed? What she ate? Who she slept with?

She smiled at the painting one more time, then turned, heading back to the kitchen where quiet conversation and the occasional chuckle of laughter was heard. Back to where "fresh-out-of-the-oven" banana bread was waiting for her.

Back to where Melanie was waiting for her.

CHAPTER THIRTY-NINE

Melanie sighed contentedly as she ran her fingers around Erin's breast, then down her stomach, drawing lazy circles on her skin before making the return trip.

"I think I'm insatiable," she admitted. "Whatever have you done to me?"

She felt Erin's quiet laughter under her hand. "What have you done to *me*? It's not even noon and we're out here sunbathing in the nude."

"Is that what we're doing?"

"Well, it's what we're doing *now*." Erin leaned over and kissed her. "Would you believe me if I told you I've never made love in the water before?"

"You have a pool. Surely you and Sarah—"

"Oh, there were some make-out sessions, sure, but we always took it inside."

"You live in the city. I guess you have to."

"I guess." She reached her hand across the rock they were lying on and rustled the water. "I like this much better."

Melanie had no reference since she'd never had a pool before, but yes, she imagined this—the creek, the mountains, the birds—was much more of a treat to the senses than a backyard pool in the city.

She should be calling an end to their playtime, anyway. They hadn't had rain in two days, but the forecast called for torrential rains by late afternoon, lingering through the night and into tomorrow. The threat of thunderstorms was there, as usual, but it was the heavy rain that had her worried. This storm would be a true monsoon. There were a hundred things that could be done in the garden to get ready, yet here she lay, soaking up the sun, feeling a bit sluggish after their lovemaking. She finally sighed, the sound making Erin raise her eyebrows.

"I must get to work. If it rains as much as they say, tomorrow will be a wasted day."

"Not really. We've got green beans that we need to can and squash to put up." Then Erin grinned. "And you said you were going to teach me how to make fresh salsa from the tomatoes that are coming in."

"I did, didn't I? Well, that means you'll need to pick some peppers too." She sat up and glanced to the sky, which was still clear and sunny. "Okay...chores." She smiled at Erin, who had sat up too. "You're getting very tan."

"I'm getting very fat."

"Honey, you've got a long way to go before we can use that word."

She stood and offered her hand, pulling Erin up too. She found herself engulfed in a hug. A very naked hug. She was smiling as her eyes closed, and she tilted her head, giving Erin room as her lips moved across her neck.

"You make me want to be lazy," she murmured.

"I'm trying to make you aroused." She felt Erin smile against her neck. "I see your mind is still on the garden."

"If there was a grocery store down on the corner, I might be inclined to blow it off." She moved her mouth to Erin's, then pulled away. "But, alas, my grocery store is my garden. You don't want me suffering through a bare winter, do you?"

Erin's expression changed as their eyes met…as, she was sure, did hers. Erin would be leaving in five weeks and two days—yes, she'd looked at the calendar. The monthly dinner with the ladies was coming up this week, then it was downhill from there. The days were flying by faster and faster, it seemed. They didn't talk about it—not really. They acknowledged it, mostly silently. She supposed at some point they would do more than gloss over it. Not yet, though. She wasn't ready to have that hovering over them for the next five weeks.

"Come on," she said after kissing Erin's cheek lightly. "We need to finish putting hay out between the rows or it'll be a muddy mess for the next month."

* * *

Erin was thankful when she saw the dark clouds inching closer and closer to the bluff behind the cabin. She surveyed her work, knowing she'd have time to finish out the last row before the rain came. Melanie had already finished her section, the hay laid out neatly between the rows and around some of the plants. She was turning the new compost pile they'd built, and Erin saw her glance to the sky, too, probably calculating how much time she had left.

She was hot and sweaty and tired, and again, she was struck by how much work it was, struck by the fact that Melanie usually tended to all these chores alone. How had she managed? Well, obviously it was usually all work and no play. Taking time out to play in the creek—and while away an hour making love—wasn't a part of Melanie's normal routine. From what she'd learned, the only divergence from work was an occasional hike she'd allow herself once or twice a week.

Of course, she had to remind herself that it wasn't like this all the time for Mel. Summer was simply the busiest. After the fall harvest and during the winter months, Melanie probably had more time—lots more time. Then what would she do? What did she do to occupy her time? Did she sit alone, wishing for spring and summer? What did she do?

"You daydreaming?"

She blinked several times, finding Melanie striding toward her. She nodded. "Yeah." She tilted her head. "What do you do during the winter?"

Melanie stood before her, resting her hands on her hips, a smile trying to form. It was obvious Mel was struggling to hide it. Erin noted that her hair seemed a little lighter than it had been when she'd first met her—bleached from the sun, maybe. Today, with the clear blue skies swallowing them, Mel's eyes seemed to be nearly cobalt.

"Do?" she asked, finally giving in to the smile. "You mean, being a hermit and all, what do I do with my time when the garden isn't active?"

"Yeah. That."

Melanie took a step closer. "Are you worried about me?"

"No. You've managed seven years without me. I don't imagine you'll miss me being around."

Melanie's smile faded. "Well, you'd be wrong." She stepped closer still, finally letting their bodies touch. The kiss Mel gave her was feather-soft. "I'll miss you." Their arms went around each other simultaneously. "I'll miss everything about you being here…from your fresh tortillas in the morning, to your singing to the twins, to your snuggling after making love. I'll miss all of it."

Erin smiled. "I do not sing to the twins."

"Don't lie. I caught you twice." Melanie pulled back to meet her gaze. "You sing quite well too."

"Are you lonely during the winter?"

"No more than any other times. I keep busy, Erin. It's not like there's nothing to do. The chickens still need tending, the goats. Meals still need to be cooked. But I have more leisure time." She pulled out of her arms. "I watch TV, I'm on the Internet… things I normally don't take time for during the summer." She touched her cheek with a gentle hand, then leaned closer for another kiss. "Let's don't talk about you leaving. Okay? It'll be here soon enough."

CHAPTER FORTY

Melanie gripped the sheet with both fists, her hips arching off the bed even as Erin tried to hold her down. The scream tore from her throat, but Erin didn't relinquish her hold. Her head hit the pillow, her eyes squeezed closed as Erin's mouth continued its glorious assault on her, finally slowing when she went limp on the bed.

"No more," she murmured, unable to open her eyes. "I'm going to pass out."

She heard Erin chuckle as her mouth nibbled against her hip, sending goose bumps down her legs. It had been so long since her affair with Courtney, she hardly remembered the act itself. She was fairly certain, though, that it had never been like this. And why would it? She'd been young, riddled with guilt even then, knowing what she was doing was wrong. She doubted she'd ever been able to fully relax when she was with Courtney. Now? She was a grown woman, single and unattached. She'd found she had no inhibitions and neither did Erin. Being together, like this, was effortless. She tugged Erin up to her, finding her mouth.

"I must sleep," she whispered after the kiss.

Erin pulled the sheet and blanket over them, then lay down beside her, one arm curled protectively across her stomach. The window beside the bed was cracked open a bit, letting in cool, rain-soaked air. The persistent showers alternated between heavy and light—the wind calm, then fierce. Lightning flashed bright enough to light up the sky and thunder crashed across the bluffs and mountains, then tranquility followed and the only sound was the steady summer rain that she loved. Far away, over the hills, she could hear the low roar and knew another storm was coming. The calm rain would be displaced again soon. She'd slept through enough thunderstorms over the years to not be worried, but the rolling sound that was drifting down the mountain tonight seemed ferocious. Unconsciously, she tightened Erin's arm around her.

"Good night, Mel."

She opened her eyes at the whispered words, smiling in the darkness. "Good night, sweet Erin."

CHAPTER FORTY-ONE

Erin woke with a start, finding Mel standing by the window, looking out. Loud thunder seemed to be still reverberating around them and she could hear the rain pounding against the glass.

"Lightning hit the bluff behind the shed."

Erin rubbed her eyes. "Can't believe I've been sleeping through this."

"It's been off and on. Lots of rain."

Melanie had her sleep shirt on and a pair of shorts. "How long have you been up?"

Mel glanced at the clock by her side of the bed. "Hour or so," she said around a yawn.

"Come back to bed."

"It's nearly dawn."

"It's storming. We won't be going to let the chickens out anytime soon. Come back to bed."

Mel moved away from the window and removed her shorts before crawling under the covers. "I'm glad we put Bandito up."

"He wasn't happy with us," she reminded her.

"I bet he is now," she mumbled as she snuggled closer.

Erin smiled and closed her eyes, listening to the rain as it splattered the glass. The piñon pine brushed the wall by their head, the wind tossing the branches forcefully against the cabin. They were safe and snug, though, and she relaxed as Mel burrowed against her, even as the storm continued to rage outside their window.

Two hours later, they were woken by a horn blaring. They both sat up, looking around questioningly. Melanie was the first to move, tossing the covers off and hurrying out of the bedroom. Erin was still naked, and she looked about for her clothes before going out too.

Stella was pounding on the door and Mel jerked it open.

"Come quick! Those two giant ponderosas fell on Rachel's house. We can't get to her." Stella touched her chest. "Lordy, we don't even know if she's okay. Her little house is nearly flattened."

"Oh, my God," Melanie said in a rush. She turned to Erin, her eyes fearful. "We'll need my chainsaw. Put on some jeans and boots." She turned back to Stella. "Angela has a chainsaw too. Have you—"

"Yes. I stopped by her house first. Please hurry, Mel. I'm so worried about Rachel."

"We'll be right there, Stella."

Erin went into her old bedroom, finding a pair of jeans. By the time she was dressed, she heard Mel start up her truck. She hurried out, glad the rain had slowed to little more than a drizzle. Judging by the dark clouds, though, their rainstorms weren't over with.

The ground was wet and muddy and she followed Mel into the shed. It was still dark inside and when she turned the light on, the chickens started clucking from their roost. The goats were standing by the door, as if waiting for it to open.

"Should I let them out?"

"Better not. There's more rain coming." Mel handed her a jug. "Here, take the gas."

Erin took the red plastic jug from her, then watched as Mel lifted the chainsaw off a hook on the wall. She took a couple of tools from the pegboard and hurried out again, Erin following behind her.

They didn't talk as they bounced along the road, the many holes now filled with water. In one spot, she wasn't even sure where the road was—it looked flooded—but Mel made it through without incident.

The little driveway beside Rachel's house was an array of colors as several of the ladies stood there with umbrellas open to ward off the drizzle. The house did indeed look flattened. Her breath caught as she stared at it. How in the world could Rachel have survived?

"My God, you can't even see the house."

Melanie slammed to a halt and was seemingly out the door before the truck even came to a stop. Angela was standing away from the others, her chainsaw resting on the ground by her feet.

"I don't even know where to start, Mel."

"Where's her bedroom?"

Stella pointed. "It's on the back side. But there are so many branches, it's just buried. I can't even see if that part is standing or not. We've been calling out to her, but…"

The giant trees, at their base, were at least five feet in diameter. She remembered them from her short stay here, guessing they were seventy or eighty feet tall. Rachel's house was somewhere buried in the branches. Judging by the angle of the trees, the house had offered little resistance to their weight.

"We'll start cutting back there then." Mel turned to the ladies who were standing by in hushed silence. "Whoever is able, start pulling the branches away as we cut." Mel turned to her. "There should be some gloves behind my seat. If you could direct them. I'm not sure how much help they'll be."

"I got it. Start cutting," she said as she hurried back to the truck.

"Hurry, Mel!" someone called.

Soon, the sound of chainsaws buzzing filled the air and the sweet smell of freshly cut pine wafted about. It was slow going and some of the ladies were more in the way than helping. When Vivian tripped on a branch and tumbled to the ground, she went to help her up, then motioned them back.

"Let me," she said. "There's too many of us. Once I get it away from Mel and Angela, you can drag it off. But we're getting tangled here. Someone could get hurt." She looked to Stella for help.

"She's right. Let the young ones work. We're just getting in the way."

Erin nodded her thanks as they moved away, some holding hands as they watched. Little by little, tree branches were removed, revealing more and more of the house. What was left of the house, she corrected herself. She tried not to think about poor Rachel, tried not to think about how mean she'd been to her at the beginning, how she'd run out on her, criticized her cooking, her coffee. Criticized everything, really.

A loud rumble of thunder brought her head up. As she looked into the sky, it opened up, hard rain falling without concern for them or their plight. No, Mother Nature didn't care, did she?

The downpour sent some of the ladies scrambling for cover. She watched as Mel wiped the rain from her face before cutting another branch. As soon as it fell, Erin reached for it, tugging it along the ground away from Mel. It was a large, heavy branch and she struggled with it, moving it to the pile with the others. They were almost to the corner of the house now. Mel held her hand up, signaling to Angela to stop. They both killed their chainsaws, the silence now broken only by rumbling thunder.

"Rachel! Can you hear me?" Mel yelled. "*Rachel!*"

Everyone seemed to hold their breath at once, listening. There was no sound.

"Rachel?" Angela tried. "Rachel?"

Erin moved between them. "I think I can get to the house from here."

"No," Mel said quickly, grabbing her arm. "It's too dangerous. The more branches we cut away, the less support the tree has. It's unstable as it is."

Yes, several large branches—stabbed firmly in the ground—seemed to be the only thing keeping the tree from flattening the house completely. Even as they watched she could see it shifting. She imagined she could hear the branches groaning against the weight of the tree. She met Mel's gaze as the rain fell harder. The dark clouds seemed to swallow them and it was as if dusk had descended upon them already. A lightning bolt sizzled over their heads and in unison, they all ducked instinctively. The loud boom of thunder made the earth shake beneath her feet. She looked at Rachel's house again. It was only going to get worse.

"It's now or never," she said.

"Erin, no!" Mel's grip was firm on her arm. "Let me. I'll—"

"No! I'm expendable. You're not."

"Oh, my God! That is crazy!"

Erin pressed against her, kissing her hard, unmindful of who was watching. Yeah, it was crazy, she thought as she ducked into the branches, feeling them dig into her skin. She pushed through, finally falling on her knees, then her stomach as she crawled along the rain-soaked ground, squirming under the pine boughs. As she got closer to the house, she could see the damage up close. The first tree had pretty much demolished the living room; the roof and walls had collapsed around the tree. The second tree, the one she was crawling under, was teetering precariously along the roof of Rachel's bedroom. Several large branches had broken through the roof and the windows were shattered. That was a plus, she supposed. At least she wouldn't have to break the glass to get inside.

The problem, of course, was trying to crawl between the thick, wet branches to get to the window. She ignored the stabbing pain as a limb dug into her back when she stood. She was drenched and she wiped her face futilely as the rain turned into a torrential downpour. A bright flash of lightning and ensuing clap of thunder hit almost simultaneously, making her feel like she was in the center of the storm.

"Rachel!" she called through the wind and rain, pausing to listen for an answering call. Nothing came.

She squeezed between the branches, sliding up the wall to the window. She could no longer see Mel; the tree totally obscured her. A strong gust of wind rustled the tree and a branch slapped against her face. She closed her eyes for a second, trying to ignore the nearly constant rumble of thunder. The lightning was dangerous—she could almost feel the static charge in the air around her. She hoped Mel and the others had taken cover. But no, knowing Mel, she was still standing out in the storm, waiting for her to return.

"Now or never."

She took a deep breath, then pulled herself up and through the broken window, taking care not to cut herself on the shattered glass. It was only slightly quieter inside. The wind whistled through the opened windows and rain poured in through the hole in the roof. As she looked around, she realized she was in the tiny spare bedroom, where she'd spent exactly one night. She tugged on the door but it wouldn't budge. The tree's weight was pressing on the rafters, putting pressure on the doorjamb. She slammed into it with her shoulder, but it still wouldn't open.

"Oh, for the love," she muttered. She leaned against the door, thinking. Rachel's room was down the hallway to the left. A bathroom separated the two bedrooms.

She spun around and went back to the window. As she hopped back out, she noticed blood on the sill. She glanced at her hands, seeing tiny cuts on both palms. She dismissed them as she fell to her knees, trying to burrow her way under the tree again. Two thoughts struck her as she slid along on her belly; one, it smelled really, really fragrant up this close and personal with the wet ponderosa pine. And two, if she found Rachel, how would she ever get her out of the house? Rachel was eighty-two years old. Could she expect her to slither along the ground like she was doing, hoping like hell the tree didn't collapse and smother her?

She found the bathroom window, broken like the others. She could go no farther, though. One thick limb, as big around as a tree itself, was blocking her path. As the storm raged, she thought she heard Mel calling to her. Between the thunder and lightning, the wind and rain, she couldn't be certain. Perhaps it was only her imagination.

"I'm okay," she yelled back, doubting Mel could hear her anyway.

She hugged the wall, reaching for the window. It was up higher than the bedroom window and after inspecting it for glass, she grabbed hold of the sill, needing all her strength to lift herself up. She balanced on her stomach across the sill, then fell inside to the floor. She looked up, thankful the roof was intact. Like the bedroom, the bathroom door frame had pressure on it from the roof and she struggled to open it. Unlike the bedroom, though, she did manage to open it far enough for her to squeeze through.

"Rachel?" she yelled in the hallway.

She looked right, into the main part of the house. The missing roof let in enough light for her to see the large mass of tree occupying the living room. To the left was Rachel's bedroom. She took a step toward it, then heard the house creak and groan around her. Was the tree shifting?

"Rachel?" she yelled again as she hurried to her room.

The door was open and she gasped. A tree limb had come through the roof and had impaled the bed. She glanced around frantically, finally spying the edge of a pink nightgown sticking out behind the overturned dresser.

"Rachel!"

She dropped down on the floor, laying flat to look under the dresser, shocked to find two eyes blinking back at her.

"I'm...I'm stuck, I think," came a quiet, frightened voice.

"Are you pinned? Is something on you? Your legs? Are you hurt?"

"I don't think so. I'm against the wall. The dresser fell and... and now I'm stuck." Her voice cracked then. "My house is falling around me."

"I'm going to get you out of here. But first I've got to move the dresser." She got into a kneeling position, surveying the situation. She wasn't certain she could move the dresser by herself. At least, not back into its original position. She thought she might be able to push it over, onto the bed, and hoped there was enough room between the legs and wall to pull Rachel out. She lay back down, facing Rachel. "Can you move back a little? I'm going to push the dresser onto your bed."

"Yes, I can move a little."

"Okay. As soon as I push and get the legs up, I'm going to hold it. Can you crawl out then?"

"Yes, I can try."

Erin was about to push when she felt the house shake around them. She looked up, seeing the roof starting to give way. The tree must have shifted or rolled.

"We've got to hurry, Rachel! No time to waste!"

She didn't pause to consider an alternative. It was this or nothing. Taking a deep breath, she pushed the dresser with all her might, feeling it tip, lifting the back legs off the floor. She pressed against it, holding it in place.

"Now! Move now!" She couldn't see behind her but sensed Rachel trying to get out. "Hurry!"

"My nightgown is caught on something!"

"Jesus," she muttered. "Can you tear it? Or take the damn thing off!"

"Take it off?"

"Rachel...I can't hold this forever." Part of the ceiling gave way, landing on top of the dresser. She turned her head away from it. "Rachel! *Move!*"

She felt Rachel's hand grab her ankle, as if for traction. In the chaos of the storm, the ceiling falling, the tree shifting... she heard the distinct sound of fabric ripping. Her arms were cramping, her fingers slipping on the damp wood. She glanced behind her, seeing Rachel now crawling on her knees, out of the way. She jumped back, letting the dresser fall back and it banged against the wall hard enough to gouge the sheetrock.

She reached down and pulled Rachel up, surprised that the older woman flung herself into her arms. Erin took the time to hold her for a few seconds, then gently pushed her away. Rachel's face was stained with rain and tears.

"Come on. Let's get out of here."

They barely made it into the hallway before the roof collapsed. She grabbed Rachel's arm and ran, pulling her down the hall and into the demolished living room. As if in slow motion, sections of the roof gave way, dropping behind them as they moved. The sound was deafening and through it all, she could hear Rachel screaming. The house seemed to be collapsing around them and she didn't know where to go. Could they make it over the fallen tree and onto the other side of the living room? That roof was already down. There was nothing more to fall on them there.

The massive tree, with its five-foot diameter trunk, blocked their escape. She ran up to it, touching its side, wondering how they could scale it. She turned to Rachel.

"I'm going to lift you up. Fall to the other side. Cover your head."

"Oh, Erin...I can't. I—"

"You have to!"

She didn't let her protest further. She stood behind her and grabbed her hips, only then noticing how small and frail she seemed. She hoisted her easily, nearly pushing her over the tree. Without thinking, she went back several feet, covering her head as sheetrock fell from the ceiling. She took a running start, bolting toward the tree, jumping at the last second. The rough bark cut into her hands and arms as she attempted to squirm over the top. Behind her, she heard a whoosh as the entire roof collapsed, the force pushing her over the tree and onto the floor beyond. She landed in a heap, her shoulder taking the brunt of her weight. Rachel was curled against the tree, her thin arms folded around her head, protecting herself from debris.

The second tree fell completely, obliterating what remained of Rachel's little house. It was over as quickly as it had begun. She looked up, seeing dark clouds still swirling over them. Rain was falling in a steady stream, but the torrential downpour seemed to have subsided. She stood up and went to Rachel, gently taking her hand.

"I think we made it."

Rachel met her gaze. "I don't know how. There's nothing left of my house."

Erin smiled at her. "The most important thing is still here. You."

Rachel smiled weakly at her. "I don't even know what happened. I got tossed from my bed, then all hell broke loose."

Erin laughed at that. "Yeah, it did. Come on."

They headed toward the base of the tree, away from the cluster of branches. Even there, though, the lumber and debris from the walls and roof blocked their way. As she stood there, trying to decide what to do, she heard the voices, the screams... her name being called.

"Erin! *Erin!*"

"We're here!" she yelled. "Living room."

It seemed like they waited hours as the ladies—all seventy-something in age—and Melanie and Angela worked to clear a path for them; cutting the tree away and moving sections of wall and roof. Mel's eyes met hers at every turn and Erin was itching to get to her, to hold her, to tell her she was okay. When the last section of wall was removed, Rachel gingerly made her way across the threshold of what was once her front door. Stella was there to greet Rachel, taking her into her arms in an affectionate hug.

Then Mel was there, arms wrapped around her tightly, whispered words that she couldn't decipher, gentle lips meeting hers. Mel pulled back then, her eyes misting with tears.

"You're a freakin' crazy woman."

"You're right. That was crazy."

"The tree fell. I thought—"

"I'm okay. We were like five seconds ahead of it," she said with a smile. Yeah, she could laugh about it now. She was a crazy woman but they'd made it out alive.

Melanie turned her hands, inspecting them. The tiny cuts were no longer bleeding but they were red and raw.

"My hero." Mel's grip was gentle as she held her hand. "Let's get you home, huh?"

"Yeah. Let's go home."

CHAPTER FORTY-TWO

"I'm not sure who is going to miss you more—me or the ladies," she whispered when they finally had a second alone.

"Rebecca must have been a prosecutor in another life. She's been grilling me." Erin motioned to her plate. "What's that?"

"I'm assuming she got the answer she was seeking, as if you kissing me in front of them wasn't enough," she teased. "This is eggplant. You want it? I'm done."

"You don't like it?"

"Very good, yes. But it's fried. In case you haven't noticed, we've had nothing fried at home. Well, other than our breakfast potatoes, but that's more sautéed than fried."

"Watching your waistline, are you?" Erin stabbed at the eggplant, scooping it onto her own plate. "I can vouch that there's not an ounce of fat there," she said with a wink.

"I'm more concerned with my heart health than my waistline, but thank you for the compliment."

"Oh, Erin—I made that chocolate cake that you liked. Save room now," Stella said, nearly beaming at Erin. They were all beaming at Erin. Her heroics with the tree was still being whispered about. "We're all so glad you joined us again." She led Erin to where the desserts were. "I trust Mel is taking care of you?" she asked, just loud enough for Melanie to hear.

She was certain she was blushing, and she turned away, only to find Angela watching.

"Oh, my! Is that a cute blush I see?" Angela laughed. "No need to be embarrassed, Mel. I think it's wonderful."

"Wonderful? I don't know what you're talking about," she said lamely as she put her plate in the sink.

Angela linked arms with her as they went back into the living room. "Some of the ladies are positively jealous."

"What does everyone think is going on?" she asked a bit hesitantly.

"Oh, don't be coy, Mel. She's cute. That kiss she gave you wasn't exactly platonic. I guess it was bound to happen, what with you two living together like that."

Melanie blew out her breath. What did she say to that? Did she deny it? And how in the world would they all know? Guessing or hoping?

"Has someone been spying on us?"

Angela leaned closer, her voice low. "Rumor has it that Stella caught you wearing each other's clothes."

"Oh, good Lord! How would she even know that?"

Angela laughed. "Erin was wearing your tree hugger T-shirt and you were wearing one she didn't recognize...and it was inside out."

Melanie grabbed the bridge of her nose, knowing her face was again covered in a red-hot blush. It wasn't so much that everyone knew...it was that she didn't want them talking about her, discussing it. Or worse...*imagining* it.

"So I've been the topic of gossip, huh?"

"Oh, Mel, these ladies haven't had anything to coo about in years. Give them this. Everyone loves you. The fact that you've got a cute hottie living with you—and you're wearing each other's clothes—has been like a fantasy for them. Top that off with Erin rescuing Rachel and they're all positively giddy!"

She nearly rolled her eyes. A cute hottie? What would Erin's reaction be to that description? She would be amused, most likely.

"So you're saying I shouldn't try to hide it?"

"Bask in it." Then Angela leaned closer. "You are having sex, right? Because, well, it's kinda written all over your face."

Another blush and a forced smile. "Okay. We can stop talking about it now."

Angela surprised her by a hug. "I'm happy for you."

"What? That I'm having sex?" Her smile faded. "She *is* leaving, you know."

"Yes, she is. I think Stella is hoping you two fall madly in love and she'll stay on. New blood, you know."

"Well, I hate to bust her bubble, but no. She's definitely leaving."

Angela touched her arm. "So no falling madly in love? That's too bad. From the looks you two were sharing, I thought it was more."

"No. Sorry."

"So just having a little fun, then?" Angela teased. "Nothing wrong with that. If I were in your shoes, I'd do the same thing." She motioned to where Erin was surrounded by no less than five gray-haired ladies. "Rebecca is a hopeless romantic and wants all the details, but I think Dianne has a little crush on her."

Melanie smiled. "Yes, I think so. When Dianne cut her hair, she was gushing over her."

Erin must have felt them watching. She turned, meeting her gaze, then smiled before being pulled back into the conversation. Melanie let out the tiniest of sighs, then smiled almost apologetically at Angela.

"We've become good friends too. I'll miss that, for sure."

"Oh, I know what you mean. I miss having someone to talk to sometimes. You and I get along well enough, but even after all these years, we haven't really nurtured a friendship." Angela held her hand up quickly. "And I'm certainly not blaming you, Mel. It's as much my fault. Even though we're closest in age, I'm still twenty years older than you are. And we both enjoy our alone time, obviously. No one sees you except at these monthly gatherings, and I only see some of them because I live within walking distance of the main cluster."

"Wish you picked a spot farther up the creek?"

"Sometimes, yes. If I'd known I was going to stay on, I'd have done like you did—built something. But at the time, this house was far enough away from the others that I felt secluded, especially after living in the city."

"There was already a garden established at your house. That alone was worth it, I'd think. Even after seven years, I'm still digging up rocks when I till."

Their conversation shifted to gardening, signaling an end to the brief personal tidbits they'd shared. Yes, they were probably both to blame for not working at their friendship more. Truth was, she never really missed having a close friend. Friends had been few in her life, close friends even rarer. Adam, that was it. And even then, she'd kept secrets from him, hadn't she? Erin, really, was the only one she'd told all her secrets to. The good, the bad, even those things she was ashamed of and others that were better kept hidden... She'd told them all to Erin.

She nodded appropriately as Angela filled her in on the happenings around the tribe, the little bits of gossip that got passed on in casual conversation, like how Rachel was adjusting to living with Stella—and how Stella was adjusting. Sadly, they hadn't been able to salvage much from Rachel's house. From what Angela had heard, Rachel was still contemplating moving into one of the vacant houses—which would need some work to get it livable. Melanie kept her gaze on Erin, though, smiling as Erin smiled. Yes, she would miss her friendship. Miss her sharing her bed. Most of all, she'd miss the feeling she got— deep inside—when Erin's eyes captured hers. That sickly sweet feeling that sent her stomach rolling and made her feel like a young girl.

A young girl in love.

CHAPTER FORTY-THREE

Erin stood with her shoulder against the railing, her gaze traveling across familiar things: the chickens making their last pass for insects before the waning light chased them to their roost, the twins eyeing her through the fence, the two magpies on the gate talking to her like old friends, the setting sun's rays glistening on the creek, the hummingbirds buzzing at the feeder, the rosebushes, the piñon pine on the corner. The shed.

There were sounds too. Sounds that she wanted to take with her: the faint splash of the gurgling creek against the rocks, the clucking of the chickens, the breeze in the trees, the call of a raven as he soared toward the bluff.

All familiar now. No traffic noise, no horns, no chatter, no clutter. She closed her eyes for a moment, trying to memorize it all, wanting—needing—to be able to recall it when she left. She wondered how long it would stay with her. She'd been here three months—less one week—and she had a hard time remembering her daily commute to work, the spreadsheets she'd pored over as if they were life or death, the endless phone conversations with clients and contractors. All of that had faded away as if they'd never been a part of her life. Would her time here—Melanie—fade away too, once she got back home, got back to her real life?

She heard the door open, but she didn't turn around. Soon, two warm hands slid up her back, then they pulled her close to an equally warm body.

"You okay?"

She swallowed, her gaze still fixed on Rosie as her little nose twitched, begging for a rub. "Are we ever going to see each other again? Talk? Keep in touch?"

"Oh, sweetie...how? There's no phone. The occasional email?" The arms tightened for a moment, then relaxed, turning her around to face her. "There's no point, Erin. We live in two different worlds. You'll get home, back to your routine." Melanie smiled quickly. "Well, I hope not your *old* routine. I hope you'll start keeping normal hours. But you know what I mean. You're healed, honey." Mel reached out, touching between her breasts. "In here, you're healed. Whatever demons you were fighting, you've defeated them. You're strong again. You'll meet someone, you'll let them in. I'll be a fond memory." She smiled again, this time a bittersweet smile that Erin knew was forced. "At least I hope it'll be fond."

"Mel—"

"Erin, we knew you'd be leaving. Let's don't pretend otherwise."

Erin studied her, seeing the sadness in her eyes that Mel was bravely trying to hide. "What about you? Have you defeated your demons?"

"I think so. I guess I won't know for sure until...well, until they don't haunt me anymore."

Erin touched her cheek lightly, letting her fingers trail across her skin. "I'd like to think I helped with that."

"You've helped in more ways than I could possibly tell you. I feel...well, I think I feel normal again."

"Normal enough to want to leave here?"

Melanie grabbed her hand and squeezed it tightly. "Wanting to leave and able to leave are two different things. This is my home, Erin. This is my life. Whether I feel healed, whether my demons have left or not, that doesn't mean I want to leave here."

"Yeah, I know. Hermit and all."

"Yes. And Stella and the ladies—they need me. They're my family. Having you here made me realize that I need a family."

Erin nodded, glad for that, at least. What had she been thinking? That Mel would want to pack up and leave with her? No. She couldn't picture Mel in a city. Actually, she couldn't picture Melanie anywhere but right here where she was.

Melanie leaned closer and kissed her...a gentle, slow, quiet kiss. When she pulled back, Melanie averted her gaze.

"I thought I'd make meatless balls from the leftover lentils. Do spaghetti and meatballs for dinner. That okay with you?"

"Perfect." She took a step away. "I'll tend to everything out here." She walked off the porch, then looked up to the evening sky. "No rain tonight."

"No. I think—like summer—our rainy season is coming to an end. I'm going to miss it."

Erin turned around, trying to find Mel's eyes in the shadows. She nodded. "I'll miss it too."

CHAPTER FORTY-FOUR

The week seemed to fly by, yet at the same time, it was nearly endless. Endless, because for nearly every second of every day, Melanie found herself counting down the hours until Erin walked out of her life. It had been both a happy week and sad, even though they'd tried to put on brave faces. They didn't talk about it. In fact, there'd been no words spoken about Erin's impending departure since last week on the porch. Maybe they thought if they ignored it, the day would never come.

Yet here it was. Tomorrow. And she supposed it was a fitting end…today. They hadn't had rain in four days, had barely even had clouds in the sky. They'd taken hikes along the now wet and flowing Mule Creek. They'd even gone up to the hot springs one morning, packing lunch with them and having a picnic on the rocks. They'd done the bare minimum in the garden, choosing instead to spend their remaining time together—together being lazy or talking or making love. The garden, and her chores, would still be there after Erin left. Tomorrow.

Today, though, another storm had blown in. So, yes, it was fitting, she thought. The skies had been as gray as her mood, dark rain clouds blanketing the bluff early that morning, like they planned to hang around a while. And they had. The rain had begun before they'd even cleaned up their breakfast dishes. The thunder alerted them that it would be a downpour and they'd scrambled to put things away and make sure the goats and chickens had taken cover. The rain had been relentless until noon, when it finally eased up, the thunder and lightning moving on past them.

The rain had lightened up enough for Erin to make a run out to the shed to check on the chickens and the twins. Judging by how long she was gone—and the dark, shadowy look in her eyes when she returned—Melanie guessed she had been saying her private goodbyes to them.

Goodbye.

Damn, but she didn't think it would be this hard. Three months ago, she assumed she'd be dancing for joy when this day came. Dancing for joy at the prospect of getting her solitude back, getting her space back. Now? Quite the opposite. The heavy rain clouds weighed on her, and the ache that had been growing all week was threatening to choke her, making it difficult to swallow. Difficult to breathe. She'd held herself together, though, forcing smiles and making lighthearted chitchat. Until she couldn't.

Erin was inside. Erin was inside packing—packing to leave—and Melanie simply couldn't stand the sight of it. She wanted to run away, escape this pain...this pain that she didn't know what to do with. She didn't know where to put it, she didn't know how to label it.

They were friends. They'd become lovers. Nothing more. It was always going to be temporary. They both knew that. The closest they'd come to *not* making it temporary was Erin wondering if they'd keep in touch when she left.

And no, they wouldn't. She'd drive Erin to Silver City tomorrow morning. She'd drop her off under the cluster of pine trees that had been planted years ago, a spot that Erin had pointed out to her on one of their trips into town for shopping. Right there, she'd said. Right there was where her sister had dropped her off. That's where Stella had picked her up. And that's where Melanie would leave her tomorrow—right there.

They would have already said their goodbyes before they got there. They would probably hug—one last time, one last look into eyes she would forever remember—then she'd get back in her truck and leave Erin standing there. She'd probably look in her rearview mirror a couple of times and... And by then, she'd most likely be crying.

Without much thought, she walked out into the chilly rain, the last rain of summer, her feet moving faster and faster, taking her away from the cabin. She wrapped her arms around herself as she headed to the creek. The creek had always been a solace for her...a friend. The sound of the creek was as familiar to her as her own breath. She stood at the edge, absently watching it flow past, the steady downpour from earlier turning the pristine water into a cloudy mess.

And a cloudy mess was a good way to describe her feelings. A mess, for sure. She lifted her head up, relishing the sting of the rain as it hit her skin, letting it mix with her tears. Letting it wash the tears from her face. She could no longer stop them. She hung her head low, feeling sobs shake her shoulders.

Erin hadn't even left yet. How could she possibly feel this lonely? She knew loneliness. She knew how to handle it. But this? This seemed completely foreign to her. This seemed far worse than mere loneliness. This felt like her heart was being ripped from her chest.

She didn't know how long she stood there. Long enough to be soaked to the bone, but not long enough for her tears to stop. Then arms wrapped around her from behind and her tears turned to sobs once again. She felt Erin bury her face against the back of her neck, and she squeezed her eyes against the pain. When Erin turned her around to face her, gathering her close, Mel clung to her, willing her tears to stop.

Their kiss was urgent...fiery and passionate. As the rain fell harder, their kisses turned frenzied and they were grasping at the other, hands moving without thought, mouths locked in a hard kiss, tongues battling. They were both breathless when they pulled apart, their eyes clinging to one another as questions flew between them.

Without a word, Erin took her hand and led her back to the cabin. They undressed in the bathroom, dropping their wet clothes on the floor. The warm water from the shower sent steam circling around them. Mel's tears fell again, and Erin wiped them gently from her face.

"Shhh," Erin whispered.

The kisses were slower now, gentler. Intense, yet sensuous. Tears forgotten, she drew Erin close, her fingers moving across wet skin, her palms pressing against taut nipples.

They said nothing—because there was nothing to say.

They said nothing—yet, with each kiss, each touch, they said plenty.

CHAPTER FORTY-FIVE

Melanie slowed her truck as they approached Stella's house, then parked behind the Suburban that Erin had ridden in that very first day. She wanted to tell Stella goodbye, even though she'd said her formal goodbyes to everyone at the August dinner last week. The fact that she and Mel were lovers was now old news, apparently. Unlike the July dinner, not even Rebecca grilled her. Mel cut the engine but didn't move to get out. She'd been unusually quiet this morning. Hell, they both had been.

"Be right back," she said as she opened the door. Stella must have heard them because she was standing at the screen door, waiting for her.

"You're heading out early, dear." Stella came out onto the porch, holding a cup of coffee. "What time is your sister meeting you?"

"Ten. She flew into Albuquerque last night. We have a four o'clock flight this afternoon, so..."

"You'll have a whirlwind of a day." She looked past her, seeing Melanie in the truck waiting. "I won't invite you in for coffee then."

"I wanted to thank you. For everything." She smiled. "I know I wasn't a poster child of what a perfect guest would be."

"Nonsense. We only had a few kinks to work out at the beginning."

"Yeah. I still feel bad about how things started off with Rachel." She glanced over her shoulder. "Mel, though—she's, she's been the best. I don't think I would have made it without her."

"Yes—the two of you seem to have bonded...Hmm?"

The look in Stella's eyes told her it wasn't really a question. She nodded. "Yes. I'm going to miss her. A lot."

"Rachel owes you her life. Don't feel bad about anything." Stella drew her into a hug. "You know my phone number here. If you ever need...well, if you need to get a message to Mel or anything."

"Thanks. But...well, I don't imagine we'll...see each other again."

"I understand." Stella squeezed both of her hands. "You look good, Erin. Whatever you've learned here from Melanie, I hope you take that with you."

"Thank you." She leaned down and kissed the older woman on the cheek. "Take care, Stella."

She bounded off the porch and down the steps without another word. When she got in beside Melanie, they looked at each other but neither spoke. Melanie finally started up the engine and drove away.

* * *

After a nearly silent drive into Silver City, one broken only by the occasional comment about anything *but* the departure that awaited them, Erin felt the fingers of dread start to choke her as they approached town. How was she going to say goodbye to this woman? How? What could she possibly say to her?

She glanced over at Melanie, finding Mel watching her. Mel moved her hand across the console and Erin's took it, their fingers entwining naturally. They squeezed at the same time, drawing smiles from both of them. Still...they said nothing.

When Melanie pulled up beside the circle of trees—the same place where Stella had picked her up three months prior—their hands were still folded together. Erin glanced around, wondering if Joyce had made it yet. It was still a few minutes before ten.

"You going to stay? Meet my sister?"

Melanie shook her head. "If you don't mind...I'd rather not." She cleared her throat and Erin wondered if Mel was trying to blink back her tears. "I'd rather be the one to leave first."

Erin nodded. "I understand."

They stared at each other for a moment, and she wondered who would speak first. They'd already said their goodbyes. Last night, this morning. They'd said their goodbyes with touches and kisses...not words. There weren't any words that would make this easier so neither of them tried. Mel finally pulled her hand away and opened the door.

They set her luggage on the curb, then they stood there, a good three feet apart, their gazes drawn together, then away, then back together again.

"I...I feel like we should talk, but I don't know what to say."

Melanie shook her head. "There's nothing to say, Erin."

Erin nodded. "There is something, Mel. There is one thing I wish for. I wish you would forgive yourself for Adam's death. Forgive. You don't have to forget...but forgive."

Mel chewed on her lower lip nervously, but nodded. "Yes. I think...well, I think I already have." She met her gaze, holding it. "And I wish...I wish for you to not ever change who you are. Don't give up yourself for someone else. Don't change for anyone, Erin. Be who you are. Show people who you are."

She watched as Melanie visibly swallowed before continuing, as if having trouble finding the words. "If they don't love the real you, then they're not worth your time. Let them go."

As their eyes held—five seconds, ten, longer—she saw so many things there. Things she wanted to memorize, things she wanted to be able to see on those lonely, dark nights that were coming. Then Mel stepped closer and they embraced tightly.

"I didn't think it would be this hard," Erin murmured into her ear.

"I know." When Melanie pulled away, she wiped at a tear on her cheek. "It goes without saying that I'll miss you."

Erin nodded. "I'll miss you more."

Melanie smiled as she wiped another tear. "No, no. You won't win this one. I'll miss *you* more." She took a step away, then another. "Take care of yourself, Erin."

"I will. You do the same."

Melanie backed up again and Erin could see the tears swimming in her eyes. "Goodbye, sweet Erin."

Erin took a deep breath, uttering the three hardest words she'd ever said. "Goodbye, my Mel."

She stood there on the curb, beside her forgotten luggage, tears streaming down both cheeks as she watched Melanie drive away. Away and out of her life.

CHAPTER FORTY-SIX

"Oh, my God! I didn't even recognize you! What have you done with my sister?"

Erin smiled as Joyce hugged her tightly. "I did what you said. I got healthy."

Joyce held her at arm's length, still smiling. "Wow. You look...you look wonderful, Erin. I *love* your hair."

"Thanks." She wiped at the corner of one eye, hoping that all evidence of her earlier tears was gone. She would never be able to explain that to Joyce.

"Like I'm looking at a ghost," Joyce continued.

Erin raised her eyebrows.

"A good ghost," she clarified. "You look like...well, like you did when you were younger. Jeans, T-shirt. Relaxed. I like it. You look like *you*." Joyce went to pick up one of her bags. "Let's blow this joint, huh? Get you back home where you belong."

Erin turned, looking around the parking lot, half expecting—hoping—to see Mel's truck speeding back toward her. But no. Mel was gone. And soon, too, so would she be. Gone.

"Come on, Erin. Got a flight to catch."

She took a deep breath, wondering at the emptiness she felt. Wondering if it would follow her back to Houston.

CHAPTER FORTY-SEVEN

She stared at the clothes that were all hung so neatly in her closet. Power suits. Black ones and gray ones and a few navy ones mixed in for good measure. There must have been twenty or more. And then there were the matching blouses. Two whole racks of them. She walked deeper into the closet, eyeing the shoe rack. God, had she actually worn those? Her feet hurt just thinking about it.

With a sigh, she pulled one of the suits out. She held it up, staring at it, trying to picture herself wearing it. Charcoal gray. Sarah would tell her to wear a white blouse with it or perhaps a blue one. She dropped it onto the floor and pulled another one out, this time black. She had countless blouses that would go with it. But it too ended up on the floor.

"Don't change for anyone."

She heard the words so clearly, she actually turned around, expecting to find Melanie in the room with her. But no. She was alone.

Joyce had told her to take a few days before coming into the office, but she couldn't stand the silence in her house a second longer. She'd ventured out yesterday—she didn't have a thing in the house to eat—and found herself at Whole Foods, pushing a cart through the produce aisle. It nearly pained her to buy things that she'd gotten used to picking in the garden. Mel's garden. She got familiar things: squash, potatoes, broccoli. Some onions and peppers for her breakfast. She'd eyed the bulk bins of dried beans and had even gone so far as to bag a pound of pintos, then decided she was being too adventurous. She opted for canned beans instead.

Her trip to the grocery store, however, did nothing to alleviate her loneliness. It only served to worsen it, if anything. Because cooking alone, eating alone, only magnified the ache in her chest.

She looked once again at the row of suits, then shut the closet door. She walked over to her luggage, which was still on the floor beside her bed. She'd put off unpacking because...well, once she unpacked, then she was back. Back here and not there. She dug out a pair of rumpled jeans and held them up. A smile lit her face as she remembered Mel taking her shopping, at Walmart, of all places. She took a deep breath, then slipped them on. She rummaged in her drawers, finally finding a wrinkled T-shirt— navy with their company's logo emblazoned on it in white. She slipped it over her head, then went back to the closet, using the full-length mirror.

"Damn...I've got boobs again." Well, sort of. If she pulled the T-shirt tight, yeah, there were definitely breasts there. She let out a sigh, then ran her fingers through her hair. She'd had Dianne give her a trim the week before she left. At first, she thought maybe she should let it go. Let it grow, get somewhat back to normal. But Melanie had run her fingers through it— much like she was doing now—and had told her how sexy she looked with short hair. That was all it had taken.

She turned away from the mirror, away from the sad eyes that looked back at her. Was she going to be able to fake it? Pretend she was happy? Happy to be back? She paused, then turned back to the mirror, meeting her gaze again.

Why wasn't she happy? She was healthy again. She was back home, back in familiar territory, back in control. There were no dark thoughts, no self-doubt, no anger. She had gotten her life back. She hadn't even considered stocking up on Red Bull when she'd been out. She didn't need it. She hadn't reached for the bottle of bourbon last night to dull her senses. Having a drink never even crossed her mind. And now? Now she was heading into the office, to a job she loved. She'd get her projects back. She'd work like she used to, normal hours, like she'd done before Sarah.

So why wasn't she happy?

She turned around and slammed the closet door. Did that question really need an answer?

CHAPTER FORTY-EIGHT

Melanie had expected Stella to come by yesterday. She was thankful Stella had given her a day...a day to get used to being alone again. A day to get used to Erin being gone. As she had stood in her garden that morning, trying to find the will to do some work, she had suspected it would take much longer than a day or two.

She moved as if on autopilot, pouring out what was left of her coffee and going about making a fresh pot, all the while wondering what she was going to say to Stella. Or maybe she wouldn't have to say anything. Perhaps Stella was simply coming by on her weekly visit...a weekly visit that had all but ceased once Erin had become entrenched in her life.

She paused, staring out the kitchen window. Entrenched. Yes. That was a good word. Erin's presence seemed to be everywhere in the house. And last night, as she'd crawled into bed alone—early enough that the sun was still hanging on, early enough that she'd had to force the chickens into their roost— Erin's presence, or its lack, seemed to fill the room.

She'd allowed herself to cry then. The room was dark and shadowy. There was no one to hear or see. She'd cried on the long trip home from Silver City too. Cried so hard that she'd had to stop on the side of the road to gather herself, afraid she'd have a wreck or run into a tree if she didn't. And when she'd gotten to Eagle Bluff, she'd sped past Stella's house, not taking a chance that she'd be out and about and would wave her over.

So Stella had given her one day. She was on her way now. Melanie could hear her old truck bouncing along the road. She'd be there before the coffee finished brewing.

She went out onto the porch to wait, offering a small wave as Stella neared. She smiled when she saw Fred hanging off the back. Stella parked beside her own truck and got out, going around to let the tailgate down for Fred.

"Thought he might enjoy a ride," she explained. Then she added, "Thought you might like to keep him a day or two. For company."

She nodded. "Thank you. I think I will."

Stella sat down in the rocker beside her. Erin's rocker. She didn't say anything for the longest, just sat and rocked. Melanie did the same. Finally, Stella spoke, but her rocker never lost its rhythm.

"Do you remember Colleen?"

Melanie frowned for a moment, trying to place the name. Then it came to her. "Yes, I do. She came every summer for a while."

"Yes." Stella's rocker slowed. "Six summers. It was by chance that she stayed with me that first time. It just so happened to be my turn to host."

"And regardless of whose turn it was after that, she always stayed with you."

"She did." Stella turned to look at her. "Do you know why?"

Melanie met her gaze. "I can only guess."

"It was the third summer. It was on a Tuesday. We were sitting in my flower garden in the back, drinking tea. There were hummingbirds buzzing around the bougainvillea and she was fascinated by them. We were laughing at their antics."

Stella was smiling now as she started rocking again. "She kissed me out of nowhere. I was so startled—no one had kissed me in thirty years!"

"You became lovers?" she asked gently.

Stella blushed bright red and she wouldn't look at her. "Not that summer, no. We kissed…"

"You fell in love with her?"

Stella glanced at her then. "I did. And when she left, I convinced myself it was all a figment of my imagination, yet I waited and waited for winter to pass, then spring…counting down the days 'til summer, hoping she'd come back. And she always did."

Until she didn't. Melanie remembered it well. She usually came in August. By September, when there'd been no word from her, the other ladies were gossiping, noting that Stella wasn't herself. By the time the September monthly dinner rolled around, it was obvious that Colleen wasn't coming that year. And yes, it had taken several months for Stella to get over it.

"Why didn't you call her? When she stopped coming, why didn't you call?"

"It wasn't any of my business, was it? Oh, that's not to say that I never picked up the phone. I did. Many times. But I never went through with it." She folded her hands together in her lap. "It was the most beautiful letter, Mel. I take it out from time to time…on those occasions when I'm missing her. On those nights when I'm feeling particularly lonely."

Melanie nodded. Yes, Stella knew about loneliness too, didn't she? How hard was it for her now? Maybe that's why Stella hadn't come around much in August; she'd been missing Colleen.

"She didn't want me to know she was sick," Stella said, almost to herself. "She didn't want me to look at her with pity, I suppose. She said she wanted me to remember her how she'd been…out here." Stella stopped rocking and stood up quickly. Melanie was once again struck by her grace, her agility, at seventy-five. "Enough of that, young Mel. How are *you* doing?"

Melanie met her gaze. "I miss her," she said simply.

Stella nodded. "I imagine so. How deep were you in, honey?"

Mel looked away then. "It…it kinda snuck up on me. I had been so careful—at least I thought I had—knowing she'd be leaving."

"Our hearts sometimes don't listen to reason, do they? I would venture to say that Erin misses you as well."

Melanie nodded. "Yes, I'm sure she does. We met at the wrong place, wrong time, I guess."

Stella shook her head. "Is there such a thing? When you meet someone, someone who lights up your world—and Erin did that for you and you for her—is there such a thing as wrong place, wrong time?"

Mel held her arms out, motioning toward the creek. "Well, definitely wrong place. I'll get over it, though. I've been alone forever, it seems."

"Mel, if it's love—love will find a way."

Melanie met her gaze. "It didn't for you, though, Stella. It didn't find a way. I think it'll be the same for me."

Stella opened her mouth to say something, then she closed her eyes briefly, making Melanie wish she'd not said those words to her. When Stella opened her eyes again, she smiled. "I almost forgot," she said as she hurried off the porch toward her truck. "I baked a zucchini cake yesterday. How about a cup of coffee to go with it?"

Mel nodded. "That would be nice. Thank you."

CHAPTER FORTY-NINE

Erin rested her forehead against the glass, her gaze fixed on the street, eleven floors below. Twelve o'clock—the lunch hour—and cars were at a standstill, everyone waiting to get through the light and hurry off to restaurants or shops, only to rush back again at one. She'd rarely been a part of that mess, only if she had a business lunch scheduled. She simply hadn't bothered with eating.

Melanie would be proud of her. She'd actually packed her lunch—half of the huge potato she'd baked for dinner last night, some steamed broccoli, and a scoop of chickpeas. She'd even thrown a banana in for good measure. She had skipped breakfast, though, and her stomach was rumbling. She didn't want to fall back into that habit, so she'd already set her alarm for fifteen minutes earlier.

Not that she'd needed an alarm this morning. She'd been tossing about in her bed for most of the night and she'd been awake, staring at the ceiling, when the alarm had gone off.

She hadn't been staring at the ceiling, really. She'd been thinking. Remembering. The ache she felt was entirely different than the pain she'd had when Sarah left her. Of course, with Sarah, there was more anger than pain, wasn't there? She should have said "good riddance and thank you for wasting six years of my life" and been done with it. She smiled at that thought. Yeah…easy to say now. Who knew her heart wasn't *really* broken at the time?

"Erin? I thought you were going to take a few days."

She jumped at the sound of her name, turning to find her father standing in her office. She hesitated only a second before going to him, hugging him tightly in greeting.

"Dad."

"Glad you're back, Erin. We missed you."

"I missed you too," she said automatically as they drew apart.

"Wow. Joyce said you looked wonderful. She wasn't exaggerating."

"Thanks."

"Still—I should apologize. Erin, what I did, what we did—"

"It was the right thing, Dad. Yeah, I was pissed at you, but it was the right thing. If I'd stayed here…Well, I needed a kick in the ass. Thank you for giving it to me." Then she smiled. "Sending me away for three months was kinda drastic, but I'm really glad you did."

"So you're back to your old self? Joyce seems to think so."

Erin shrugged. "I guess so." She pointed to her laptop. "Taking things slow. I haven't done much more than poke around."

"Poke around faster. I'm ready to dump those projects back in your lap." He headed to the door, then stopped. "Why'd you do it?"

She raised her eyebrows.

"Working the hours that you did? Making the demands that you did? What were you trying to prove? Something to me? Something to yourself?"

She frowned. "Prove?"

"You were already top dog, Erin. You brought in more money, more clients than them. You completed more projects. What else were you trying to prove?"

"I don't know that I was trying to prove anything." Then she smiled. "I had time on my hands, I guess." She walked back toward the window. "I needed to be good at something. I apparently wasn't good at anything in my personal life, so…"

She stared out the window, not really seeing the cars on the street. Was that it? Was that what it had all been about? Not a broken heart. Not Sarah leaving. She needed to have something she was good at. Something she excelled at. Because she was a failure…in her relationship, she was a failure. She turned back around, seeing her father's quizzical expression. She smiled.

"Thanks, Dad."

He nodded. "Not sure what I did, but okay. Damn glad you're back, Erin. I don't know how you did it. I don't know how you juggled ten projects and kept your sanity."

She laughed. "Obviously I didn't keep my sanity."

He laughed too. "Well, to say the least, some of them are running on fumes, some are so far behind schedule, you'll probably scream. And a couple of them, the buyers are calling almost daily, wanting updates. One of them, I don't think there's been any work done in over a month."

"Okay…I'll get everything back on track."

"I have no doubt you will." He shook his finger at her. "Don't go overboard, Erin. Take it easy. It's not the end of the world if we don't meet deadlines."

"I'll keep that in mind."

"Good. See that you do. When you're settled, we'll plan dinner one night."

After he left, she stared at her laptop for a moment, then turned to the window, looking out past the tall buildings and the congestion on the streets, seeing a sliver here and there of the blue sky between the high-rises. She tried not to, of course, but thoughts of Melanie flooded her mind. What was she doing? Was she out in the garden already? Had she remembered to throw scratch out for the chickens? Was Rosie looking around, wondering where she was?

She turned away from the window at that thought. Damn. Worried about whether a goat missed her or not. She sat down at her desk and pulled the laptop closer. With a heavy sigh and without much enthusiasm, she pulled up her accounts.

She really didn't see the numbers, though. She saw a tiny black nose sticking between the slats of a fence—and quiet laughter coming from behind her as she rubbed that tiny nose.

Damn.

CHAPTER FIFTY

Melanie wondered if she'd ever be able to make tortillas in the morning and not think of Erin. How long would it take for her memory to fade? She placed the ball of dough onto her tortilla press and squeezed it flat. For that matter, when would she go back to cooking for one? It seemed at every meal, there was always enough for two.

Fred had been the beneficiary of that. It had been four days since Stella had dropped him off. He didn't do much more than lay under the rosebushes, but she could tell he was getting restless. She supposed she'd need to run him back down the creek to Stella's soon. In fact, she might do that today. Stop and visit her and Rachel, take them a bag of veggies since Stella was cooking for two now. Rachel had been living with her since the storm and, according to Angela, it seemed to be permanent. Maybe she'd stop by Rebecca's place too and see if she needed any help with anything.

She smiled a little as she stared out the kitchen window. Maybe it was true what she'd told Erin. The ladies were her family and she needed to think of them that way. She needed to spend more time with them other than only popping over for the monthly dinners. But was it fair to use them as an escape from her thoughts? From her loneliness?

Yeah. But she needed more than that to escape. She needed to do something. Mid-September was already sneaking past them. She needed some physical exertion. What better way than to cut and haul firewood down from the mountain? She'd ask Angela. It was a little earlier than she normally cut wood but only by a few weeks.

She took her breakfast—Erin's favorite of spicy fried potatoes and scrambled eggs—to the bar and poured another cup of coffee. As she ate, she called upon old habits, mentally going over her chores, planning out her day in silence. She tried her best to muster up some enthusiasm—as she'd been doing since the day Erin left.

It mostly didn't work. When Erin left, she seemed to have taken all the joy with her. Again, she wondered how long it would take for her to get back to normal. How long until she snapped out of this funk she'd been in?

How long before she stopped missing her?

CHAPTER FIFTY-ONE

"Hey, you want to get lunch?"

Erin looked up, frowning. "Lunch?"

Joyce came into her office. "Yeah, lunch. You've been back over two weeks. I figured you'd be caught up by now. We could walk to Ralph's, get a burger."

Erin shook her head. "Don't eat burgers."

"What? You love burgers."

"Kinda don't anymore. I'm eating…well, vegetarian."

"*What?*"

Erin smiled. "I spent three months eating that way. I guess I'm used to it now."

"You ate vegetarian while you were away? Why on earth?"

"You really didn't read their website at all, did you? Yeah, imagine my surprise to find out not only was there no cell service, no Internet—but they were all vegetarians."

"Oh my God! Like you didn't even eat chicken?"

"Eat the chickens? They were like pets. No way I could eat them. But farm fresh eggs are the best things ever."

"Wow. You're full of surprises, aren't you?"

"Am I?"

"Yeah. You've been so calm since you've been back. David Hale called me, wanted to know if you were okay. He said he told you it would be another ten days before he could start on cabinets and you didn't scream at him."

Erin shrugged. "He got delayed at another project because the guys doing the drywall had a supply issue. Not his fault."

Joyce put her hands on the desk and leaned down, meeting her gaze. "Are you *sure* you're Erin Ryder? Have you been body-snatched?"

"Funny."

Joyce smiled at her. "So? Is that a no on Ralph's?"

"I brought my lunch."

"Good God—who *are* you?"

Erin glanced up from her spreadsheet. "I'll call around, find someplace that has decent veggie burgers. Maybe we can go another day."

"Okay. Let me know." Joyce paused at the door. "I'm glad you're back, Erin. Really, I am."

She nodded. "Yeah. Thanks."

She'd like to say that she was glad to be back too. But that wasn't the case, was it? As soon as Joyce left, she spun around in her chair. She'd closed the blinds today, using the bright morning sun as an excuse. Truth was, she couldn't find any motivation to work, not when she was staring out the window, wishing she was anywhere else but closed up in this bare office. Not true either. Not anywhere. She knew where she wished she was.

She'd taken to making Melanie's fried potatoes and onions and peppers for breakfast. She'd bought a dozen eggs but found the taste lacking after eating fresh ones for so long. She'd bought a package of flour tortillas, but they, too, paled in comparison to the homemade ones she'd grown accustomed to. Even adding green salsa—from a jar—didn't help much. She should have stolen one of the pints of salsa that Mel had canned from her garden veggies.

Two weeks. Seventeen days. So, almost three weeks. The days—the nights—had simply crawled by. She'd officially taken back all ten of the projects from her father. Two weeks. It had taken two weeks to get them back on track and running smoothly again. All without yelling or throwing tantrums or threatening the contractors. She'd calmed down the buyers who were starting to panic at the delays, she'd called in a couple of favors, and she'd hired a new contractor—a plumber who was just starting up a new business—to work on a house that had been at a standstill for three weeks. Things were running smoothly again.

She stood up and opened the blinds, noting that clouds now shrouded the sun. Would they have thunderstorms today? Rain? She thought it funny that she had never really bothered—or cared—about the weather before. She went from her garage at home to the parking garage here at the office. Rain only affected her by slowing her commute. She didn't consider that trees and grass and, yeah, people's gardens needed rain to survive. Creeks and rivers. The birds. She smiled. Goats and chickens.

She took a deep breath, then blew it out—as if she could blow away the images in her mind.

Unfortunately, they stayed. They were as fresh and crisp as ever.

CHAPTER FIFTY-TWO

The path along Mule Creek was dry, the dirt starting to crack again from the sun. Once the summer rain ended, the characteristics of the desert started to show again. The cabin, which was along Eagle Creek, was at the edge of the foothills, the trees and terrain more mountain than desert. Here, closer to the bluff, where Mule Creek now flowed, desert plants dominated.

She paused beside the large yucca, the tall stem of the flower starting to lose its petals. She had such a clear vision of Erin bending close to smell the fragrance, she had to blink several times to chase it away.

She turned her attention to the creek, its water flowing steadily by, gurgling past the rocks on its way to meet up with Eagle Creek past the cabin. The little creek would lose steam as winter approached, lessening to only a trickle in places, until the snowmelt from back in the mountains filled it again. It would go dry as the spring flowers bloomed and stay dry until July when the cycle started all over again.

"Mel…look at that!"

She whipped her head around, hearing nothing but the breeze as it carried Erin's voice away. She closed her eyes, letting imaginary fingers caress her cheek, soft fingertips glide across her skin. She smiled as quiet laughter whispered in her ear, warm lips nipped at her neck, demanding hands pulled her close.

The smile faded when she opened her eyes. It was the creek flowing, the breeze whispering, the piñon pine brushing her arm.

Damn… How long was she going to do this? Would she be like Stella, years from now still hanging on to a memory of a long-lost love? She couldn't decide which hurt worse—the guilt she clung to over Adam or the emptiness in her heart where Erin used to be.

Because, yes, she could admit—now, she could—that she'd fallen in love with Erin. She'd convinced herself that their relationship, while emotional to some extent, was mainly physical. And, of course, temporary. That was something they'd both known going in. Temporary. Yet they'd become friends. Rare for her. Rarer still, they'd become *close* friends. Erin knew all her dark secrets. Erin never judged. It was simply too easy. After her initial fear, it was so easy being with Erin. Being lovers.

Easy. Natural. They were open and free with each other. There were no outside distractions, no ulterior motives, no games. And she fell in love.

She tapped her hiking stick on the rocks a couple of times, then walked on. She had tons of things she could be doing. *Should* be doing. The green beans were all but spent, so she needed to pull the plants while they still had some life in them. The goats were in for a treat. And it was time to collect pine needles. The nights were getting colder and if she wanted to harvest sugar snaps before a hard freeze, she'd need to protect them. And she needed to stack the firewood she'd cut last week. Most of it was still on back of her truck. So many little chores that had occupied her days for the last seven years. Yet she was out hiking as if she hadn't a care in the world. Hiking, because, in the garden, she saw Erin in every corner. In the garden, in the shed, in the kitchen, in the bedroom... There was no place left for her to go. Even out here, in the wide-open spaces, the deep, endless sky, all she had to do was listen.

She tilted her head now, smiling again as the breeze carried Erin's voice, tickling her ears as it passed by, lingering for only a second before disappearing into the trees.

CHAPTER FIFTY-THREE

She tapped the steering wheel absently, the song on the radio barely loud enough to register. She'd left earlier than usual and now was regretting it as traffic had slowed to a crawl. While she had taken to arriving at the office after nine to avoid the morning rush, she normally stayed until six thirty or so, letting the five o'clock traffic die down. Today, though, she'd made a point to leave earlier. She'd found she was staying longer and longer and she was adamant that she would not fall back into old routines that kept her at the office until nine or ten at night. So she'd head home early, she'd make dinner. Then she'd watch a little TV. That medical drama that she and Mel had started watching was on tonight. She could kill an hour or two in front of the tube.

Then start all over again tomorrow.

"Your life sucks," she muttered to her reflection in the mirror.

Yeah, it did. She knew what she needed to do. She needed to try to hook up with some of her old friends. Try to reconnect with them. Hell, she needed to go out and *do* something. Maybe it was time to start dating again. Real dating this time. Not just quick hookups to try to get over Sarah. Because it wasn't Sarah anymore. It was Mel.

How had Melanie gotten so deep into her heart? When had that happened? And why the hell couldn't she kick her out? It was like she followed her everywhere…to work and back home. At the grocery store, she walked beside her in the produce aisle. She hovered over her while she cooked. She sat beside her on sofa. And she crawled into her bed at night.

She recognized the similarities. When Sarah left, yeah, the house seemed empty. Her bed seemed empty. She knew now that it was mostly with anger that she missed Sarah. She'd stumbled around her empty house, wondering where she'd failed, trying to picture Sarah in happier times. Sometimes she could convince herself that they'd been ecstatically happy together, but she knew deep down that that was only in her imagination. She and Sarah had a superficial relationship only. She couldn't remember a single time that they'd talked from the heart. Shared secrets and dreams. They were never friends. They met, they became lovers, they moved in together. There was never anything to bind them, other than that. If she hadn't been so busy with work, surely she would have seen that, recognized how lacking their relationship was. Busy with work, busy with trips to New York and Mexico. Hard work and hard play, nothing in between. Everything was fast. Hard and fast. Nothing was ever slow and easy.

She met her eyes again in the mirror. Things had been easy with Mel, hadn't they? They worked side-by-side, but it wasn't hard and it wasn't fast. It was almost a lazy kind of work. They teased and played in the garden. They snuck off to the creek on occasion. They took time for hikes and for picnics. It was slow and easy and damn near perfect. So perfect were things with Mel, the difference was absolutely glaring when compared to Sarah.

Things felt perfect there with Melanie.

How was she ever going to find that here?

By the time she got home, the stress of sitting in traffic for an hour had frazzled her nerves. So much so that she very nearly hit the strange car that was parked in her driveway. She pulled up beside it, but there was no one inside. With a curious shrug, she opened the garage door and pulled in, closing it behind her again.

As soon as she went inside the house, she knew someone was there. She could feel it. She took out her phone, ready to call 911 when it occurred to her that if someone had broken in, the alarm would have gone off. Would burglars park in the driveway?

"You're home early."

It was so familiar…she thought surely, she was dreaming. She turned, finding her standing just outside the kitchen. Her blond hair was longer than she remembered, long and silky. She put her phone back in her pocket, trying to string some thoughts together, enough to make a sentence. Why hadn't she gotten her key back? She knew why. She'd always hoped that Sarah would come back.

Sarah walked up to her then, wrapping both arms around her in a tight hug. Erin stood stiffly, only pulling away when Sarah moved to kiss her.

"What are you doing here?"

Sarah's smile was as brilliant as she remembered. "I missed you, Erin. So much." Sarah's gaze moved to her hair. "I hardly recognized you, though. That's a bit extreme, isn't it?"

Erin moved past her into the living room, heading to the bar. She stopped when she realized what she was about to do—pour herself a drink. She spun away from the bar.

"What do you want, Sarah? Did you forget something?"

Sarah's smile was confident as she came up beside her, her hand running smoothly up her arm. "I forgot you, darling. Did you miss me too? I heard from some of our friends that you had a rough go."

Erin met her gaze, wondering why she'd ever thought she was in love with this woman. Her blue eyes had a coldness to them. How had she not seen that before? Cold and calculating.

There was no warmth there. At least, no genuine warmth. She knew what that looked like now and she wasn't seeing it here. Sarah was trying hard to convey some, though, wasn't she? How had she not noticed that before?

Maybe because she'd had nothing to compare it to. Erin looked into Sarah's eyes, their blue not unlike that of Mel's. But it was what was inside the blue that held the difference. Truth, honesty... Love. Things she'd seen in Mel's eyes. Here? No. Those things were missing. She supposed they'd always been. Joyce's words rang true. Sarah was a taker, not a giver.

When she didn't answer, Sarah moved closer, close enough that they were touching. "I can see that you did miss me. I'm so sorry, Erin. I made a mistake. I realized after I left how much I loved you. How much I *still* love you." Sarah ran her hands up her arms, pulling her closer. "You feel that too, don't you?" She lifted her head, her mouth close to her own. Erin let Sarah kiss her. Her lips felt foreign to her. There was nothing there. She felt nothing. She could have just as well been kissing the rim of a scotch glass. That thought made her smile, and she pulled away from Sarah. Kissing scotch glasses was her forte, wasn't it? Or it had been.

She moved away from Sarah, wondering why she wasn't angry. She turned to face her. "So you still love me, huh? What happened to...What was her name again?"

Sarah's smiled turned a bit coy. "It doesn't matter, darling. She wasn't you. She could never be you."

"She wasn't me?" Erin gave a humorless smile. "That's funny, isn't it? Because with you, I wasn't me either." She shoved her hands into the pockets of her jeans. "I like myself a bit better now."

Sarah's gaze traveled over her, as if seeing her jeans and the polo shirt for the first time, the polo shirt with their company name on the left pocket. She drew her brows together in a frown.

"Were you at work? Like *that*?" She moved closer again. "Darling, I told you a hundred times, you've got to dress the part. What? Did you completely fall apart when I left? Your hair? Your clothes? Erin, we worked so hard to get you where you were. Why would you throw that away?"

"Unbelievable," she whispered. "You are unbelievable. Sarah, *we* didn't work hard. *I* worked hard. You tried to zap the life out of me and you nearly succeeded." She walked toward the front door and opened it. "I'll need your key, Sarah." She held her hand out. "If you come to the house again, I'll call the police."

Sarah's mouth dropped open in disbelief. "What…What are you saying?"

"Do you need it spelled out for you? I want you to leave. I don't want to ever see you again. Ever."

"Leave? Erin, I love you. I—"

"Spare me the bullshit, Sarah. It's not going to work this time. I've wasted enough years on you." She pointed to the door. "Get out."

The loving smile Sarah had plastered on her mouth changed into a vicious snarl. "You were nothing without me! Nothing! Look at you now! It didn't take long. You're already starting to fall apart! You are *so* going to regret this, Erin. I'm the best thing that *ever* happened to you. Now you're throwing me out? As if I mean nothing?" Her laugh was bitter. "You need me, Erin. I don't need *you*."

"Then why the hell are you here?"

"I took pity on you. I'd heard you were having a hard time. But you know what? Forget it. You can go to hell! I wouldn't come back to you if you *begged*!"

Erin arched an eyebrow. "It didn't work out with your new girlfriend so you thought you'd slither your way back into my life, huh? You know, if you were like four or five months earlier I might have been stupid enough to let you back in." She held her hand out. "I'll take my key now."

Sarah twisted it off her keychain, then threw it at her, hitting her in the cheek. "I hope you have a miserable life!" she spat as she strode out the door. "Loser!" she tossed over her shoulder.

Erin closed the door and leaned against it. "Wow," she murmured. "Didn't see that coming."

She went back into the living room, her gaze drawn to the bar. If she was ever going to drink again, now was the time.

Sarah seemed to do that to her. She picked up the key, then went into the kitchen instead. Maybe she'd make some of Melanie's spicy burritos for dinner. Top them with that enchilada sauce she'd picked up at Whole Foods.

She paused as she was cutting up the onion and stared off into space. If it had been four or five months ago, would she have really let Sarah back in? In the state she had been in? She really didn't know.

She put the onion into the pan, then paused again. What was she doing here? How long was she going to pretend she was happy being back?

I miss her.

Yeah, she missed her. She missed the cabin and the creek and the goats and the chickens and the garden and… and she missed the rain. She missed all of it. Since she'd been back, she'd been doing nothing more than going through the motions. Going through the motions of living. She had an ache inside her chest that wasn't going away, it seemed.

Because I miss her.

CHAPTER FIFTY-FOUR

She leaned against the window, her gaze fixed on the traffic below. She heard someone approach, sensed that it was Joyce. She glanced at her, then back to the window.

"I never realized how busy everything is. There's so much movement. Cars, people, planes flying over. Everyone's in a hurry."

Joyce walked up beside her. "You spend an awful lot of time staring out the window."

"Do I?"

"You know you do. It's like you're here but you're not really here."

Erin shrugged. "I can't seem to find my groove."

"What are you talking about? I checked the status on your projects. Everything is humming right along as if you'd never been gone. Dad was frazzled the whole time. He couldn't wait for you to get back. And when you did…You snap your fingers and it's all running smoothly again."

Erin continued to stare out the window. "Nothing feels right."

Joyce came closer to her. "Are you okay?" she asked quietly. "This whole month, you've been...I don't know. Distant."

Erin turned away from the window then, considering the question. Was she okay?

"No. I mean, yeah, physically, I'm fine. Great, in fact." She took a deep breath. "I miss her."

Joyce frowned. "Who. Stella?"

Erin smiled and shook her head. "No. Not Stella. Melanie."

Joyce's frown deepened. "Who is Melanie?"

Erin turned back to the window, looking out again. She no longer saw the cityscape that bustled with activity. She saw a lazy creek, she saw a blue scrub jay land on a low branch of a piñon pine, she saw hummingbirds feeding at a red and yellow flower. Saw the twins kicking up their heels as they ran from their stall in the morning, saw the chickens gathered around her feet, waiting for the scratch she was about to toss down. And she saw Mel in the garden, on her knees, dirt streaked across her face, her straw hat blocking the hot sun. Her blue eyes would be twinkling at her, smiling...teasing. She smiled back at her, then realized that Joyce was still there watching.

Erin pushed the images away and turned back to the office once again. "Sarah came to see me."

"*What?* When?"

"I don't know. Last week, I guess. She still had a key to the house. She was inside when I got home. Guess I forgot to change the alarm code."

"What the hell did she want?"

"Said she still loved me. Said she missed me."

"Oh, good Lord. Erin—"

"I finally saw it, Joyce. I finally saw it—in her eyes—that she'd been lying to me all along. It was right in front of me, her pretending. It was like before. Like when we first met. I heard the words and I didn't look deeper. I heard the words this time, but her eyes were saying something completely different. They always had probably...I just never saw it before. I never looked for it."

Joyce touched her arm. "She wanted to come back?"

"Yeah. I guess she thought she could simply waltz back in like nothing ever happened. I think she wanted to pick up where we left off." She shook her head. "I felt nothing for her. Nothing. No anger, no apathy. Certainly no love. Nothing. What I did feel was a sickness inside me. Felt sick that I let her leaving affect me like it did. Like I was the first person in the world to ever have a broken heart. Damn stupid of me, Joyce."

"Is that what it was all about? A broken heart? Or maybe you thought you needed to continue on like you were, be the person she wanted you to be, so that you could attract someone else like her. Or maybe you were holding out hope that she'd come back."

"I don't know anymore. It scares me to think that if this was five months ago—would I have let her back in?"

Joyce met her gaze. "Yes, I hate to say it, but I think you would have. You were in a very bad place, Erin. I don't think there's any question that you would have let her back in."

She let out a breath. "I don't know. I'd like to think that I would have been smarter than that."

"Smart like you are now?"

Erin smiled. "Yeah. I've seen the light and I know it's not her."

Joyce raised her eyebrows. "So who is Melanie?"

Erin looked away. She didn't know how to tell Joyce about Mel. For that matter, she didn't think she *wanted* to tell her. Not yet. "Nobody, really. Someone I made friends with." She looked at her then. "As you know, all of the ones here kinda disappeared on me."

"You kinda disappeared on them. You should give them a call."

"Yeah. I should."

CHAPTER FIFTY-FIVE

She couldn't remember the last time she'd been to Joyce's house. Years. Sarah hadn't liked Joyce and her sister certainly hadn't liked Sarah. Joyce had always voiced her opinion of Sarah to her, but as far as she knew, Joyce had never said anything to Sarah directly. In fact, whenever they'd gotten together—birthdays, backyard barbeques, Christmas—Joyce was always cordial to Sarah. A little cool, maybe, but pleasant. She wondered if Sarah hadn't felt the underlying tension. Or maybe Sarah could tell that Joyce had seen through her deception, could see that Sarah was nothing but a fraud. Regardless, it had gotten to the point where Sarah had refused to attend family gatherings and Erin had gone along with it, distancing herself even further from them. Their only interaction was at the office, and even then, it was downright frosty.

After Sarah left, nothing changed. It got worse, if anything. Admittedly, it was her fault. She withdrew even more, so much so that her relationship with Joyce was hanging by a tattered thread. Joyce apparently still cared enough about her to finally intervene when she was near rock bottom. She smiled at that. *Near?* Oh, she had hit the rocky slopes, all right. Flat on her face, she'd landed.

She rang the doorbell. She knew now that it was Joyce who had put things in motion, not her father. He'd simply wielded the iron fist, forcing her to leave. But it was all Joyce's doing. For that she would be eternally grateful.

Carl opened the door and the surprise was evident on his face. "Erin? Everything okay?"

She smiled at her brother-in-law. "Fine, Carl. How are you?"

"I'm good, thanks." He stepped back, allowing her to enter. "It's been a while."

She nodded. "Too long. Joyce around?"

"Yes, sure. Come on back. We just finished dinner." Joyce was in the kitchen, rinsing a dish at the sink. "Honey, your sister is here."

Joyce spun around, her wet hands dripping water onto the floor. "Erin!" Then she frowned. "What's wrong?"

"Nothing. I just wanted to talk if you've got a few minutes."

"Of course." She looked at Carl. "Can you finish loading the dishwasher?"

Joyce poured them each a glass of iced tea and they went outside to the back deck, sitting down at the patio table.

"It's still so warm, isn't it? It's nearly Halloween. We should at least have a hint of fall in the air by now."

She nodded. "I miss the cooler nights, for sure. And no humidity. That was great."

"You're talking about New Mexico, I'm assuming. You haven't said much about it, you know."

She nodded. "I miss it." She smiled at Joyce. "Considering how much I was dreading it, I loved it there. It was a farm. Where I lived. A cabin. She had chickens and goats. Two cute little twins. And a huge garden. Practically everything we ate came out of the garden."

"She who?"

"Melanie. The way the place is set up, Stella is...the matriarch, really. It's her land, she started it. The ladies who live there, most are on the other side of sixty. Most in their seventies, actually. And Rachel," she said with a smile. "Rachel is eighty-two. They take turns hosting guests. That's what they call women like me. Guests. It was Rachel's turn. I lasted one day with her. So Stella moved me to Melanie's."

"Why one day?"

"I was having caffeine withdrawals big time. She served diluted decaf with cream." She made a face. "Then there was her unseasoned beans. At every meal, including breakfast." She laughed. "She wanted to teach me to knit."

Joyce laughed. "Oh, I would have paid to see that."

"Yeah...I wasn't very nice to her." She looked out into the backyard, seeing the water in their pool glistening from the lights. "Melanie is...thirty-seven. Stella put me with her. We got off to a rocky start." She glanced at Joyce. "My fault. I was a total bitch." She stood up and walked to the edge of the deck. "I miss her."

Joyce came up beside her. "What's going on, Erin?"

She took a deep breath. "I guess...I guess I fell in love with her."

"*What?*"

It felt good to say it out loud, she noted. She turned, smiling at Joyce. "You heard me."

"So you were...*involved* with her?"

"Involved? Yeah. We became friends. Good friends. And then...We became lovers."

"With the woman you were staying with?"

"The woman I was living with," she corrected. "It changed somewhere along the way. And somewhere along the way, I fell in love with her."

"Is that why you sent Sarah away?"

Erin shook her head. "No. Mel and I...Well, we knew it was only temporary. We both knew I was leaving. Something she said to me, though. She said I shouldn't have to change for someone to love me. She said if they didn't love the real me, they weren't worth my time."

"That's true, of course."

"Sarah never loved me. It didn't take her coming back for me to see that. Seeing her, hearing her words…That only reinforced it. I was simply her meal ticket." She walked off the deck toward the pool and Joyce followed. "Being with Melanie, the way we interacted, the way we were together, the way we lived together…Well, it's made me question everything about my life, not only my relationship with Sarah, but everything."

"What do you mean?"

"I didn't know it at the time, but I was never really happy with Sarah."

"I could have told you that. It's like you quit having fun. You quit laughing, quit smiling."

"I know that now. I didn't see it then." She sat down in one of the pool chairs that surrounded a small, round table. "Being out there—away from here—opened my eyes to a lot of things. One of which is my happiness. Or lack thereof. What makes me happy? I thought the job made me happy. I was devoted to it, as you know. Being away, though, then coming back…" She shook her head. "I'm not happy, Joyce."

"Oh, my God. What are you saying? You want to *quit*?"

"I'm saying I don't feel like I belong here anymore."

"Here Houston? Here the office? What?"

"Yes. Both." She met her gaze. "I think I want to go back."

"*Back*? To New Mexico? A place you said was in the middle of nowhere? No cell service? No nothing?"

"Yes."

Joyce sat down beside her. "And do what?"

"Live. Love."

"Oh, Erin. Did they…did they brainwash you or something? Were they a cult? I knew it! I had a feeling—"

Erin laughed. "They're not a cult, Joyce. They're a group of women who wanted to escape society for various reasons. The older ones all moved out there thirty and forty years ago, when being gay wasn't acceptable in society and they wanted to live someplace where they could be open. They created their own little community. And they welcomed me like one of their own."

"But why would you go back? You don't want to escape society."

"I feel kinda lost now. Like I have no purpose."

"You have a purpose. What are you talking about? You have a job. The company depends on you. You're like…what drives it."

"No. You made out just fine when I was gone."

"Fine? Dad was frazzled. I thought he was going to have to go on blood pressure medication," she said with a laugh. "We weren't fine. I was worried sick about you."

"I think you were feeling guilty. Not worried."

"Okay, yeah. I did feel a little guilty. I mean, we forced you. It was underhanded what we did. Dad threatening to fire you and all." She leaned closer. "You know he never would have gone through with his threat if you'd called his hand."

"Doesn't matter. It was the right thing to do."

Joyce sighed. "Are you serious, Erin? I mean, about wanting to go back? Is it because of this woman or…"

"Melanie. Yes."

"How does she feel about it? About you going back?"

Erin smiled. "I haven't talked to her. As you know, there's no cell service."

"So what if she doesn't feel the same way? I mean, you were there for only three months. That's hardly enough time to forge a deep, lasting relationship. What if you go back and you find that…Well, that you rushed into things? Then what? And I don't mean 'then what' the job. You know you'd always have a place here. I mean—'then what' *you*? After Sarah…"

She hadn't really thought about "then what" or whether or not Melanie would want her to come back. She didn't need to. They hadn't talked about it. They hadn't talked about anything regarding their future. Because there had been no future to talk about.

She could close her eyes, however, and still see Melanie out in the rain, crying. She knew then what her tears meant. Melanie's heart was breaking right there in front of her. She'd known it that night when they'd made love, the way Mel had clung to her, the way she'd tried to hide her tears.

And the next day, when Mel had driven away—wanting to be the first to leave—she'd felt her own heart break as she watched

Mel's truck disappear from view. Watched Mel disappear from her life.

"She does feel the same way." She smiled a little, knowing it was the truth. "I want to go back. I *need* to go back."

Joyce shook her head. "Erin, no. You can't just rush into something like that. You've got to—"

"It's not rushing, Joyce. I've been thinking about it since the day I left." She leaned forward, tapping the tabletop with her index finger, trying to make her understand. "I was *happy* there. I felt like I was a part of something. Like I belonged. It felt right being there."

"For God's sake, you don't even know if she wants you back."

"Her tears told me she didn't want me to leave in the first place. I should have listened to my heart. Instead, I did what I was supposed to do. I packed up my things and left. Came back here." She shook her head. "I didn't pack everything, though. I left something behind." She touched her chest. "I left something behind."

Joyce smiled at her. "My God…You're getting all sappy and romantic on me. Whatever in the world has happened to you?"

She smiled too. "I found my home. I found the person I'm supposed to be with. And it may sound corny and—and sappy, as you called it—but I think everything that happened before… it was supposed to happen that way. Everything. And it led me to her." She spread her hands out. "Think about it. What are the chances that you'd stumble upon their little obscure website? I did a search and it was like on the third page, buried. And once you open it, it's so ambiguous even I didn't know what they were offering and I'd *been* there! Yet you found it, you called them, and you booked a stay for me."

"Are you saying that there was some higher power guiding me?" Joyce laughed. "You don't even believe in that sort of thing."

"I don't. Or I didn't. I never believed in fate or the old 'everything happens for a reason' saying." She shrugged. "Maybe I was wrong."

"You'd really leave here? Your home, your family, your job? You'd leave all that to go back?"

"My house doesn't feel like a home. My family is what? I see you and Dad at the office, that's it. I think Brent and I have had all of two conversations since I've been back. My life here is the job, nothing more."

"We used to do things as a family. We used to—"

"I know. It was my fault. I won't even blame Sarah. I let her put a wedge between us. It doesn't change things, though."

"You're right. We stopped getting together for birthdays, holidays. That doesn't mean that we can't pick it up again."

She shook her head. "My heart's not here anymore, Joyce. And most of the time, my mind isn't here either."

"So you've already made the decision, huh?"

She took a deep breath. She had, hadn't she? She wanted to be back on Mel's little farm, nestled in the foothills between the mountains and the desert, a long hour's drive to the nearest town of any size. She looked out into the night, past the pool, past the privacy fence, past the neighbor's house and the one beyond that. Looked up into the city sky where not a single star was visible. She wanted to go back, where she could see a million stars. As much as she'd felt like an alien in foreign territory when she'd first landed at Eagle Bluff Ranch, she knew now, in her heart, that it was *home*.

If she closed her eyes—like she was doing now—she could hear Melanie calling out for her, calling her to come back home. She could hear Melanie's soul calling to her. A bit fanciful to think that, yes. To an outsider—Joyce even—that notion would be mind-boggling and totally unthinkable. It would have been to her too. Before. But now? Now she could *hear* someone calling to her. As crazy as that sounded, when she closed her eyes, it wasn't crazy at all.

She opened her eyes then, finding Joyce watching her curiously. She smiled and nodded.

"Yeah. It's where I belong. It's where I want to be."

Joyce stared at her. "That's it? There's nothing I can say to—"

"No." She stood up quickly, thinking of all the things she needed to do. "Realtors? You know any?"

Joyce's eyes widened as she stood too. "So you're going to sell your house? Without even talking to her first? Erin, you're rushing things."

"I don't think so, but even if I am, that house isn't where I want to be." She pointed back toward the deck and house. "Listen, I'm going to take off. Thanks for listening." She surprised herself—and most likely Joyce—by hugging her tightly. "Thank you for everything. I hate to think of where my life would be right now if you hadn't intervened."

Then Joyce surprised her by kissing her cheek. "I do love you, sis. When you get settled—*if* you get settled—I expect an invite."

"If?"

"You were born and raised here in the city. I'm still trying to wrap my mind around you out there," she motioned. "On a farm, of all places."

Erin laughed. "I know." Her smile lingered. "It's so peaceful, Joyce. I hope you will come visit me."

Joyce nodded. "You'll be at the office tomorrow? Gonna tell Dad?"

"Yeah. Gonna tell Dad."

As she drove back to her house, she so wished she could pick up her phone and call Mel. It was going on two months. She'd be lying if some of Joyce's warnings weren't nagging at her. Two months? For her, it had been an eternity. What about Mel? She'd had to get back to her life, thinking they'd never see each other again. How had she managed? Was Melanie feeling as lost as she was?

Probably.

Lost and alone both. Mel knew all about being alone, didn't she? So did she, for that matter. Even when Sarah was around, she'd spent most of her time working alone. But no more. Life was more than long hours at the office, big houses, and expensive vacations. Life wasn't supposed to be fast. It was supposed to be slow. Slow and enjoyable. So she was going to go back. Back to Mel. Back to where things were slow and easy. Where sunshine on her face could make her smile, where the antics of twin goats could make her laugh, and where a long, drawn-out kiss could make her heart race. Back to Mel. Back to where she belonged.

Back to Mel. Back to where things were easy and slow.

And she couldn't get there fast enough.

CHAPTER FIFTY-SIX

Melanie rocked quietly, the chair making rhythmic sounds against the boards of the porch. She was staring out into the darkness…waiting. She didn't know if it was her imagination—or if she was simply more aware—but it seemed like Goldie and Rick were coming around more often lately. She'd even caught sight of them during the day a couple of times. One day they'd been down by the creek, lying side-by-side along the bank, in the shade of one of the pines. Goldie had kept a watchful eye on her as she moved about, but Rick didn't seem concerned that she'd spied them. Another day, while she'd been walking aimlessly in the back along the bluff, she'd come upon the coyote pair as they were traversing down the rocky slope. They'd stopped, watching her as she watched them. Neither had seemed concerned with her that day; they'd sat on their haunches, ears flicking back and forth as she passed below them.

The tea in her mug was still warm and she took a sip. The nights were getting colder and winter would be upon them soon. She tugged the afghan up higher across her lap, smiling at the sight she must make. It didn't matter. There was no one to see her. Unconsciously, she glanced to Erin's rocker. The empty rocker. She wondered how long she would keep referring to it as Erin's.

What was Erin doing tonight? Was she alone too? Or had she sought out old friends? Had she met new ones? She closed her eyes. Was she dating? She opened her eyes again, not wanting to think about Erin with someone else. She didn't know why it bothered her so. In the long game of life, she and Erin were but a blip on each other's radar. Three months. Hardly worth bothering with.

Yet it was. *Everything happens for a reason.* Did it? She'd never been a big believer in that saying. She'd had a shitty childhood. Was there a reason for that? Her mother was an addict. Was there a reason for that too? Adam? Was there a reason she'd met Adam? Was there a reason she'd torn his world apart and caused his death?

Was there a reason Erin's life spiraled out of control? A reason her sister picked this place for her healing? A reason they were thrown together? So many things had to have happened in their lives for them to meet out here at this creek...of all places.

Everything happens for a reason. Did she believe that now?

Maybe if Erin had stayed, then she'd believe it. But Erin had left. What could the reason be then?

She stared up into the sky, watching the twinkling stars. Her guilt? Was that the reason? Did Erin come so that she could examine her guilt? Take it out of its hiding place and put it on full display? Did Erin come so that she could make peace with her past and do as Erin had suggested? Forgive herself?

Or maybe it wasn't about her at all. Maybe it was all about Erin. Maybe she was simply a bit player in Erin's journey. Maybe she wasn't supposed to fall in love with her. Maybe the joke was on her.

Maybe it had been all along.

That thought drew a weary sigh from her and her chest suddenly felt very heavy with the weight of loneliness. Was this to be her life now? Living out here, alone. Knowing what it felt like to have someone—a partner—if only for a brief time. How was she to get past that now? How did she forget what that felt like? How did she go back to the way things had been before Erin?

A single howl made her lift her head, her gaze going to the dark shape of the shed. The howl seemed lonely too. Was it Rick calling for Goldie? Why weren't they together? She waited, listening. Then it came again...the long, drawn-out wail. Her heart clutched in her chest. Had something happened to one of them? She was shocked that the thought brought tears to her eyes.

She stood up, letting the afghan fall to the porch. She went to the steps, holding onto the railing, listening, hoping to hear an answering call.

The sound was much louder now, directly behind the shed. The chickens and goats were probably stirring nervously. Where was Bandito? He rarely let the coyotes get this close. The howl turned to a chortle, then barks. She stared into the darkness, wondering if they'd chance coming around the shed. Wondering if she'd get a glimpse.

She jumped when the howl sounded again, the pitch becoming higher before turning into a series of yaps. She saw movement at the edge of the shed, and—in the light of the half-moon—she caught sight of Goldie's beige fur as she headed toward the creek. A few moments later, she heard Rick greet her with barks and yips. They sang together for a moment, bringing a smile of relief to her face. She leaned against the railing, her eyes closed as she listened to them.

She wasn't alone after all. Nothing had changed, really. Her life was here, as it had been before Erin. She had her garden, the chickens and goats. She had an old donkey who patrolled the creek and a pair of coyotes to serenade her at night.

She wasn't alone.

She went back inside, pausing to pick up the afghan that had fallen. She turned around once, smiling as the night quieted, the coyotes moving on. She opened the door, then heard them again, as if they were talking to her. She nodded.

"Good night. See you tomorrow."

CHAPTER FIFTY-SEVEN

She was nervous, but it was a mixture of nerves, she noted. Anticipation and anxiety both were rolling around in her mind. She was nearly giddy at the prospect of seeing Melanie again, but since there'd been no contact, it would be a total shock to Mel. Was that fair to her? She'd thought about calling Stella, but she didn't know what she'd say to her. She certainly didn't want Stella to relay a message that she was on her way. Part of that was fear that maybe Melanie didn't want her to come.

She'd been able to push that fear away easily enough—she still remembered the tears when she was leaving—but the closer she got to Eagle Bluff, the more that fear resurfaced.

What if Mel didn't want her? What if Mel was feeling none of what she felt? What would she do then? Would she turn around and leave? This time, for good? Would she go back to Houston? Go back and sit in her lonely office and try to make sense of her life?

No. She'd been doing that for more than two months. They were on the back side of November already. Thanksgiving was but two days away. Joyce had asked her to stay—she and Carl were hosting dinner. But she wasn't even tempted. Her house had been on the market less than a week before it sold. She'd kept nothing. An estate sale took care of the furniture, and her clothes she'd donated. The Lexus, a luxury car that Sarah had said made her seem regal, had been traded for a four-wheel-drive SUV—a Toyota Land Cruiser. She'd paid more than she'd intended, but she'd wanted something that was both comfortable—okay, luxurious—and practical for where she'd be living.

She glanced in the mirror, meeting her eyes. *Hoped* to be living, she silently corrected. She let out her breath as she gripped the steering wheel tighter. She should have called. She should have asked Stella to have Mel call her. They should have talked. She shouldn't just show up out of the blue like this.

Too late now. A quick look at the vehicle's navigation system showed the Gila River fast approaching. She'd turn to the right. She'd follow the river for a bit, then where Eagle Creek dumped into it, she'd turn again, this time onto the road that would take her to Eagle Bluff Ranch. She only hoped that Stella hadn't taken to locking the gate. It would be quite a hike in, if so.

It was two in the afternoon. The sun was bright. The air cool—cool enough for a light jacket. What would Melanie be doing? Had they had a freeze yet? Were there still plants in the garden that needed tending? Had she cut firewood for the winter already? Had she been to Silver City for her monthly shopping?

She smiled at that thought as she remembered her shopping trip at Whole Foods three days ago. She'd gotten a variety of dry beans, some Japanese sweet potatoes, some wild rice, oriental noodles, and other things that she thought Mel might like. She didn't want to show up empty-handed.

She slowed as the road approached and she looked in the mirror. There were no cars in either direction. She turned onto the river road. Ten more miles, she thought. Ten more miles. What would she say to her? Well, before she got to Mel, she would have to stop at Stella's. What would she say to Stella? She shook her head. Stella didn't matter.

What would she say to *Mel*?

CHAPTER FIFTY-EIGHT

Mel looked up at the sound of a vehicle bouncing along the road that led to her cabin. She stabbed the pitchfork into the compost pile, then shielded her eyes to the sun. She could tell by the sound that it wasn't Stella's old truck. A crimson red vehicle—an SUV of some sort—approached. She had a moment of panic, thinking once again that Stella should start locking the gate. It wouldn't be hard for someone—a stranger—to breach the property. She rolled her eyes. And then do what? Attack seventeen elderly ladies and rob them blind? Still, her hand wrapped around the handle of the pitchfork, just in case.

As the vehicle got closer, she released the handle. Her heart started beating triple-time, and she felt a damp nervousness coat her palms. When the vehicle stopped, parking appropriately next to her truck, she knew it wasn't a stranger. She moved around to the garden gate, sliding the latch back before opening it.

A dark-haired woman got out and she felt her throat close up completely. She held on to the gate for support, feeling light-headed as she locked gazes with Erin Ryder.

* * *

Erin could see the shocked look on Mel's face. Of course, Stella had warned her that Melanie might faint dead away. Stella had suggested that she come along, but Erin had been adamant that she didn't want their reunion to be witnessed by anyone. She wanted them to be able to talk freely, to show emotions—good or bad—without an audience. Now, though... As she looked at Melanie, saw the disbelief in her eyes, she wished she'd taken Stella up on her offer.

She walked around the truck slowly, her gaze never leaving Mel's. Mel finally pushed off from the gate, taking a hesitant step in her direction. In her dreams, she'd pictured them running toward one another, flinging their arms around each other tightly, kissing passionately, vowing undying love. Instead, Mel stopped and put her hands on her hips, looking at her a bit warily.

"What are you doing here?"

Erin bit the corner of her lip. "Well, I...'I missed you' doesn't seem quite enough right now," she said hesitantly. "I did miss you, though."

Melanie nodded. "I missed you too." She arched an eyebrow. "What are you doing here?" she asked again, her hands still planted firmly on her hips.

Oh, boy. This *so* wasn't how she envisioned their reunion. She scratched the back of her neck nervously, wondering if she could run back to Stella's and reconsider.

"Are you like here to visit...or what?"

Erin swallowed. "Well...Do you *want* me to visit?"

Melanie shook her head. "No."

That one word was like a dagger to her heart, a blow to the chest hard enough to knock the breath out of her. Melanie took a step closer.

"I can't do it again, Erin. I can't go through you leaving again. I...I can't do another goodbye."

Erin nodded. "Okay. So...so what if I didn't leave?"

"What are you saying?"

"What if I stayed?"

"Here?"

Erin licked her dry lips. "Well, I kinda thought here. I guess maybe..." God, this wasn't how it was supposed to go. "Maybe..."

Melanie walked closer to her. "What are you really doing here, Erin? Just tell me."

Erin met her gaze, seeing the familiar blue eyes that she'd looked into a hundred times before, it seemed. She took a deep breath.

"I'm in love with you. And I'm miserable without you... and...and," she motioned behind herself. "I didn't belong there. I felt like...I was all messed up and it was all weird and I...I wanted to be here with you. I felt like this is where I belong. This feels like home." She pointed behind herself again. "That...that didn't. I wanted to be here. With you."

Melanie tilted her head thoughtfully. "You fell in love with me?"

Erin nodded. "I did." She held her gaze. "You fell in love with me too." Then she cocked an eyebrow. "I mean...you did, didn't you?" she asked hopefully.

* * *

You did, didn't you?

Melanie stared at Erin for a long moment, wondering if this was real. Was it the middle of the night? Was she in deep sleep? Was Erin haunting her dreams again?

"I did," she finally said. "So...you came back?"

"Is that okay?"

Melanie closed her eyes. "Is this for real?" she whispered.

"I love you, Mel."

She opened her eyes. Erin was still there. Her hair was blowing in the breeze. Her eyes were as she remembered—deep and dark and full of emotion. She'd thought it before—that Erin loved her. She'd thought it that last day, for sure. Before that too. When they made love, when they cuddled afterward. When they talked. She'd thought it then. But Erin still left. Even after she'd gone, she still thought it…when she dared. She could see it now, fully. Erin wasn't trying to hide anything from her.

"You love me." It wasn't a question. Erin smiled and nodded. Melanie took a step closer. "And you want to stay?" Erin nodded again. "Stay for…a while?"

Erin's expression turned serious. "Stay forever, Mel."

Melanie felt a tear slide down her cheek, saw Erin's gaze follow its path, saw Erin's expression soften.

"I missed you being here," she managed. Her tears fell freely now. "I tried so hard to get back to normal, but…" She wiped at her tears. "I kept seeing you, hearing you, in everything I did." She tried to laugh. "It was driving me crazy."

Erin drew her into the circle of her arms. Melanie sank against her and weeks—months—of frustration, of sadness, peeled away. She felt fresh, new, with a lightness to her spirit that she hardly recognized. She held Erin tight, her eyes squeezed closed.

"I…I love you." She pulled back enough to meet Erin's eyes. "I love you," she said with certainty. The kiss Erin gave her was almost one of relief and Melanie smiled against her lips. "Were you afraid?"

"Yeah. The closer I got, the more I doubted everything." Erin laughed lightly. "Yeah. So I sold my house, sold everything I owned…bought this thing," she said, motioning to the vehicle. "Thought it'd be good on our monthly shopping trips. I bought some jeans and boots and all kinds of other stuff." She kissed her again, then brushed at the remnants of her tears. "And then I thought, what if she doesn't want you? What the hell are you going to do then?"

Mel laughed. "So what was your fallback plan?"

"I was going to see if Stella would let me move into one of those vacant houses. Then I was going to court you." She grinned. "Use my charm until you couldn't resist me."

Melanie held tightly to her hand. "I can't believe you're here."

Erin looked around, her glance going to the cabin, the shed, the garden. "I…I left my heart here." She met her gaze. "I felt like I left my soul here."

"How do you feel now?"

"I feel whole again."

She nodded. "Yes. That's how I feel. Whole."

CHAPTER FIFTY-NINE

Melanie squeezed her hand as she climaxed, her sounds of pleasure lingering in the bedroom long after her body had stilled. Erin stayed where she was, her fingers still buried inside her, Mel's thighs clenched tight, holding her there.

The first time they touched, it had been intense, as if they were trying to make up for the lost weeks and months that she'd been gone. As they got reacquainted, their touches became gentler, their actions slowed, their lovemaking was like before—unhurried and deliberate. Slow. Relaxed.

She smiled against Melanie's lips. Enjoyable. Easy.

"Why are you smiling? I just had the orgasm. I should be smiling."

Erin pulled back, watching Mel in the waning afternoon sunlight that still poured through the window. "And so you are."

Melanie did a catlike stretch, relaxing her legs finally, a contented smile on her face. Erin withdrew her fingers and Mel jerked slightly, then sighed.

"I had wondered if maybe you'd started dating again." Mel opened her eyes. "When you left here, you were healthy, healed. Beautiful. I…imagined that you were dating again."

"Is that what you thought?" Erin pulled the sheet and blanket over them as she settled down beside Melanie. "You didn't picture me alone, staring at my walls, dreaming of you?"

Melanie shook her head.

"Did you picture me at Whole Foods, in the produce aisle? Or perhaps cooking potatoes and peppers for breakfast?"

Melanie smiled. "Did you?"

"I did. Although store-bought potatoes and eggs are the worst. You've ruined me."

"Are you saying you didn't go back to your old eating habits?"

"I'm not sure if it was because I felt good—physically, at least—or if it made me feel close to you. But no, I didn't."

"I'm so proud of you!"

Erin smiled as her fingers traced one of Mel's nipples. "I…I saw Sarah."

"Oh, yeah?"

"She came to the house. Actually, she was *in* the house when I got home one evening. I never got my key back from her." She met Melanie's gaze. "I guess maybe I'd hoped that she'd come back one day…so then she'd have a key."

"So *did* she come back? To you?"

"She did. She said she still loved me. Said she missed me. Said she'd made a mistake." Erin felt Melanie stiffen a little, but she said nothing. "I was surprised that I wasn't filled with anger. I really felt…well, not much of anything." She paused. "She kissed me."

"And…you kissed her?"

"No. There was nothing there, Mel. I felt nothing. Her words were hollow. She has blue eyes, much like yours. The similarities end there. She said she loved me. You never said those words to me. Your eyes, though—I didn't *need* you to say the words." She leaned up on an elbow, looking at Melanie fully. "I had been missing you so much and feeling like I was drifting aimlessly…not knowing in which direction to go. Sarah shows up—literally out of the blue—and it all became crystal clear. She was saying these words to me, yet there was nothing in her eyes. Mel, there'd *never* been anything in her eyes. And I never…I never knew that it *should* be there."

She swallowed. "You never said the words to me." She met Mel's gaze. "But it was there in your eyes. I saw it…I did. But I didn't know what to do with it. I'd never seen it before. Once I did… Well, I knew that it was supposed to be there. Sarah…" She shook her head. "It wasn't there, it had never been there."

"You saw it, huh? I thought I hid it well. I didn't even dare admit it to myself until after you'd left." Melanie gave her a quick smile. "I hope you told her to never, ever kiss you again, right?"

She nodded. "I kicked her out, told her I'd call the police if she came to the house again. She called me a loser. That was her parting shot: I was a loser." Erin leaned down and kissed her. "With you, I think I'm the winner."

CHAPTER SIXTY

"You don't know how much I missed this little goat."

"Judging by how long you've been rubbing on her, I'd guess it was more than you missed me."

Erin laughed. "I think I rubbed on you quite a bit last night."

"So you did."

Erin pointed to the small oak tree near the cabin. "Hummingbird feeder is gone. They all leave?"

"They did. Most left… Well, not too long after you did."

"I wish I hadn't left, Mel, but I needed to leave. At the time, I needed to leave."

"I know. You needed to leave in order to…to *know*."

"Exactly." Erin held her hand out to her. "Walk to the creek? I'd like to say hello to it."

Melanie nodded. "I love that about you."

"What?"

"That you think of everything as more than just an inert object…or a stupid farm animal."

Erin's eyes widened dramatically. "Are you calling the goats and chickens *stupid*?" She lowered her voice. "They'll hear you!"

Melanie took her hand and swung it between them as they headed to the creek. "I think the chickens missed you. I don't throw out nearly as much scratch as you did. And Rosie? She always looked past me, like she was waiting for you to come up behind me."

"And the ladies? Did they grill you after I left?"

"Yes, but they were very sweet. They could tell that I was hurting. At the monthly dinner in October, Rebecca told me that you'd be back." The smile she'd had on her face faded somewhat. "I didn't believe her. When I got home, I crawled into bed and cried."

"I'm sorry, Mel."

"I'm sorry I didn't believe her." She linked arms with Erin as they stood beside the creek. "Thanksgiving is tomorrow. We always have a big feast at Stella's. Takes the place of our monthly dinner."

"Good. I'll look forward to it. Be nice to see everyone."

"Yes. You can help me cook. Angela and I bring the meatless loaves. Two each. Everyone else brings a side dish." She grinned. "Rachel will cook the beans."

"Oh, goody," Erin said dryly. "How I've missed them."

"Stella bakes pies. And now that you're here, I would imagine there'll be a chocolate cake at the table too."

"Did I pick the right time to come back or what?" she teased.

"How was Stella? You never said. Was she surprised to see you?"

"I don't think so, no. She wanted to know what took me so long."

Melanie nodded. "She came to see me a couple of days after you left. Brought Fred over for some company for me." She leaned her head against Erin's shoulder. "You're not going to leave again, right?"

"I'm not going to leave."

She lifted her head, looking at Erin. "Are you going to get bored being here?"

"Bored?" Erin frowned. "What are you worried about, Mel? Tell me."

"I'm worried that you're used to living in a city and you're not used to being on a farm." There. She'd said it. Her worst fear—that Erin would grow bored here and leave again.

Erin cupped her face for a moment, then her thumb moved gently across her cheek. "I was here three months. Did I look like I was bored?"

"Not counting the first week? No, not really. But you knew you'd be leaving. There was an end date, an end in sight. It's a lot different here during the winter than during the summer."

"I'll find something to keep me busy." Erin took a step away, then glanced back toward the cabin. "I'm used to building things. Maybe I'll enlarge the shed or something. Or build new stalls and we can get more goats! Or some horses or something."

She smiled. "Horses? Have you ever ridden a horse?"

"No. But I'm thinking it would be a lot of fun." She smiled at her. "Point is, I'm not going to get bored. And I've been on construction sites since I was old enough to walk. I'm pretty handy with power tools. I'd guess that there are a lot of odds and ends that the ladies need help with."

"Like a handyman?"

Erin smiled. "Handy*woman*," she corrected.

Melanie took her hand and tugged her back toward the cabin. "Handywoman," she repeated. "I like it. And speaking of getting more goats, guess what day it is?"

Erin gave an exaggerated groan. "Ah...come on. I just got here. You can't possibly expect me to muck the goat stall."

"Uh-huh."

"Ah, Mel...that's such a shitty job."

"I know it is." She grinned. "That's why I'm so glad you're here, my handywoman."

"Oh, I don't mind mucking the stall. Little Rosie gives me love taps while I do it." Erin stopped walking, her gaze drawn to the sky. "It's so blue. Like...bluer than I've ever seen before." She turned to her then. "Beautiful. Everything is beautiful. I'm looking forward to a real winter...cuddling by the fire. And

spring, when everything blooms again and the birds come back."
She smiled. "But I'm mostly looking forward to summer. Play
days in the creek, the hot springs." Erin reached out and touched
her chest, running her finger down between her breasts. "You
out in the garden, topless. The summer rain chasing us into the
shed…"

"So you can steal a kiss," she finished for her.

"Lots of kisses." She leaned forward and kissed her then.
"I'm very happy, Mel. I feel like my heart is smiling."

Melanie nodded. "Me too." She moved into her arms. "I love
you." She felt Erin squeeze her tight, heard the softly spoken
words repeated to her.

Yes, her heart was smiling too. Erin was home. Everything
was perfect now. She found Erin's mouth again and let the kiss
deepen.

"Maybe the goat stall can wait," she murmured after a while.

Erin laughed lightly as she led her away from the shed and
toward the cabin. "You're too easy."

"Are you complaining?"

"That you'd rather make love than clean goat poop?" Erin
looked past her to where the twins were watching them from
between the slats in the fence. "Sorry, girls. You'll have to wait."

Melanie was smiling as she went into the cabin. She paused,
glancing back outside, finding only Rosie still staring after them
with a somewhat accusing look on her face. Then, in typical
young goat fashion, she kicked up her heels and did a spinout in
the chicken yard, scattering the hens in the process.

With a contented sigh, she closed the door and let Erin lead
her purposefully into their bedroom.

Bella Books, Inc.

Women. Books. Even Better Together.

P.O. Box 10543
Tallahassee, FL 32302

Phone: 800-729-4992
www.bellabooks.com